SCHOOLED

SCHOOLED

A NOVEL

TED FOX

LAKE UNION
PUBLISHING

Published by Lake Union Publishing, Seattle

www.apub.com

Amazon, the Amazon logo, and Lake Union Publishing are trademarks of Amazon.com, Inc., or its affiliates.

ISBN-13: 9781662505454
ISBN-10: 1662505450

Cover design by Philip Pascuzzo

Printed in the United States of America

For Jenny.
Obviously.

CHAPTER 1

Nothing good ever comes from going into work on Saturday.

We had even made a rule against it. It was a couple of weeks after a giant gadget site named us best electric toothbrush—the exact phrasing was "The Toothbrush That Will Make You See the Face of God"—and our sales had taken off. Finally confident Scrub wouldn't go out of business anytime soon, we'd sent a company-wide email announcing the office was from that point forward closed on weekends so that no one would feel pressure to come in. Everybody had worked hard to get us there, and we could at last afford to hire more people so that we all could go back to having lives.

But that was before we got bought. Now we were being told to streamline, to get more "efficient," firing instead of hiring. Nothing could be more un-Saturday.

I walked through the silent floor full of cubicles into my office. The blinds on the window were closed, and I didn't bother turning the lights on. Artificial twilight seemed appropriate.

I was supposed to have had this done two weeks ago, which itself was an extension of the original deadline. But I kept putting it off, hoping that it would magically get easier. Magic having failed, I was now onto plan B: sifting through past performance reviews in a vain attempt to make the patently unfair as fair as possible.

My computer didn't seem any more eager than I was, informing me as soon as it powered up that it needed to run a variety of system updates. It was just as well. Kayla, my wife, had let me take the last of the lasagna leftovers for lunch so at least one part of this epically terrible day wouldn't be quite so terrible, and now I had good reason to eat them while I still had an appetite.

I opened the third drawer of my desk with my free hand to retrieve my emergency pack of cigarettes (an ironic vice for someone at a toothbrush company, I know) and then headed for the kitchen. It was narrow, galley-style, and even darker than my office, but I didn't need the lights there either. That microwave had furnished me with too many perplexingly reheated lunches to count (how does the top stay cold when the bottom is hot?), and I could find my way to it in my sleep.

I popped open the door and immediately caught a whiff of the ghost of seafood past. Philip. He was always reheating fish in there, despite repeated interventions by at least a dozen of us.

"Is that layoffable?" I wondered out loud as I reached into the shopping bag and grabbed the container, dropping my cigarettes onto the dark floor in the process.

I shoved the lasagna unceremoniously into the microwave and closed the door before going into a squat to feel around for that familiar rectangle. I hadn't smoked regularly since college, but occasionally, when work got crazy, it was one of the only things that could help me slow down and breathe (again, ironic). And now that the image of Philip packing up his desk was stuck on a loop in my head, it would have been fair to say I wanted all the cigarettes. All. Of. Them. But especially the seven left in that pack on the kitchen floor.

So my search felt a little more frantic than it otherwise would have been. And just as I was about to concede to the gross inconvenience of walking the 15 feet back to the door and turning the light on, I found them.

I stood up and briefly wondered where I had set the lasagna. Right. Already in the microwave. The slice was especially thick, and I was determined to heat it all the way through even if that meant turning some of the layers molten. I set the timer for eight minutes and walked out, intent on enjoying a moment of carcinogenic calm before the storm.

As the first drag penetrated my insides—God, that sounded sexual, and God, it almost was—I stared out at our parking lot, empty except for my car and two squirrels chasing each other into the dumpster, and replayed how we had gotten here, as if that might somehow make the ending turn out differently this time.

The greatest-hits version? One of our largest competitors, one with what they liked to call "a full suite of oral hygiene products," including much-higher-priced electric toothbrushes with far inferior battery life, had gotten tired of losing market share, so rather than try to get better, they had done what any aspiring monopoly would do: they bought us.

It was a great deal for Janice Daughtry, the founder and owner of Scrub, and a nice piece of validation for me, our director of corporate strategy. Because five years earlier, when Janice and I and a few others had been making plans in a coworking space that smelled like a damp dog burping ramen, the only thing that had seemed certain was that our future wasn't. She and I had met and hit it off at a conference I was attending in service of a consulting job that was tolerable at best. So when she pitched me on coming to work for her, I had gone for it, even though I had a pile of student loans and had already crossed that invisible threshold into the second half of my 20s, when you're supposed to be settling into a career. I called my parents to tell them, and my dad's only reaction had been to ask, "What's wrong with normal toothbrushes?"

The amount of time I had spent back then debating whether I could use a Ring Pop to propose to Kayla and play it off as a romantic gesture suggested he wasn't wrong.

And yet there I was, now early 30s, smoking that cigarette, in charge of our whole team, which as of our acquisition by Mouth Inc.—Mouth Inc., for God's sake—numbered 200-plus people.

I owed the promotion to Janice, who had gotten eight figures in the sale and was moving to Arizona. As part of the deal, she had insisted that the Mouth people, as they had come to be known by all of us, put me over all that had been Scrub. So they had. My first day at the new company, they'd told me I needed to lose 50 of our employees.

"These people are my friends," I'd said. "You can't expect me to just cut them all loose for no reason."

The HR rep had looked horrified. "Oh, of course not; we'll do that. We just need you to identify who's nonessential."

"You think twenty-five percent of our staff isn't essential?"

"Why? Do you think it's higher?"

Crap, the lasagna. I pulled my phone out of my pocket to check the time and only then realized I hadn't paid attention to when I'd started the microwave. All the more reason to stay out there until the cigarette was done, I thought. Because it wasn't like the lasagna wouldn't still be delicious if it sat for a few minutes. That recipe had been handed down to me from my nonna, and while I was proving completely inept at picking people to be fired, I knew my way around the ricotta backward and forward.

While I was finishing my smoke, I realized I'd need a reinforcement snack for later in the day. I was 85 percent sure there was a Chocsplosion! candy bar in the car and 50 percent sure it wasn't melted. Not great odds, but good enough to get me walking in hopes of finding the candy that implored me to "Blow up chocolate with every bite!"

I didn't know why chocolate needed to be blown up, but the anthropomorphized cocoa bean with the dynamite on the wrapper was strangely compelling.

I'd driven Kayla's car in case any of my employees happened to pass by while I was there. That no-weekends rule had become baked into the culture, and if they knew I was at the office, they might get paranoid that something was wrong. Which obviously it was, so they'd be right.

Kayla didn't give me a hard time about the intermittent smoking, but I didn't want to push that by funking up her car, so I opened the door and leaned in while keeping my hand with the dwindling butt outside.

"Yes!" I said as my outstretched fingers once again found what they were looking for, and I momentarily forgot why I was there on a Saturday in the first place.

I was standing next to the car, examining the wrapper and noting with relief that its contents were still (roughly) in the shape of a candy bar, when I first heard them. Sirens.

Not that I thought much of it. Our building was close to the fire station, so hearing those trucks was almost a daily occurrence. I started back toward the office, determined to make that butt last until I got to the front door.

I was halfway there when the first fire truck came lurching into our lot.

Cigarettes and firefighters being natural enemies, I instinctively dropped what was left of mine to the ground and stamped it out with my foot. I'd like to say I never littered when I smoked, but anyone who says that is lying. And in my defense, it now seemed I had bigger things to deal with than how I disposed of my trash.

"I'm really sorry," I said, walking up to them as they got out of the truck. "I was at my car and didn't even hear the alarm go off." Our building had the kind that alerted the fire department as soon as it got triggered. Pro: it saved money on the insurance. Con: if no one was there to answer the phone—say, because they were outside smoking— fire trucks showed up for burned lasagna.

"Any idea what it might be?" one of the four asked while they started unloading. He was at least six inches taller than me and looked like he could use me as a Wiffle ball bat.

"Uh . . . yeah." This was embarrassing. "I was heating up my lunch, and it probably just started burning a little."

"Is there anyone else here?"

"No, just me."

"What were you heating—"

That's when we heard the explosion.

Our heads whipped toward the building, where the second-floor window closest to the kitchen had been blown into nothing. I heard the other three yelling things to each other, and I was vaguely aware of a second truck barreling into the lot. Meanwhile, the enormous man next to me seemed to grow another six inches. I was a planet about to be consumed by a supernova.

"What were you heating up?" he shouted over all the other noise.

"Huh?" I watched the flames lick the gaping hole where a window had been, unable to process what I was seeing.

"What was in the microwave?"

"Oh—*lasagna*!" I yelled back, thinking for the briefest of seconds that maybe I had exonerated myself. But then: *"Shit—and aluminum foil!"* My stomach bottomed out as I said it.

He shook his head in disgust. *"You can't put metal in a microwave!"*

"I know!"

"It catches fire!"

"I know!"

"Clearly!" he shouted and left. I just stood there. I had been so distracted by the layoffs and Philip's lunches and my cigarettes that I had completely spaced on what I was pulling out of that bag and igniting—all within kindling distance of some aerosol cans (those ones that blow lint out of your keyboard) and extra rolls of paper towels. Doing it in the dark hadn't helped either. Regardless, none of this figured to matter much when it came to my defense.

I knew I should be letting someone know what had happened, but that someone was no longer Janice, and I was paralyzed at the thought of telling any of the Mouth people, whom I'd worked with for all of three months. But ready or not, I got that chance 20 minutes later, right at the same time the TV news crew was setting up.

"Oh my God, Jack, are you okay?" the CEO of Mouth shouted to me as he disembarked from his SUV. His name was Sidney Edmonds, and we were supposed to meet on Monday to go over my list of cuts. Mouth HQ was 700 miles away, in New York, and he was coming in person to make it harder for me to miss another deadline. It seemed he'd gotten to town a couple of days early and was driving by when he saw the building on fire.

Lucky me.

"Oh, Mr. Edmonds. I'm, uh . . ." No point in trying to spin it. "I'm so, so sorry, sir." He was right in front of me now, and I paused and looked from him to what remained of the second floor and then back to him, doing my best to hold down the nausea I felt milling around somewhere between my stomach and the back of my throat. "I really screwed up," I added for some reason. As if the flaming building hadn't provided enough context.

"What happened?"

"It was, uh . . . a mishap with the microwave, sir."

He grunted. "That's one helluva mishap. And stop calling me *sir*. But you—you're all right?"

I had to be hallucinating. Was I all right? What did he care? I had charbroiled the building. His building. Not the whole thing, certainly. But enough.

"Yeah, I'm good. I was outside. Having a smoke." I admitted the last part sheepishly, because I felt I had to, but it didn't faze him.

"What were you even doing here?" he asked. He was about 50 and dressed in a navy-blue Mouth polo shirt, which made me wonder if he always wore that on weekends or only when traveling on official Mouth business. "I know all of you take that Saturday thing pretty seriously."

"I was . . . well, to be honest, si . . . Sidney, I'm still trying to . . . finalize . . . the list." *Finalize* sounded better than *start*.

"You still haven't done that?"

I shook my head.

"Look, I get it," he said. "But it's part of being a leader, Jack. And that's how we see you: as a leader."

"So, wait." I was doing my best not to look dumbfounded, but pulling that off in front of a smoldering building that you set ablaze is just as hard as it sounds. "Am I not, like . . . fired?"

"No, you're not fired. That said, it's not exactly a point in your favor, either, so you can show me your gratitude by actually doing the job we're paying you to do."

I didn't know how to respond to that. Thankfully, we were interrupted by the reporter from the TV station asking to speak with him.

I watched Sidney from behind the camera, hating myself for how grateful I felt. Not just because I didn't have to stumble through an interview but because I still had a job. Because of him. And yet none of that changed that he was going to make me lay off 50 others.

The stress of everything had brought my appetite back with a vengeance, so I cracked open the Chocsplosion! while he talked.

"One of our many dedicated employees was just here on a Saturday," Sidney explained after confirming there weren't any injuries. "He wanted to get some extra work done, and there was . . ."

He stopped midsentence. I would've thought that he'd frozen up, but he was staring straight at me, my mouth full of candy bar.

"Jack, what is that?" The camera was still rolling. I could see the red record light when the camerawoman turned it to me.

"Whuh whuh?" I mumbled through the chocolate.

"What are you eating?"

I swallowed. Hard. "A Chocsplosion!?"

He didn't say anything for about five seconds, but his face turned somewhere between red and purple. The camera swung back to him just in time to catch it.

"A *Chocsplosion!*?" He was practically spitting. "Are you effin' kidding me?"

I'd later come to wish he'd actually sworn because it being a livestream, they probably would have cut the segment right there. As it was:

Camera pan to me. "Uh . . . no?"

Back to Sidney. "You have the nerve—no, no, the audacity—you have the *audacity* to disrespect me by stuffing your mouth with that *crap*? Right in my *face*?"

If you had told me that morning there was going to be trouble at the office and asked me to guess why, the safe bet would've had to do with the layoff list. Torching a wing of the building with my lasagna? The million-to-one long shot.

"Grown man verbally assaulting me over my choice of candy bar" would've ranked somewhere below "zombie apocalypse."

But the red light was on me again, so I had to say something.

"You . . . uh . . . you don't like Chocsplosion!?"

"No, *Jack*, I don't like Chocsplosion!" The camerawoman was in serious danger of whiplash by this point. "Would *you* like the company that *you* gave seventeen years of *your* life to, only to be passed over for CEO because you *allegedly* had a history of making people quote-unquote uncomfortable?"

Allegedly was the only part of that sentence I took issue with. But he appeared to have convinced himself it was appropriate.

"And if that *were* you, Jack, and they expected you'd shut up and smile and be happy with your big salary and vice president status, do you think you'd have the *balls* to leave? To leave the place where *you* were the one who came up with 'Blow up chocolate with every bite!'? Would you leave to take over an oral hygiene company and make it your sole mission in life to lay waste to that unholy, mouth-rotting, tooth-corroding union of caramel and eleven different chocolates that disrespected you like that? Because I did, Jack: I had the balls. But you? You can't even grow a pair to make a few"—he hesitated on his word choice—"changes here and there. So let me do what you apparently can't and make it real easy for you: don't bother coming back on Monday. You're done."

With that, he stormed off. The camera returned to me for my reaction, but the only thing that came out of my mouth, I discovered upon later viewing, was a long strand of caramel. Touché, universe.

So that was it. I had been fired. On camera. Eating a Chocsplosion!

Any hope I had of the video fading into the ether dissolved that afternoon when a woman in Kansas tried to rob a bank by pretending the Chocsplosion! under her shirt was a gun. Two equally bizarre yet unrelated Chocsplosion! incidents in one day were just too much gold for the internet to pass up. The video of me went viral, typically accompanied by either some variant of "Blow up your office with every bite!" or a joke about Choco (the cocoa bean) having rage issues. It wasn't a total loss, though; it basically made that reporter's career. He works at one of the networks now. Sends me a Christmas card each year.

I got in Kayla's car and drove to the gas station up the road. She had just gotten a big promotion and was out for a celebratory lunch with one of her friends, but this didn't feel like the kind of thing I should sit on for too long, nor did it feel like a phone call I should make while driving.

"You sound surprisingly okay with everything," she said when I was done. Based on the background noise, she was near the restaurant's kitchen. She had excused herself from her friend, no questions asked, as soon as I said hello. I knew she'd be able to hear it in my voice. And while I had grown steadier throughout the course of the call, she wasn't completely buying it; I had just caused a fire and been fired in the same hour, after all.

"Well, I mean my career is probably ruined," I said. I was sitting on the hood of the car, smoking another cigarette. "So that sucks. And while I was watching it burn, I was so sick to my stomach I thought I was going to puke on the firefighter. Sidney too."

I paused to take a long drag. "But I don't know. It's like . . ."

I stopped again, searching for what I was feeling, and Kayla nailed it for me: "It's like if your new boss is going to fire you over having a soul, maybe it's better to get out now?"

I felt the relief wash over my body. "God, I love you."

She laughed. "I know."

"Seriously, how are you this cool?"

"Well, I just made partner, so I had been planning on asking you to be my trophy husband, regardless." I laughed, and I could hear her smile through the phone. "And also, while you were off wasting those leftovers, I got some news of my own this morning."

I sat upright. "What news?"

"I wanted to tell you in person when you got home."

"Okay, now you have to tell me."

She was quiet for a second or two, but the smile sounded like it might swallow her entire face.

"Kayla? Kayla, what is it?"

"I'm pregnant, Jack."

CHAPTER 2

No matter how long I've got on this earth, I won't have too many moments better than rolling through a drive-through at 9:07 a.m. on a sunny Tuesday, singing along with my five-year-old daughter at the tops of our lungs. We were rocking out to some Lizzo—I love my kids more than anything, which is why I never subjected them to Kidz Bop—and even in the radio edit, I still had an "as hell" to navigate.

"Feelin' good, as well!" Lulu belted from her booster seat.

I don't think I had ever been as convincing in a meeting at Scrub as I was the day I got her to believe that those were the words. Although she wouldn't even have been familiar with the concept of hell, like most five-year-olds, she was surprisingly good at detecting when you were scamming her.

"Hey, there are my favorite customers!" a barista named Sammi said. She peeked in through the open back window. "What's up, Klay and Lulu?"

Klay was two and in prime "stranger danger" mode, so he just tried to bury his head, but Lulu managed a little wave, clearly pleased to be recognized.

I handed over my reusable cup. "Actually, can we change it to a small? I'm trying to cut back now that certain someones are sleeping through the night. Most of the time."

"Ha, no problem. Just a sec."

The kids and I were on our way to the playground, which had been a Tuesday ritual almost since Kayla went back to work after her first maternity leave and I needed excuses to get out of the house. We hadn't planned on it being just Lulu and me for quite so long; actually, we hadn't planned on me staying home at all. It sort of just happened. Because any time I thought about going back to work that first year or two after I got fired, I couldn't summon the motivation to pursue anything. I didn't want to lead if leading meant canning people just to improve some corporation's P&L, but I worried that taking anything other than a director-type position would make it look like my career was moving the wrong way. Then there was reliving the humiliation. The longer I went without a job, the longer the gap on my résumé, and the more likely it became I'd have to explain why I hadn't been working. And for what? I'd put all of myself into Scrub, bet on it succeeding when success had been far from assured, only to see the place that I loved get snatched away. The fire was the send-off, but the damage had been done well before that microwave caught fire. I couldn't escape the feeling that none of it—the vision, the camaraderie, the people—none of it mattered. My procrastination about the layoffs had only gone so far in protecting my employees, and I hadn't been able to protect myself or do my job. Instead, I choked under the pressure. That realization began to settle over me like a cloud in the months after the fire, and once it had, it was hard to picture ever going back to the life I'd known. Eventually I'd stopped trying.

Of course, my retreat from the work world was possible only because I'd married someone who continued to kill it at her own job. By the time Kayla got pregnant the second time, my metamorphosis from director of corporate strategy into stay-at-home dad was complete. Living on one income with four people after having lived on two with two had presented its challenges, but those had eased recently when Kayla got promoted again, this time to senior partner.

"Here you go!" Sammi said, returning with my iced coffee. I held out my phone for her to scan. "Playground today?"

"Good memory. I gotta squeeze in as many of these as I can before she goes to kindergarten in the fall."

I'd been thinking about Lulu starting school—not her cozy, few-mornings-a-week preschool, but school-school—more than I expected. Having all this time with the kids over the years was its own reward (or punishment, depending on the day), but it also wasn't the worst thing that it gave me some cover for my decision to flee gainful employment. Although there were still plenty of people who couldn't wrap their minds around the idea of a dad staying home, it was something concrete that I was doing and that I was good at. And sure, even with Lulu at school, I would still have Klay with me a few more years. But soon he'd go, too, and then what would be my purpose every day from 8:00 a.m. to 2:20 p.m.? I had no clue. And yet any time Kayla brought up the idea of me going back to work at that point, I just acted like it was too far away to think about and changed the subject. Our jokes about my trophy-husband status notwithstanding, she'd fallen in love with me when I'd had big dreams of corporate success, and now I was relying on her to support all of us. I knew it, and she knew it, but I couldn't bring myself to say out loud that I'd come to prefer it that way.

"Can you two say bye-bye?" I said, looking over my shoulder to the back seat.

"Bye," Lulu said in a voice that only I could hear. Klay sounded like he was sucking on his hand.

"Aww, have fun! Bye, Lulu! Bye, Klay!"

"Have a good one," I said as I started to pull forward.

We had gone approximately seven feet when Lulu asked, "Daddy, can we watch?"

I sighed. The trip through the drive-through had been so easy.

"Not in the car, Lulu. You know that."

"My friend *Bird's* parents let *her* watch TV in the car."

Yeah, your friend Bird's parents also named their daughter Bird. "That's fine. It's just not something that we do."

Before my lie about the Lizzo lyrics, convincing Lulu that the screen in my minivan was just a shiny blackboard that we could never, ever use because "chalk makes Daddy sneeze" had been my greatest act of parental deception. Like I said, though, they're little lie detectors, and the day she finally called me out on it, I'd resigned myself to years of fighting over how mean I was.

I've got a real thing about screen time.

"But you *never* let us watch!"

"Watch doggies?" Klay added hopefully.

"No, Klay, we're not watching doggies. And Lulu, you just watched last night."

"That didn't count! That was Mommy's idea!"

"That literally makes no sense."

We litigated all the way to the playground. On most days it would've taken almost 10 minutes to get there, but the two of them harmonizing on their whining was enough to convince me to drive by the old Scrub building, a route I typically avoided, to cut the trip down to 6.

It had been months since I'd gone by there, and seeing it never failed to make me wonder how different my life might have been had Janice never sold.

Because I'm not going to lie: I did miss parts of working sometimes. Not toothbrushes specifically—I don't think that would be possible—but just the going in and making plans and getting stuff done. And while on the whole I'd say kids are a far superior brand of human being than their grown-up counterparts—I have yet to see a 30-year-old find their life's calling splashing in a puddle, for instance—there really is no substitute for regular conversation with other adults you like or, short of that, don't hate. I mean, the day I sold Janice and the finance people on moving to 100 percent recycled packaging, even though it would cost a little more, I felt like I had accomplished something meaningful. With parenting, you often have to satisfy yourself with smaller victories—or just not losing too badly.

"Lulu—seriously, no throwing the mulch!" I'd said this at least four times in the three minutes since we'd arrived at the playground.

"I'm *not* throwing mulch, Daddy!"

"Oh really? Then what're you doing?"

"I'm putting it back in its spot."

"Aah. And I suppose your brother isn't trying to eat it so much as he's checking for indications of dry rot."

"What's . . . incations?"

"In-*di*-cations are signs for something. Like that smell coming out of Klay's diaper is an *indication* I need to change him. Dude, Klay, drop it." I stopped. "Great—now I'm talking to you like a dog."

"Doggie? Where doggie?"

"No, Klay, no doggie. Just cool it with the mulch, okay?"

"Daddy."

"I mean, it can't taste good. It's wood covered in dirt."

"Daddy."

"And that one has bird sh . . . poop on it. Okay, we're putting this down now, bud," I said, scooping him up.

"Daddy."

"What, Lulu?"

"What's *cool it*?"

"You're five. You don't need to tell anyone to cool it."

"I'm five and a half!"

"My mistake."

Being a stay-at-home parent is like this paradox: on the one hand, you're never alone, because your kids always need something, but on the other, it's easy to feel completely isolated. I had tried asking my mom about that a few times because she had stayed home with me and my brother. But there was being thrown off by the idea of a man taking care of his own children, and then there was my mom. Not that she ever said it directly.

"You mean *you* give her her bath?" she had asked over the phone when Lulu was about six months old.

"Uh-huh."

"By yourself?"

"Uh, who else do you think is here?"

My dad was even worse. I was pretty sure he just told his friends I was self-employed. Or doing time. The only thing better than your boss saying into a camera that you have no balls was guessing your father was thinking the same thing.

I was in no place to complain, though. I had two awesome kids (mulch issues aside), a rock star of a wife, and an 801-day streak of not wearing a tie. Life was good. I didn't even have emergency cigarettes anymore. Although my firstborn starting school all day did make me wonder if I should pick up a pack.

"Hey, aren't you that Chocsplosion! guy . . . you know, from the fire?"

Plus by then, I was only getting called "Chocsplosion! guy" maybe once a week. Two times, tops. These were the perils of the video continuing to make the rounds thanks to World Chocolate Day and the equally necessary National Chocolate Day.

The kids and I had moved to the swings. Lulu was 75 percent self-powered at that point, so I was pushing Klay and his percolating diaper in one of the three little baby bucket swings with the leg cutouts, and the mom who had recognized me had her daughters in the other two.

"Yup, that's me," I said over the rhythmic squeaking of the chains. Sometimes I denied it because there are only so many times you can relive the story with yet another complete stranger who feels entitled to ask you about it. But this woman was dealing with twins who couldn't have been more than 18 months, so it was the least I could do.

"Amazing," she said with a laugh. I just smiled and kept pushing.

"I hope this isn't weird," she continued after about three more back-and-forths of the swings. I glanced at her, and she was blushing a little. "But our senior year of college, my husband went as you for Halloween. He even did the caramel."

"That's charming," I said in a way I hoped made it clear I wanted to push in silence.

"So what do you do now?" she asked.

I had long since lost track of the number of people who had assumed there was no way the dad at the playground—or the grocery store or the zoo or the Chipotle—could possibly be the one who stayed home with his kids. I usually just shrugged it off. But that Halloween story had sapped all the goodwill she had accrued via her twin toddlers.

"Uh, this," I deadpanned, motioning in the general direction of my two swinging children.

"Oh." It surprised her, but she recovered quickly. "Do you, like, like it?"

"Yeah, it's good overall. I mean, it has its moments."

"Tell me about it. My husband's always like, 'I wish *I* got to just hang out at the park today.' I think he thinks they magically entertain themselves while I sit on a bench texting or something."

"Husbands," I joked, and she laughed again.

"What does yours do?" she asked, taking a break from pushing to adjust her ponytail. I couldn't tell if she was making an assumption about my sexual orientation because I was a stay-at-home dad or simply responding to my choice of the word *husbands*. It was probably the latter, but the sociocultural dynamics of the playground can get pretty twisty. Just like the slides.

"Wife, actually," I said. "She's a senior partner at Elder and Berry." I got proud of Kayla all over again whenever I said it, just like I did every time the three of us waved goodbye to her in the mornings.

"The accounting firm?"

"Yup."

"Wow, impressive. And, you know, cool of you."

"Cool of me what?"

She was working the two swings simultaneously now. "You know. To let her do all that."

"I don't *let* her do anything. She's my wife."

"You know what I mean. A lot of guys would have a hard time staying home while their wife worked. Especially a big job like that."

"Yeah, I guess. We've set a real high bar as a gender."

She laughed one more time. "Wait until I tell Kurt I met Chocsplosion! guy. And that he's hilarious."

"It's Jack, by the way," I said, right as her phone rang, prompting her to turn away from her kids and loudly answer: "Oh my God, Clare—you'll never guess who I'm standing next to at the playground!"

I looked over at my daughter, whose swinging motion had become an aimless drift.

"All right, Lulu—I need to change Klay on one of the benches, so why don't you go on the slide now."

"No thank you, Daddy." She had a real knack for being polite while basically telling you to go to hell. I would've respected it if it weren't directed at me.

I lifted Klay up and succeeded in getting only one of his feet stuck in the leg hole. "Okay, well, take your last swings, and then we're going to go over there by the benches."

"I don't *want* to take my last swings."

I could ratchet up to scary-dad voice and demand that Lulu follow me across the playground, which in theory would reinforce that she couldn't pick and choose when to listen. This was likely to cause a meltdown, regardless of whether it succeeded in getting her off the swing. Because in reality, that was still a big if, and if it didn't work, I'd then be faced with the follow-up decision of whether to pick her up and off the swing and give her one more chance to walk on her own, escalating our parent-child arms race to a whole new level in the process.

So what about acquiescence? What if I caved this time and let her stay on the swings? It would be a dangerous precedent to set, but I didn't let her get away with *whatever* she wanted. Just look at our fight in the car on the way over.

"Fine," I said with just enough edge to make it clear she wasn't winning. "You can keep swinging. I'm going to take your brother and change him. You can come over when you're done."

"But I don't want to swing *by myself!*"

And screaming.

I sat Klay down next to me on a bench and dug my changing pad, wipes, and a new diaper out of my bag. By the time I had him on his back, I noticed I couldn't hear Lulu crying anymore, so I did a quick scan to make sure she was still there. She was—not on the swings, but over near some bushes, which, whatever. She wasn't screaming. That was a win.

My attention turned back to Klay, who was grinning like he was holding on to the best secret of his life. Which could mean only one thing: I was going to need extra wipes.

"Daddy," Lulu said, appearing out of nowhere at my side when the cleanup was basically done.

"Lulu."

"I can't find my underwear."

"What do you mean, you can't find your underwear?"

"I can't find my underwear."

"What underwear?"

"*My* underwear!"

I hadn't secured the diaper yet and held it in place with my hand as I looked up at her for the first time since she'd come over. My face was pinching itself inward, trying to squeeze my brain into comprehension.

"You mean the underwear you were wearing?"

"Uh-huh."

Before I could ask another pointless question, I was interrupted. But not by Lulu, and not by Klay or Kurt's wife. It was a man's voice.

"No way—Jack Parker? Is that you?"

I didn't need to see his face to know who it was. Not even after all those years.

Chad Henson.

CHAPTER 3

Here's all you need to know about Chad Henson: he sucked.

All right, so that's not fair. You deserve to know all the reasons why he sucked. But first I needed to know something for myself:

"What are you doing here?" I asked, sitting Klay up and putting my things away.

"Ha, great to see you, too, Jack!" he laughed, flashing a smile that was as good as any we had ever put in a Scrub ad. He had had it even when we were in high school, and I knew for a fact that he had never suffered through braces to get it. No acne, either.

Reason number one for the sucking.

"Yeah, sorry," I said. "It's just been a while. And, you know, you live, like, across the country." We didn't follow each other on anything, but maybe a year before I had seen a post online of him and his wife on the beach during this ridiculous sunset, which he captioned with "Just another perfect night in Malibu #datenight #blessed."

Reading it felt like being bathed in body spray.

His smile grew even bigger. "Not anymore—we moved!"

I think I stopped breathing for a second. It was basically dread apnea. Chad didn't notice. Because of course he didn't.

"Cassie and I wanted to be closer to our parents. For us and for the kids."

"Your parents live here?" I asked, barely above a whisper. Kayla's mom was in Albuquerque. My parents were just under four hours away, in South Haven, Michigan, where they had retired right on the lake. Either would have been an acceptable destination for the Hensons. So would Mars.

"No, they're still back home. Same house, actually. But a two-hour drive is a lot better than a four-hour flight. So when Cassie got offered a job here, we decided to sell my startup, take the plunge, and move back to the Midwest. She just started yesterday. Isn't that awesome?"

He paused, I thought maybe to locate his kids. Mine were taking it easy on me at the moment, Klay sucking his hand again and Lulu returning to the bushes. But Chad wasn't looking for anyone. He was doing this thing. An unmistakably Chad thing.

I had first observed it the fall of our sophomore year, when we were up against each other for class president. I hadn't had a burning desire to run, but my dad had pushed me to because he had been student council president when he was in high school and said it would look good on my college applications.

The forensics teacher thought it would be great if we had a town hall–style debate where the other students got to ask us questions. And J. D. Briggs stood up and went—I'll never forget this—"Would you support making all tests optional?"

I laughed because I assumed it was a joke. Because needless to say, changing the *entire school's* grading policy was well beyond the scope of the *sophomore class president's* realm of influence. I knew that. Everyone else knew that. I'm pretty sure even J. D. knew that. But Chad put on this really thoughtful expression where he squinted his eyes and kind of stroked his chin and started doing this little nod, like he was really mulling it over, before launching into this speech about how anything was possible if we worked together, the absurdity almost spilling out of his ears.

He won the election. And throughout the rest of high school, whenever he needed to convince you of his sincerity or just wanted to play dumb, he would bust out that squint-stroke-nod thing before talking. I had seen it on at least a dozen more occasions by the time we graduated.

I was seeing it again on the playground.

"You know something, Jack. I think . . . I think Cassie's at *your* old company." I felt the blood drain from my face. "The one before *the fire*, I mean. It was Mouth, right?"

Hey, terrific—he had seen the video. Which meant he knew *exactly* where I had worked. That shady, girlfriend-stealing mother—

"Daddy, I found them!"

"Daddy's talking to an old . . . Daddy's talking to someone, Lulu," I said, trying to wave her off without looking down. It was a standard parenting move that allowed me to confirm that Chad's smug smile never left his smug face.

"But, *Daddy*, I found them." She was pulling on my hand now.

"Found what?" I sighed before instantly regretting it. Please be something else, please be something else.

"My *underwear*!"

I was looking down at my daughter now, but I could practically feel Chad's eyes enlarging.

"Don't you want to know *where* I found them?" she asked proudly.

"Not really, no."

"That squirrel has them." She pointed toward the bushes.

I'd been worried I hadn't prepared Lulu enough for kindergarten—her *elementary* school would have more kids than my *high* school—but apparently some of that energy should've gone toward teaching her to keep a respectful distance from wildlife.

"I think that's our cue . . . ," I started. I never got to the "to go" because she was gone again, headed for the fort next to the slide. Reluctantly, I turned back to Chad.

"Looks like you've got your hands full," he said.

"Ha, yeah. And yes, it was . . ."

"Go with Lu," Klay said, twisting himself around and desperately scootching to get off the bench. I picked him up and set him down on the ground, and he zigzagged away to chase after her.

"Yeah, Mouth," I tried again. "That's where I was. But really Scrub for most of it."

"What's Scrub?"

"It was a company that got bought by Mouth. You know, right before." No way he was letting me off that easy.

"The fire?"

"Yes, Chad, the fire."

"I'm so sorry about all that, BTW." He literally said *BTW*. And he didn't look very sorry. "Especially since *everybody* saw it. In a weird, roundabout way, it kind of reminded me of what happened in high school."

Wow, any excuse to bring that story up, huh?

In reality, there were several contenders for the title of what "happened" in high school. But I didn't have to guess what he was talking about. No one in our class would've.

For instance, it wasn't about the clown costume. That was a hazing thing for the soccer team. I'd had to wear it to school for an entire day and ask at least three girls for their phone numbers. Even though Chad and I were the same year, he had been the only one to make varsity as a freshman, and by the time I got there as a junior, he was a captain and the ringleader for this sort of thing. But as obnoxious as it was, I certainly hadn't been the first or the last kid to get hazed at Lakeside High School.

What "happened" wasn't about Maria Flores either. My girlfriend for almost all of junior year, she'd used our first slow dance at prom to tell me she had been hooking up with—guess who?—Chad for two months. She left with him that night and dated him most of our senior year, until she caught him with someone else. But despite getting that news in a public place surrounded by all of our classmates, I hadn't started the uncontrollable, full-body dry-heave sobbing until I was well off school grounds.

Then there was the election for senior class president the following fall. Chad had won every year since we were freshmen, and I still remembered Dad's reaction two years before, when I had come home and told him I lost. He'd looked like someone coming to grips with the term *safety school* for the first time.

But senior year was different. I was reasonably well liked, and the Maria story had dulled Chad's shine with enough people that I had a real shot at beating him. Then, a week before the election, this rumor started. Had I heard? Chad had cancer. Or Chad's mom had cancer. Or maybe it was Chad's dog. The point was: Chad. Cancer. There was a not insignificant number of people who thought I should drop out of the race and let him have it because of "what he was going through."

And despite the Maria thing and wanting to prove something (still not sure what) to my dad, I was one of them. I hated Chad, but I didn't hate him that much. So in the end, he ran unopposed. He was our class president all the way through high school. And curiously, he didn't set the record straight that he and everyone in his family, including his dog, was perfectly fine until after all the votes had been counted. By then, though, everybody was so happy that he was okay, what did it matter if the rumors hadn't been true?

I never found out for sure where they had started, but when I congratulated him that day, he'd smiled at me and winked. "You're too nice to ever win anything, Jack." I had spent years telling myself that wasn't true until Sidney more or less said the same thing when he fired me. Ever since, I'd doubted I had what it took to have the sort of career I was supposed to want.

But Chad and I had been the only witnesses to that postelection conversation, and a number of people actually commended me on what a decent thing I had done. So yes, his cancer gambit was sketchy, and yes, I had some emotional scarring from feeling like a chump, but what "happened" in high school? No, that was something else altogether, which, amazingly, was the one thing that hadn't involved Chad.

"Well," I said, "lucky for me, I've never met anyone before or since who possessed the wit of Tripp Zelich."

Tripp's coup de grâce had been switching the script the notoriously absentminded Mr. Lyons used to read everyone's names at graduation with one where I was listed as "Jizz Parker," which was how he announced me to an auditorium full of people. Including my 80-year-old grandma.

"God, Tripp," Chad said, shaking his head. "Why did he call you that again?"

"Because—and this is a direct quote from sophomore year—'I'd call you Jackoff, but Jizz is way funnier.'"

Chad tried, unconvincingly, to smother a laugh. "It kind of is. But everyone chanting 'Jizz! Jizz! Jizz!' when you walked across the stage to get your diploma—didn't see that coming."

"Yeah, well, I talked to a few people afterward who thought I was in on it, so . . ." I trailed off as his last sentence caught up to me. "Wait, what'd you say?"

"About what?"

"The chant. Did you say you didn't see it coming?"

"Uh-huh." He took a sip from the travel coffee mug he'd been holding the whole time. "Totally spontaneous."

"But . . . you knew about the other part?"

"Mr. Lyons? Oh yeah. You didn't know that? I mean, it was Tripp's idea, but he didn't have any way to get to the list of names. So I was the one who switched out the real one with the Jizz Parker one—man, even you have to admit that was funny. I swapped the lists after I gave my speech." He stopped, I thought maybe to apologize or at the very least to acknowledge this was all news to me. "Because, you know, I was class president."

I couldn't say anything. Like, physically. No words would come.

It wasn't so much that I was shocked he had masterminded the whole plot that had my nonna asking me postceremony what *jizz* meant, a question my little brother, Scottie, in eighth grade at the time, was only too happy to answer on my behalf. If anything, I was disappointed in myself that I hadn't pieced that together in the course of the previous 20 years.

No, it was his complete and utter lack of concern in telling me. His arrogance. His nonchalance. His disregard. Everything about him, from his tone to the way he was sipping that coffee again, was a big ol' middle finger pointed at my entire existence. Like I should just be so *thrilled* to have the startup king of Malibu talking to little old me right here on the playground—and on a workday, no less! Guys like Chad and Sidney—they'd played the game and won, made something of themselves, and we were all supposed to get down at the altar and worship at the feet of their success. Whether they were terrible human beings or not was beside the point; they *mattered* in the ways I didn't, apparently.

"Jack?"

My eyes drifted back to his face. I was tempted to take a swing at him even if his jawline could probably break my fist.

"I asked what you and your wife do," he said. "By the looks of things, you've been at this stay-at-home-dad thing a lot longer than me."

Wait.

"You're a . . . what?"

"A stay-at-home dad too! Newly minted since I sold the company. We just didn't need the two incomes anymore. But clearly I'm not battle tested like you."

"Huh?"

"Well, for starters, you seem unfazed by how long you've been holding that dirty diaper."

I looked down at my right hand. Sure enough, there it was. I took a step to the side, tossed it into a trash can, and got a pump of hand sanitizer.

"Right." I was still reeling. "Uh, well, yeah, I guess I've stayed home since Lulu was born," I said, leaving out the months before, when Kayla was pregnant and I initially spent my days hunting for jobs. Any time I saw something that looked like it might be a fit, I'd come up with a reason it wasn't, when the truth was I was scared my best wouldn't be good enough. "And Kayla, my wife, she's a senior partner at this accounting firm, Elder and Berry."

"Hey, good for her. Are they local?"

"Kinda. They've got a few offices throughout the state. I think they're up to, like, five now, with a couple more coming." Their business was really taking off, which was great, even if it meant we were seeing each other less than we'd like.

"That's super. Sounds like the company Cassie was at. You know, before Mouth recruited her and put her over an *entire* region."

What an ass. The digs at me were one thing, but insulting my wife was enough to snap my brain fully into motion for the first time since he had told me they moved.

"Yes," I said, "and as everyone knows, every international company always assigns its best people to the Midwest. Has she made the trip to Cleveland yet? It's the Malibu of the Rust Belt."

I'd like to think he got the message, but the small grin that crept across his face suggested he knew he had found a spot he could provoke me with and that he was filing it away for future use.

"Well, I can tell you one thing, and I'm sure you'll agree: getting to stay home with your child is such a blessing."

"Where *are* your kids?" I asked, realizing I hadn't seen them once since he'd showed up next to me.

"Kid, actually. Crispin's an only child. We really wanted to focus on him." He let that linger for a good couple of seconds before adding, "Not that your two kids don't seem great, though."

"Klay, stop biting me!" Lulu yelled from under the slide. "Daddy, Klay's biting me!"

"Klay, stop biting your sister!" I yelled back, then looked at Chad, who was enjoying our exchange immensely. "You were saying? About Crisper?"

"Cris-*pin*," he corrected. He was clearly annoyed, which was the point. "He's around here somewhere. We don't believe in a lot of direct supervision, per se. We find it stifles self-actualized expression."

It was my turn to laugh. At last.

"So wait: you only had one kid so you could focus just on him, but then you don't watch him because it will make him less . . . what was the word you used . . . self-actualized?"

"You know what I mean, Jack," he said with a condescending smirk.

"I do know one thing," I said, grabbing my diaper bag and slinging it over my shoulder like it was filling me with a superpower. "I know that you're just as full of it now as you were twenty years ago."

He made this dismissive *pfft* sound, like I was accusing him of having a second head or a conscience.

"C'mon, Jack. You're not actually mad about all that stuff, are you? We're dads now. High school is, like, ancient history."

"You're right, Chad. High school is ancient history. And you know what the best part about that is? The part that you still haven't figured out?" I leaned in toward him. "You don't get to matter anymore. Like, at all. Now go find your kid."

I didn't wait for a response. I just turned and walked. When the Underpantsless Wonder and her brother, Bitey McStinkpants, saw me coming, they got excited and shouted, "Daddy!"

And I have to say, all of a sudden, I was feelin' good, as well.

CHAPTER 4

"Why don't we do this more often, again?"

"Because collectively we have four kids under the age of ten."

It was a Saturday night in July, a month after Chad's and my regrettable high school reunion at the playground, and Kayla and I were with our best couple friends at dinner. Kayla and Brooke had been each other's work wives for years, and sometime after Kayla's first maternity leave ended, the two of them decided not only they but also their spouses needed to be friends. The first time we had dinner, Brooke's wife, Tori, and I spent a half an hour feeling out the dynamic. But by the second glass of wine, I'd known on a fundamental level that I liked being around these people—even if, as Tori had just reminded me, our kids made it difficult to get together more than once every three months or so.

It also didn't hurt that the first and only time the video had ever come up, Brooke had said, "Screw that guy—Chocsplosion! is delicious."

"Oh, babe—you've got to tell them about Chad," Kayla said as the appetizer arrived.

"They don't want to hear about Chad. Actually, let me rephrase: *I* don't want to hear about Chad. As in I don't want to hear the words about Chad coming out of my own mouth."

"This is getting more intriguing by the second," Brooke said, getting the cheese plate started.

"Can't we just talk about our kids slowly chipping away at our sense of self-worth? I've got a great story about Lulu questioning whether I really knew how to get to Target yesterday." I preferred to focus on anecdotes like this rather than my brewing identity crisis as a stay-at-home parent to two kids, 50 percent of whom would soon not be needing my services to the same extent as before, potentially freeing me up to start pursuing a career I had no interest in resuming.

"In a minute," Tori said. "First: Who's Chad?"

"Jack's high school nemesis," Kayla interjected a little too quickly. "And spoiler: he's here."

Tori started surreptitiously scanning the restaurant. Brooke made no effort to hide that that was what she was doing.

"No, not *here* here," I said, resigned to the fact that I was beaten. "Like, in town. He and his wife and their kid just moved here."

Brooke's face scrunched in confusion. "But you guys didn't grow up around here, right?"

"No. It's an amazing, fantastic coincidence. And that it was a job at Mouth that brought them here is just the secret sauce on top of the crapburger that is his renewed presence in my life."

Tori and Kayla laughed while Brooke shook her head and gestured at her wife.

"This one," Brooke said, "tried to toss some Mouth toothpaste into our cart last week, and I was like, 'Put it back—we're not doing that to Jack.'"

"You're a good woman, Brooke Owens," I said, grabbing a piece of cheese and a supposedly baked-from-scratch cracker that bore a suspicious resemblance to a Triscuit.

"So wait," Tori said. "Did he get the job at Mouth, or did his wife?"

"His wife. Cassie."

Brooke rolled her eyes. "Oh God. *Cassie and Chad.* I'm imagining staged photos on the beach and lots of linen."

I almost choked on my gruyère laughing.

"Says the woman who ordered the forty-dollar cheese plate," Tori joked, which prompted Brooke to teasingly flick her off. "Anyway, pre-conceived mental pictures aside . . ."

"It was a strikingly accurate image," I noted before clearing my throat.

"Sure. But what elevated this guy to nemesis status? I mean, I doubt he was taking all those staged beach photos growing up in Indiana."

Now that I was in it, they weren't going to get the abridged version. I laid it all out, from the girlfriend stealing and what happened at graduation up through him trying to troll me about Kayla's job on the playground. For the most part, I delivered it as a monologue, with Brooke and Tori listening and shaking their heads and/or offering short exclamations like "No!" and "He didn't!" at all the spots you'd hope your friends would.

My wife, of course, had heard all of this before and reheard various pieces countless other times. She liked to tease me about being a grown man who would freely admit to having a nemesis, but whenever she had listened to it all strung together like that, she started to feel bad for me all over again. This night was no different. And it was always the same story that took her over the edge.

"No, seriously, let that sink in," she said after the server had walked away from putting our entrées down. "He pretended he had *cancer.* To win an election. *A high school election.* That's, like, borderline psychotic."

On previous occasions when I had felt the need to clarify that the rumor's specifics had been hard to pin down, Kayla had waved me off, so I let it go this time. And as I thought about it over my risotto, I wasn't sure why I had tried to correct her before. She was supporting me, and there was no reason I shouldn't support her. Because for Kayla, who had lost her dad to cancer when she was 12, the precise details of that rumor weren't what mattered. Chad had crossed a bright-red line and had done so in the name of screwing with her husband. She didn't care that she hadn't known either of us back then or that she still had never met him. He was irredeemable.

And in the end, that's all you can really ask for from your significant other when it comes to a high school nemesis.

When I had finished telling all the Chad stories, the table was silent.

"Well, seems safe to say we're dealing with a Hall of Fame prick here," Brooke said after several seconds had passed. "I mean, it's not like your entire school shunning you after you tell them you're gay. But still."

I felt my stomach tighten, and the feeling quickly shot up into my face too. What was wrong with me, talking about how hard this guy had made high school for me—a straight white male? It wasn't like I had had to come out to anyone.

"Brooke, I had no idea. I'm really sorry. I wouldn't have . . ."

She busted out laughing, and Tori pushed her lightly on the shoulder. "If by 'entire school' she means three girls she didn't like to begin with, then yes, Brooke was shunned by her whole high school."

"I still maintain Lyndsey Shelton had a thing for me," Brooke said, pointing a forkful of her salmon at Tori.

"So I've heard," Tori said. "But this Chad thing really is fascinating. Like, my best friend from middle school through senior year got completely weirded out when I told her I was gay. And on the one hand, it was devastating. But on the other, at least I knew *why* she was being like that."

"Because she was an asshole," Brooke said, suddenly serious. This was her hating her wife's nemesis sight unseen, and it occurred to me that this might be one of the most telling indicators of the strength of a relationship.

"True, although I don't think I thought about it like that at the time. I was just hurt. But again, it wasn't a mystery what was going on. With this Chad guy, though, he kept going after you and kept going after you. And yet he wasn't so much pushing you around as he was sabotaging you."

"Not sure I see how that distinction makes it any better," I said. "Either way, it felt random. Unprompted."

"Not unlike a CEO having a visceral reaction to his popular manager's choice in candy bar," Tori said.

"Right. Like, what about me is so fundamentally disagreeable that my mere existence invites that kind of treatment?"

I stopped, surprised at the emotion that roused from somewhere inside me. Because I heard them again: Too nice. No balls. They were deemed winners while I was a punch line. Chad reappearing after all those years had made that impossible to ignore.

Kayla put her hand on my thigh, and Tori waited several seconds before continuing.

"It's because he's insecure around you, Jack. You're a threat."

"That's what I've always said to him," Kayla said.

I laughed. "Chad Henson? Insecure? Chad Henson hasn't been insecure a day in his life. And that's a big part of the problem." Just the day before, he had captioned a video of himself doing crunches in a tank top with *#dadbod*. (I still wasn't following him, and on principle, I refused to start, but now that every day brought a small yet nonzero chance of running into him again, not stalking his timeline would've been gross negligence.)

"I'm with Jack on this," Brooke said. "Sometimes people just suck. And this guy is clearly one of them." She waved for the server to come over, and I was grateful for the distraction. "So I propose we do a shot to celebrate."

"Uh, to celebrate?" I asked.

"Yes, to celebrate. To celebrate that this town is big enough that you haven't seen him since and that he and Cassie are undoubtedly sending their child to some bougie private school that is in a completely different universe than the one inhabited by folks like us—the many, the proud, the just disengaged enough: the public school parents."

Tori gave her a side-eye. "I noticed you left out that it's one of the best school districts in the state, so maybe hold off on our Nobel Prizes."

"Nevertheless," Brooke pressed on, "we shall revel in our unrivaled awesomeness."

"But shots?" Kayla asked. "I don't think a place like this even does shots. Plus I've got to drive to Springfield tomorrow morning. I'd prefer not to be hungover."

I took a quick look at her, but she didn't notice. I could've sworn her trip to Springfield wasn't until Monday. She had been traveling more and more, though, so it was getting easier to lose track. Or maybe my brain had just been trying to will her departure back a day. I hadn't told Kayla, but earlier in the week, Lulu had asked me if Mommy would be there for the first day of school. It was still almost a month away and hard to know, so I'd said yes and hoped for both Lulu's and my sake I'd be proven right. Because we were both going to need her.

"Ugh, fine," Brooke said as Michael, the server, arrived. She turned to meet his expectant gaze. "Can we get some dessert menus? Oh, and coffee." She looked back to the three of us. "Unless the rest of the table is worried the caffeine will keep them up past their bedtimes, that is."

"Actually, I think I will do some decaf," Tori said to him.

"Oh for God's sake, Tor," Brooke said as Michael smiled and left to retrieve the menus. "Decaf? Really? What happened to the woman I married?"

"Is she like this at work too?" Tori asked Kayla, pretending to ignore the question.

Kayla laughed. "I think you know the answer to that."

Brooke was clearly amused but still undeterred. "What possible reason could you have for ordering decaffeinated coffee?"

"Well," Tori said, "I was going to offer to be the one to get up with the kids tomorrow so you could sleep in. But you know, if you'd rather I stay up later tonight and let you deal with them at six in the morning, just say the word."

Brooke's face softened, and her voice got quiet. "Sleep in? Really?"

"Uh-huh."

"You are a saint among women, and I withdraw my objection," she said, giving Tori a peck on the lips.

"Mm-hmm. And don't you forget it."

Kayla grabbed my hand under the table, and the rest of the night went on in much the same mood as it had before. At least that was my intention. Kayla had a habit of seeing through me, though.

"So you got pretty quiet after dinner," she said in the car on the way home.

"Oh yeah?" I asked. I didn't have Chad's chops when it came to playing dumb, but I couldn't decide if I wanted to do this right as she was about to leave for four days—which, up until an hour before, I had thought would only be three. Four days—that was a first.

"Yeah," she said, peeking at me from behind the wheel. "Did the decaf-coffee thing strike a nerve?"

She was trying to be playful, and I quickly realized how not in the mood I was. "Something like that."

"Anything you want to talk about?"

I sighed—as much from my inability to keep it to myself as from my exasperation with the actual situation.

"I didn't think you were going to Springfield until Monday," I said as I stared out the passenger window.

"It was supposed to be Monday, but then it got bumped up. Remember? I told you last week."

There was no doubt in my mind she had, even if I couldn't remember. Kayla didn't forget things like that, and she always made a point of telling me as soon as she found out. And in the big picture of our lives, there was no difference between Sunday morning and Monday morning.

But in the confined world of our car on that Saturday night, anticipating yet another day of solo parenting—of having to be responsible and fun and firm and nurturing and present and patient and, most importantly, never alone, not even when trying to go to the bathroom—in that moment, I felt completely overwhelmed. And when you're overwhelmed, you say dumb things.

"Was that the night you didn't get home until seven or the night you missed bedtime altogether?"

Kayla started and stopped a few times. "That's really not fair, Jack," she said finally.

"You're right." I still wasn't looking at her. "It's not."

"We knew the promotion to senior partner was going to mean more work. And at least one more trip per month, specifically. Especially this first year."

"You're right. We did."

"We also agreed that the extra money would be helpful. That has to come from somewhere, right? And the last time we talked, you said you weren't ready to go back to work yet. Has that changed?"

"No. It hasn't." The way I was acting had as much to do with my uncertainty about my own direction as it did with her schedule. Not that I managed to express that.

"So—what?" Kayla asked.

"It just sucks. That's all."

"I don't know what I'm supposed to say to that."

Neither did I.

CHAPTER 5

Brooke and Tori had tried to prepare me for the Willow Road Elementary "All In for Alpacas!" Parent and Guardian Welcome (Back) Orientation. What they told me could be boiled down to "No, really—their mascot is an alpaca."

I was still at a loss why an elementary school needed a mascot in the first place, but when the teacher at the double doors of the gym greeted me with a "Welcome to the herd!" with no trace of irony, I realized our friends had given me a far better sense of the place than I had thought.

Speaking of friends, Tori waved to me from near a table covered in green-and-white folders as soon as I walked in.

"There's the newbie," she said with a smile. Her and Brooke's two daughters were going into third and first grade, and I couldn't imagine how I'd feel about all the herd metaphors by the time Lulu and Klay were that old.

"How did the teacher at the door know I was new?"

"Your name tag—new parents get green." I looked down and saw that she was right. Around us, there were a whole bunch of plain white ones.

"Where's yours?" I asked.

"I'm not big into the whole 'name tag' thing."

"So this was optional?" I said, pulling mine up between my index finger and thumb.

"Depends on who you ask. C'mon, let's get you your folder."

I grabbed the one that said "Lulu Parker" off the table and, a little alarmed by its heft, followed Tori toward the back to find seats. It was 5:50 p.m., and things didn't start until 6:00, but the rows were pretty crowded.

After we sat down, I opened up the folder and started flipping through. Classroom rules. Playground rules. Lunchtime rules. School rules. Teacher bio. Principal bio. A history of the school. The Wikipedia entry on (I kid you not) alpacas.

I closed it back up. Not because I didn't want to know more about where I was going to be sending my kid every day. I absolutely did. Probably too much. And that was why—and this is going to sound stupid—holding it all there, in my hands, knowing that I wouldn't be a part of Lulu's days in quite the same way as before, I just . . . I don't know. It was hitting me hard.

Obviously, there was a piece of me that was looking forward to no longer being outnumbered every morning while Lulu would be at school and it would only be Klay and me. Fights over how much screen time is too much screen time have a way of making that appealing. Plus Klay and I had never had that same one-on-one time Lulu and I had those first three years, so that would be fun and different.

But yeah, different. I couldn't believe she was ready to go to school five days a week. The terror of that first day when Kayla had gone back to work and left me on my own with a baby who was basically still a newborn wasn't a distant memory, and the subsequent discovery, over the months and then years that followed, that, all right, I was pretty decent at this dad thing wasn't just edifying as a human being; it was what had brought me back from the fire. I wouldn't go as far as saying it saved my life, but it had retaught me how to think of myself as something other than a failure.

Lulu taking this step away from me, it was the way things were supposed to go. And she was going to kindergarten, not packing up to move out of the house or take a cross-country road trip with her freshman-year roommate who "only *smells* like pot, Dad." But it was a step nonetheless, and her absence for those six-plus hours every day would be a shot across the bow, reminding me that the demand for whatever skill I had at taking care of her and Klay was only going to wane over time.

Staring at the outside of that folder with the name that we had given that little 6-pound, 11-ounce bundle, I wondered why there wasn't some way to have your kids always need you without them being so needy all the time.

I suppose there's more than one paradox when it comes to parenting.

"How are things with you and Kayla?" Tori asked.

"Uh . . . good?" I said, confused by the question but thankful for the opportunity to think about something else.

"Brooke told me you had a fight that night after we all had dinner."

"Man, they really do talk about everything, don't they?"

Things had still been tense when Kayla and I went to bed that night, and they were only marginally better when she left for Springfield the next morning. We didn't fight often, but we had more since her promotion to senior partner seven months earlier, and the fights invariably involved her job in some way. As we had covered on our drive home, me going back to work would've given us two incomes and eased the pressure on her to keep rising through the ranks. Part of me felt guilty I wasn't providing her that, but another part questioned whether she wanted me to. Kayla liked her job. She didn't want to stand still or move backward in it. She was always looking forward. And I understood. It's how I had been too.

When Kayla was in Springfield, we'd talked the night before she got home. I mean, we talked every night when she was gone, but this was an actual talk, without children or dishes or deadlines distracting us. I had apologized because I knew I'd been a dick. She'd told me she had made sure she'd be home for Lulu's first day. It had helped, even if it felt like there were some things we still weren't saying. She also hadn't had to do much traveling over the ensuing four weeks, which let us settle into a nice rhythm, and she had been able to come home early enough the night of the orientation that we didn't have to waste a sitter on something as alliterative as "All In for Alpacas!"

It did qualify as a night out for me, though, and as sad as that sounds, I took them wherever I could get them.

"No, we're totally fine," I said. "The traveling just gets to be a lot sometimes, you know?"

"Yeah, it's got to. It's hard enough on us when Brooke goes out of town, and I don't even have the kids during the day. It must feel like an eternity to you."

"I mean, I adore my kids—but exactly. But I also know it's not like Kayla's choosing to be gone, so how frustrated can I really get?" Not frustrated enough to ask my mom to make the drive in to help, I can tell you that. She'd recently suggested I ask Scottie, my little brother turned investment banker, to help me set up an "In Link" account to see who might be hiring.

<You mean LinkedIn?> I'd typed back.

I don't know. Ask your brother.

Tori thought about my question while bending down to dig around in her purse.

"Gum?"

"Sure, thanks," I said, taking a stick of spearmint.

"What I'd say is there's a difference between getting frustrated with Kayla and getting frustrated with the situation, right? There are a lot of cases when the latter is justified, but getting pissed at the person wouldn't be. And it sounds like that's what this was, you getting frustrated with the situation."

"That's probably true. Although I was still kind of a jerk to her about it."

"Well, welcome to marriage."

We both laughed, and then Tori's phone dinged. While she responded to a text, I took another shot at the folder and began skimming the rules particular to Lulu's kindergarten classroom. I was about halfway through, in the midst of what could only be described as an uncomfortably impassioned paragraph about the unforeseen dangers of all non–glue stick adhesives, when a woman who definitely looked like she kept her LinkedIn up to date stepped to the podium.

"Good evening, everyone," she said over the low rumble of a roomful of voices. The mic was turned up too loud, with the feedback serving to help call everyone to attention. She motioned wordlessly toward the back and waited a few seconds before starting again.

"How's that?" She beamed. "Is that better? Good. Now let's try this again: Good evening. My name is Ms. Weekler, and I'm the principal here at Willow Road Elementary. It is my pleasure to welcome you to a new school year at WRE."

About a third of the gym started to applaud, at which point most of the rest of us joined in out of a sense of obligation. You could practically feel the Alpaca Pride™!

I scanned the seats around me for other green name tags but didn't see any; apparently there weren't that many new parents slacking off in the back rows. It did make me feel cooler to be hanging out with the people (a distinct majority of them moms) who had done this before— *cooler* being a highly relative term at elementary school orientation.

Ms. Weekler—I knew her name was Deidre, but good luck not referring to someone as Ms. or Mr. Whoever, even in your own head, when they've introduced themselves that way—started with a brief overview of the school, including the story of how eight years earlier, they had held a school-wide competition to select a mascot and the students had voted for the alpaca in a landslide. It made me feel better to know that if you were going to choose to have your school represented by a creature chiefly known for the usefulness of its hair, at least you had left the choice to the kids themselves. And when Ms. Weekler explained that the other two finalists, also put forward by the kids, had been a guinea pig and bacteria, we all laughed in approval that the electorate had decided wisely.

She then transitioned to telling us "a little bit" about herself, which did not seem like an unreasonable thing to do. I quickly discovered, however, how misplaced my rookie optimism was.

"Wait until she gets to Spain," Tori said under her breath.

I raised my eyebrows, looking for more information, but she just smiled.

Five minutes into Ms. Weekler's junior-year study-abroad experience in Barcelona—which she of course made a point of pronouncing "Bar-theh-lona" every chance she got—I understood all too well.

After Ms. Weekler, it was brief introductions of the teachers, who were behind her on the stage and stood one by one, beginning with the three kindergarten rooms.

"Who did Lulu get?" Tori whispered to me as the three of them waved awkwardly to all of us.

"Uh, Ms. Sandra," I whispered back.

"Oh, good. Both of our girls had her. She's the best."

That was reassuring, even though Tori had no basis for comparison since they hadn't had experience with either of the others. Then again, Ms. Brianne and Ms. Alexa looked like they couldn't have been more than five years removed from college, and I did like the idea of Lulu's first teacher having been at it a little longer. For her part, Lulu was equal parts excited they might have a class pet and nervous she wouldn't be able to remember the teacher's name. Oh, and that we'd never come back to pick her up.

Kindergarten was a real mixed bag.

The teachers stayed standing until all their colleagues had been introduced and then filed offstage to a series of tables around the perimeter of the gym, one for each class. Ms. Weekler encouraged us to visit them when she was done as well as sign up to volunteer in the room.

We, the assembled parents and guardians, began shuffling in our seats and murmuring in anticipation of inundating our kids' new teachers with all sorts of largely irrelevant information, so much so that Ms. Weekler had to call us back to attention.

"I do have one last bit of housekeeping before you head over to the tables," she said once we had quieted back down. "As some of you know, Elena Choi has served as president of the Active Alpaca Parent Board for the past three school years and was elected to a fourth term in June. However, over the summer, Elena's husband, Steven, accepted a job in Boston. He and their daughter, Leslie, are already there and staying with his parents, while Elena will be here another month, taking care of the move."

Several people around us put down their phones for the first time since Ms. Weekler had started talking.

"While we are, of course, happy for the Chois," she continued, "we are also very sad to see them go. But it does mean we have an opening for a new president."

Knowing glances were suddenly bouncing across rows and over the aisle. It appeared elementary school politics were a lot more exciting than I would've given them credit for. Even Tori, who was not someone easily intrigued by parental posturing, perked up in her seat.

"Now, I don't have to tell all of you these are big shoes to fill," Ms. Weekler said. "Elena was our first three-term president in my time as principal and, as I said, was elected to a fourth. What she's accomplished during her time here has been truly extraordinary."

She ran through some of Elena Choi's contributions: There was improved communication between the teachers and parents, facilitated by a monthly coffee. A candy sale that had allowed for the purchase of new playground equipment without making a dent in the school's budget. A revamped end-of-day pickup system that had reduced congestion in the parking lot.

This all sounded well and good enough, but it was pretty obvious Ms. Weekler was playing fast and loose with the term *extraordinary*. It was an elementary school, not the UN.

"For all these reasons," she noted, "we normally look to one of our returning parents to take on this critical role. But a week or so ago, I received a call from a Mr. Henson—Chad Henson, where are . . . oh, there you are. Would you please stand up?"

"Oh my God, Jack," Tori whispered. "That's not . . . is that *the* Chad?"

I didn't answer. Later, she would tell me I looked like I was watching the *Titanic* go down. Not in the movie but in real life. Like if I had been there in 1912 in one of the lifeboats.

"Anyway, Mr. Henson just moved . . ."

"You can call me Chad," he boomed from his seat in the third row. "Mr. Henson is my dad!"

More than a few people laughed at that.

Tori leaned in a few inches. "Okay, so you weren't exaggerating."

"Oh, terrific," said Ms. Weekler. "*Chad* and his wife, Cassie, and their son, Crispin, who will be in kindergarten, moved here this summer from Malibu, *California*. Chad just sold his *very successful* startup company and, with his newfound free time, asked if there was any way his leadership experience might be helpful to me and the school. We only had the chance to speak for a few minutes, but I can already tell he would make a wonderful president. Call it a principal's intuition."

More laughter. I couldn't look away from the two of them, but I couldn't believe what I was seeing either.

"This can't be happening," I finally muttered to Tori, who was a wall of black hair in my peripheral vision. "And can she even do that? Shouldn't she be, like, neutral?"

"Elena is so far up her butt, I think she just wants loyalty."

Ms. Weekler was already onto talking about her plan to formally install Chad as our Patagonia-wearing overlord.

"Elena has graciously agreed to keep serving until she leaves, so we'll hold a special election in late September—although I can't imagine we'll find a more worthy successor than Mr. Hen . . . oops, did it again! I can't imagine we'll find a more worthy successor than *Chad* between now and then."

"Seriously, what the hell?" I whispered to Tori, finally turning to look at her. "Are we in, like, North Korea?"

Her brow furrowed.

"You know . . . the whole dictator-succession . . . thing?"

She nodded in approval. "I'll allow it."

I looked back up to the podium. Ms. Weekler, looking very pleased that her grand plan was now in motion, was wrapping up by assuring us what a godsend Chad would be when it came to not only fundraising but also managing the volunteer activity of all the school's parents. I could already hear him telling us he had picked Chocsplosion! for that year's candy sale and was asking me to head it up because I was the resident expert, and then all these yahoos around me—who seemed anywhere from relieved to happy to have had this decision made for them—laughing right along with him.

So I did something. Something I had never seen coming when I stepped into that gym that night. Something that would alter the course of my life from that moment on.

"Screw it," I said to Tori.

"*Yeeess!*" I heard her draw out as I rose from my folding chair.

"Excuse me, Ms. Weekler?" I hollered. The whole gym turned to face me.

Chad turned to face me.

"Uh, yeah, hi, everyone. My name is Jack Parker, and my daughter is Lulu Parker. Are there any, like, requirements for running for president of the Parents of Alpacas Board?"

No one said a word as they all turned in unison back toward the principal. Except Chad. He was still staring at me, that same grin from the playground creeping across his face.

"Well, welcome, Mr. Parker," Ms. Weekler said into the microphone, adjusting her glasses to size me up, her tone noticeably cooler than it had been 10 seconds before. "It's actually the *Active Alpaca Parent Board*."

"Aah, my mistake. At least I didn't say Guinea Pigs, right?"

That got some laughs, which she did not find amusing.

"You're a new parent, yes, Mr. Parker?"

I was pretty sure a guy two rows in front of me mouthed to his wife: *I think that's the Chocsplosion! guy*, a well-timed reminder of why I hadn't made a habit of putting myself out there the past five or six years.

"I am," I said. With no mic of my own, I basically had to keep shouting everything. That was okay because it helped me hear over my heart, which was pounding with adrenaline.

"Well, as I mentioned before, we don't typically encourage new parents to run for the position of president."

"Uh, Chad's a new parent."

"Yes, that's why I said 'typically.' However, the only formal requirement is that one be a parent or guardian of a Willow Road Elementary student. Which of course Mr. Henson is."

"Ha, you did it again!" Chad said, snapping out of his grin and facing her.

She smiled at him. "So I did. And I think all of you will find *Chad* to be an exceptional candidate. As for you, Mr. Parker, we weren't really looking to solicit nominations tonight. There will be a time and place for that, I can assure you."

"Good to know. In the meantime, I just wanted to make sure everyone here tonight knows."

"Knows what, Mr. Parker?"

I broke eye contact with her and zeroed back in on Chad, who met my stare.

"That Mr. Henson's not running unopposed."

CHAPTER 6

"What're you looking at, babe?" Kayla asked, sinking into the couch next to me, laptop in hand. An episode of *The Office* was on the TV because just letting it play with no intention of stopping, even with the sound turned down, had long been my version of comfort food.

"Pictures of Lulu," I said. I didn't look up from my phone.

Kayla put her head on my shoulder. It was after seven at night, but she still smelled like her shampoo. "Aww, I always loved this one," she said and pointed at the screen. "I still remember your text: 'First trip to the zoo a success despite lack of talking animals.'"

I smiled weakly. "Eleven months old. She . . ." I quickly realized I wasn't going to be able to finish that sentence on the eve of Lulu's first day of school. Kayla could tell and snuggled me for a minute, waiting until I was ready—which I always was, eventually. I was the talker.

"I was up there putting her to bed," I continued, staring off at the TV without really taking any of it in, "and I started counting the years until she leaves for college."

Kayla sat back up. "Oh. So it's all the emotions right now, huh?"

"Uh-huh. And you know, when you think about it, it's not really *that* long. I feel like you just had her, and that was already almost six years ago. And it's only going to speed up now that she's in school."

"Can it speed right through ages thirteen to fifteen? Because in hindsight, I was a real pain in the ass for those three years."

I didn't want to, but I laughed through a sniffle. "You know what I mean," I said. "I just always thought I'd be one of those people who would really come into their own as a parent when the kids were older. It was the baby stuff I was clueless about. But now that she's going out . . . there"—I gestured to the world outside of our cul-de-sac—"I can't stop thinking about this one picture, from this one day, from a time I'm never going to get back with her. It's like I finally get those parents whose kids get older, and they all of a sudden want to have another baby."

She squinted at me. "Do you even remember that day? How she had a blowout all over her clothes, and you had to throw them out and drive her home in just a diaper, literally with her poop on your hands? Then she proceeded to cry the whole afternoon because she was teething and you couldn't find her stuffed elephant?"

"Ah, Trunky. Under my seat in the van the whole time."

"Right. And when I got home, you handed her to me and just said 'Here' and then went to Coffee Brewers for an hour?"

"Hey, it was a long day," I said, feigning annoyance.

"I'm not judging," she said and put her hands up in defense. "I'm simply pointing out that those early days weren't quite as idyllic as you seem to be remembering."

"So are you saying you *don't* want to have another baby?" I joked.

"Not unless you're the one who's going to have it surgically removed from your uterus."

She was about to open her computer but reached out and touched my hand first.

"Does this have something to do with why you're running for the parent board?" I had come home from the orientation two nights before pretty revved up about it, and to say my wife had been confused by my sudden Active Alpaca presidential bid would be a gross understatement.

"What? Oh. No. That's still because I hate Chad."

Kayla smiled at me.

"And maybe ten percent because I don't know what to do with my life if my children don't need me anymore."

"Don't need you? Jack, she's five. Your relationship with her is still just getting started. And did our son ditch the diapers and move on to medical school while I was at work today?"

"I know," I admitted with a sigh.

"It's also okay to do something for yourself, you know. It doesn't have to be a job. Just an outlet to give you something new to think about. It could be, like, a hobby or a project."

"A project? I hope you're not asking me to build a deck. Because we all remember the birdhouse debacle."

"No, nothing like that. Ooh, remember when we first started dating, you were always talking about one day, you were going to read the complete works of Shakespeare? You could do that."

"I'm going to let you in on a little secret: I just said that to impress you."

"Really?" she said, chuckling. "That's sweet. Although I would've been a lot more impressed if you'd said Jane Austen."

We sat there in comfortable silence for a minute or two, the only sounds the dryer running in the distance and some semiaudible Steve Carell.

"Do you know what Lulu told me before she fell asleep?"

"What?"

"'Daddy, I'm scared I won't know where to go tomorrow.' I asked her why. She said, 'Because you won't be there to help me.'"

My wife—who had cried when her uncle walked her down the aisle at our wedding and maybe three times since—looked like she might spill out of her eyes.

"I'm getting wine," she said, standing abruptly. "Can I interest you in any?"

She could, and while she was gone, I decided to distract myself with something even more unproductive than torturing myself with baby pictures:

I checked Chad's feed.

At the top, posted less than half an hour earlier, was a picture of him and Crispin in what appeared to be matching pajamas, captioned with "Big day tomorrow—for both of us!" I almost gave myself a headache rolling my eyes. And that was before I noticed it already had 17 likes. So of course I had to see *who* was liking it.

I didn't recognize most of them, but with minimal digging, I figured out at least a dozen of them were Willow Road parents. How did they already know him? Had they just started following him after the other night? The only new follower I'd picked up since the orientation was the friend of a friend from college who I was pretty sure was trying to recruit me to a pyramid scheme.

"Look at this," I said, handing Kayla my phone in exchange for some Target-bought rosé.

"'Hashtag first day of cool'? Well, if it makes you feel any better, it's only a matter of time before Crispy grows to hate him."

"I prefer *Crisper*. In other news, we're both going straight to hell for dunking on a five-year-old's name."

A little spark flitted across her eyes. The first time I'd seen that look was at the party where we had met. I was 26 and about to start at Scrub; she was 28 and had been at Elder and Berry for a few months, and she was about to tell me her conspiracy theory that ostriches and emus were really the same bird. Whenever she hit me with those eyes, I knew that she didn't quite believe what she'd be saying next and also that I could never imagine being with anybody else. I had asked her to marry me one year to the day later.

"That's a flawed argument," she said as she gave my phone back. "For one, either of those names would be better than the one they gave him. *Crispin* makes it sound like he's a brand of reduced-fat potato chips. Two, precisely because he is five, it's not like we're dunking on him; we're dunking on his parents' pretentiousness."

"Even so, I should probably cool it so I don't slip up and call the kid the wrong thing during a debate or something. Political suicide."

Kayla's eyes got wide over her drink. "There are debates?"

The wine in my mouth kept me from laughing. "Oh, yeah," I said when I had swallowed. "They get Anderson Cooper to come in and moderate. It's a whole thing."

She punched me on the arm.

"Can you imagine?" I said. "A debate for the parent board? It really would be just like high school. Maybe I should pretend there is one just to tell my parents and see their reactions. 'Hey, Mom and Dad, guess what? I'm running for president of the parent board at Lulu's school!' My dad would start pretending I died in the fire."

Kayla's wine almost came out of her nose.

"And your mom," she said when she had at last swallowed but was still hardly able to contain herself, "your mom would be like, 'You know how to find Lulu's school? By yourself?'"

We laughed for a good two minutes. God, my parents. A month or so after I got fired, Kayla and I had been ready to tell them she was pregnant and they were going to be grandparents. It was going to be our one chance to deliver that news in person since her mom was across the country. We had also felt like doing it face to face would let us reassure my mom and dad we were okay in the wake of my unceremonious exit from Scrub. And not just okay but happy and excited about both the baby and Kayla's promotion.

We had gone to their house for the weekend (they were still in the town outside Indianapolis that I grew up in then), planning to do it that first night at dinner but knowing full well we wouldn't be able to keep it in that long. But I hadn't even put our bags down when the full-court press about my job situation started. Did I have any leads? What about references? Maybe Janice knew someone? Or Scottie? Had I thought about how I'd handle the questions about what happened? Was I sure Mouth wouldn't take me back?

When we finally had managed to tell them we were having a baby, they were, of course, thrilled.

In their way.

Quickly they were onto how proud they were of Kayla but how no one would fault her if she wanted to stay home now, which added even more urgency to the conversation around my job. My dad had sounded like he was delivering an 11th Commandment: "You have a mother and baby to provide for now, Jack." When Kayla practically leaped out of her seat to say, no, she actually planned to keep working, they were confused into silence.

As for me, while I hadn't formally given up looking for something new at that point, the appeal of being a stay-at-home parent had been growing by the day. A baby wouldn't ask me what I'd been doing since the fire, and I could invest my entire being into her or him, confident that being a dad wasn't something that could be sold out from under me. I wouldn't have to try to save someone's job or make the impossible decisions about whom to let go. I'd just have to love my kid (and develop a burping technique).

But there was no way Kayla and I were going to discuss me staying home for the first time with Ward and June Cleaver looking on from the other side of their doilied dining room table.

And yet it had been abundantly clear right then how any conversations with my parents about me assuming the role of primary caregiver would go. I mean, I think I had always known. But that weekend had changed things. Kayla's desire to keep working wasn't about me directly, but their faces when she told them rendered their hypothetical disappointment in me real. And I hadn't wanted to disappoint them, even if I thought their reasons were representative of a bygone way of thinking. So my relationship with my parents, somewhat strained to begin with, hadn't been the same after that. I'd shared even less with them going forward. Which made telling them about the Active Alpaca Parent Board a nonstarter. Scottie—or Scott, as we were supposed to call him now—his life, they understood. Mine? Not so much.

"Regardless, you should be prepared for that optional-testing question this time," Kayla said. "Just to be safe."

"Actually, all these people are already so invested in proving their kids are better than everyone else's kids that I think the idea of going test optional would cause them to riot."

"Good point," she said. An ad started playing, and we remade eye contact. "And hey, look at you, already knowing your constituents. Cheers."

She clinked our wines. Our cans of wine. Obviously.

"It's clearly not enough, though," I said. "Chad's already got a groundswell of support online. It's like 2008 Obama, without all the hope and inspiration."

"I don't know if I'd call seventeen likes a groundswell."

"Still. I'm going to need some help."

"Well, I'm going to Chicago next week. Want me to see if Barack's available to stump for you?"

"I was thinking more like a campaign manager or adviser or something."

More to the point, I was thinking Tori.

CHAPTER 7

I had been weighing asking Tori to run my campaign ever since we left the orientation. She was the vice president at a small marketing agency and had lots of experience with social media. This was also going to be her fourth year as a Willow Road parent, which would be helpful in navigating the race. And then there was the fact that if I were going to do this thing that I normally wouldn't, I should at least do it with a friend. Because Tori had started to feel like more than one-half of a couple Kayla and I were friends with; she felt like *my* friend, and I didn't have an abundance of those anymore.

After college I'd moved right into having coworkers, and then I'd had Kayla, and then I didn't have coworkers, with any bonds I would've had frayed when the people from Scrub learned I had been there that Saturday to lay a number of them off. That I never did and got fired myself in the process hadn't seemed to help. I would've felt like I'd let them down regardless for not figuring out a way to save everyone's jobs, and the sense even among those who hadn't been let go was that I'd betrayed their trust by not telling them what was going on. When I went to watch our softball team—a team that I'd started—a few months after my dismissal, most of them wouldn't acknowledge me.

"It's all still too fresh," Frida, one of the engineers, told me. "Maybe give them some more time."

They had left to go celebrate at a bar. That was the last time I had gone to see them play.

Then I'd had kids, which eventually shrunk my world down to the other parents on the playground or at story hour. Every time I thought about trying to strike up a conversation with one of them, I knew I'd either get pulled away by one of my children or walked through a kindergarten-search process so confoundingly thorough you wondered whether they had noticed how consummately devoted to his nose-picking their little genius was.

You might think having the whole parenting thing in common would make it easier to establish a platonic connection with someone you've just met, but it doesn't; if anything, it makes it harder. Because at the end of the day, no parent looks forward to sitting around and talking about someone else's kid.

Probably not my best argument as to why I should be president of a parent board. As I said, my campaign could benefit from some marketing help.

"I love it," Kayla said. "You and Tori—that would be so great. You're always talking about how you wish you had more friends to do stuff with."

"I don't know if I'm *always* talking about it. And I believe the exact phrasing is *a friend* to do things with. My friending life post-Scrub has taught me to think small."

"I know, but I didn't want it to sound so sad."

She pretended to cringe, and I laughed. "I appreciate your concern. So you think it's a good idea?"

"Absolutely. I think she'd love to help you, and she'd be great at it."

"Awesome. I'll ask her tomorrow."

I took another swig from my rosé and held the can to my lips for a few extra seconds. There was something else I wanted to talk to Kayla about, but given how our conversation about her traveling and working late had gone the last time, I was trying to be as thoughtful as I could in how I approached it.

"So the only other thing I've been thinking about is the timing," I started out.

"Didn't you say the election was in late September?"

"Oh. Yeah. That's not what I mean, though."

She looked at me more closely. I think she could tell I was unsure of what I wanted to say and maybe that I wasn't entirely convinced I should even be saying it. She set her wine down, pulled her left leg onto the couch beside her right, and waited for me to continue.

"It's just, I'm guessing a lot of this stuff would be late afternoon or early evening. Like the orientation was."

"Right . . ."

"So, with your schedule and everything, do you . . . I mean, if I were to win . . ."

"When you win," she corrected me.

"Ha, right. At least I know I have one vote I can count on. Anyway, *when* I win, do you think you'll be able to get home close to five? You know, on the nights we have meetings or whatever?"

I wouldn't say she looked impatient with my question, necessarily. But she did appear anxious to answer.

"Jack, have I ever not gotten home when you needed me to get home?"

"No, of course not." That was true. It was also true that in the last five-plus years, I had hardly ever had a reason to ask her to get home by a certain time. In fact, I did my best not to put that pressure on her. But pointing all this out could've taken the conversation to a place neither of us wanted it to go. I'd been feeling myself becoming more passive-aggressive about her absences. The night she had come in when I was already in bed and I had rolled over and asked her why she hadn't just slept at her office wasn't my finest moment. She, in turn, was getting more defensive. Had we gotten frustrated with each other about her schedule in the past? Occasionally, sure. But it'd been rare. Now whenever we started talking about something to do with her job, it felt like one or both of us were gearing up for a fight, just in case. Like we knew a big one was coming, even if we didn't know when. I could feel that tension starting to hang around our house more and more. And that wasn't us. Especially because her drive was one of the things I loved most about her.

"I'm just worried because it'll happen more often," I said, pretty sure I was sidestepping the worst of it. "Me needing you here earlier, I mean. I don't want that to be a problem for you or become one."

"So," she said while I congratulated myself for how artfully I had navigated all that, "if I told you running wouldn't work with my job, would you still do it?"

"Huh?" I said.

"Hypothetically," she said, picking her wine back up, "if I told you I wasn't sure how I'd make it work, what would you do?"

"I wouldn't run," I responded matter-of-factly.

"Really." She said it as a statement, not a question. "And would you resent me for that?"

"I . . . uh . . ."

"Because I would resent you," Kayla said. "If the situation were reversed, and you told me I couldn't do something I wanted to do because you couldn't get home by five or five thirty, I would one hundred percent resent you for it. Whether that was rational or not."

She took a drink from her can, so I picked mine up and took one too.

"My point," she said, "is that telling you that you can't do it is not an option for me. Because I love you. I love that you want to do something for Lulu's school. And I love it even more that you want to do it to screw over Chad. So I will make it work. And yes, you do have one vote you can count on."

She tipped back her can and finished it and then snuggled back into me, her hand on my chest. The dryer had stopped, and the house had gotten quieter. I kissed her on her head.

"Thank you," I said.

"I got you. Also, I should say I wouldn't *hate* being able to whisper 'Give it to me, Mr. President' when we're . . . you know."

In the category of awesome things your wife can say to you, that was pretty awesome.

"You know, I bet we could push through a *stimulus package* right now."

"And you made it weird," she laughed, patting my chest and hopping off the couch.

"I know. I heard it as soon as I said it."

"I'm getting us two more cans of this truly exquisite wine. You pick something for us to watch." She took two steps and stopped. "Oh, and Jack?"

I looked up at her with raised eyebrows.

"Chad doesn't stand a chance."

CHAPTER 8

Kayla never did get around to opening her laptop. Instead, we spent the next few hours watching TV, sometimes talking about nothing in particular, but for the most part slowly drifting toward sleep, our legs intertwined on the ottoman.

We reluctantly pulled ourselves upstairs just before 11:00 p.m. On a normal night, I'd have been out within seconds of my head hitting the pillow. Not being awake is a rare luxury when you're responsible for small kids, so your body learns to shut down as quickly as possible whenever it gets the chance.

But this night was different. I climbed into bed and proceeded to toss and turn for two hours, imagining Lulu unable to find her classroom or alone on the playground or getting picked on by someone, and me, despite all the years we'd spent building that bond, being powerless to help her. I think I did eventually fall asleep, but it was hard to tell for sure because when my eyes popped back open to the sound of Klay crying and I checked the time, it was only 17 minutes later than the last time I had looked. I grabbed my phone to take my alarm with me and spent the rest of the night curled up in a ball next to him in his toddler bed. The alarm proved unnecessary. My son flopped like a fish on the deck of a boat, so between him and worrying about his sister, there were only so many times I could be kicked awake and then nod back off.

So I scrolled through all my feeds. I read a few articles that were way longer than anything I would've normally undertaken on my phone, including an exhaustingly deep dive into the cinematic universe of Nicolas Cage. I deleted a bunch of random photos, responded to an email I had been putting off (no, I wouldn't be interested in joining your "Daddy Issues" dads' group, guy from Kayla's office), and subscribed to two podcasts. And when I had done all of that and still found myself waiting for the sun to come up, I revisited Chad's post. It was up to 31 likes. I didn't bother trying to verify how many of the new ones were Willow Road parents. No matter the number, he was already winning.

I lay there thinking about that, whether for a few seconds or a few minutes, I didn't know. Chad hadn't just been terrible to me in high school; he had been a terrible president. Senior year, for instance, there had been a tradition that everyone did a Habitat for Humanity build funded by whatever was in our class treasury. But he hadn't wanted to do that. He had wanted us to take a trip to Chicago instead, insisting there'd still be enough money left over to make a donation to Habitat. I'm a little embarrassed to admit it didn't sound like the worst idea to a lot of us, but the school wasn't having it—until, that is, Chad's dad, who had paid to have the soccer field resodded, started throwing his weight around, saying the school had no right to tell us how to spend that money (which they of course did). But the principal had relented, Chad got his trip, and I, like everybody else, had a great time on it. Plus at least we were still making a donation. Everybody had won.

After graduation, I had overheard him tell Tripp that our "donation" had consisted of two Lakeside High blankets and a $25 gift card to Lowe's. He had sounded so proud of it.

That was how Chad worked: him first, everybody else, whatever. If he'd changed since high school, he didn't seem particularly concerned with showing it. The more I sat with it, the more I realized this election wasn't just about me beating him, as satisfying as that would be. It was also about keeping him from having any kind of influence at my kid's school.

So I did something rash there in the dark, something I knew even as I did it that I wouldn't be proud of when I was done.

I followed every person who had liked his post. Some wouldn't be Willow Road parents, but this way, I wouldn't miss any who were.

Doing it at 4:58 a.m. only made it feel more awkward and sad—yet somehow not as sad as four of them following me back by 5:10. But, glass half-full: four new followers! My campaign was taking off.

God. This was going to be a long month.

And it was only getting longer when Lulu, Klay, and I found ourselves in our first drop-off line outside the school three hours later.

She had been fine, a little excited even, from the time she'd woken up through breakfast and Kayla helping her get into the van.

"This is Mommy's special pen," Kayla had said, putting it in the front pocket of Lulu's backpack. "I use it at work every time I have a big meeting, and it makes me brave. So if you feel nervous today, I want you to remember that you have it, that even grown-ups get scared sometimes, but that it always gets better. Okay?"

"I will, Mommy."

"Good. I love you, Lulu."

"I love you too."

"Thank you," I'd said to my wife outside my door in a way that I hoped conveyed how much I meant it. In so many ways, she was our glue, which made it doubly noticeable when she was gone.

"It's going to be okay, Jack. Promise." We'd kissed each other good-bye, and then I'd gotten in.

The tide had turned as soon as I started backing down the driveway.

First came the uncontrollable screaming. That lasted the entire ride to school before turning into loud sobbing punctuated by a Festivus-style airing of grievances once we were in the parking lot.

"But I'm too *sad* to go to school, Daddy!" Lulu wailed from behind me.

"I know you're sad, Lulu," I tried. "And that's okay. We all get sad about things. But I bet you'll be having fun before you know it."

"How could I be having fun when I don't even know it?" More tears.

"Lu sad," Klay offered helpfully.

"Yes, Klay, Lulu's sad. It's her first day of school, and that's a little scary, just like Mommy said." We were sitting still, about 15 cars back from the school's entrance, and I turned to look at them. "But Mommy and I are so proud of her for being so brave. Aren't you proud of Lulu, Klay?"

"Lu sad," he repeated. Again, super helpful.

"It's not fair," she said, composing herself a bit. "Klay doesn't have to go to school. Why do I have to?"

The car in front of us started to creep forward, so I switched to watching her as much as I could in the rearview mirror.

"Well, Klay's not even three yet. When you were that little, you didn't go to school either."

Her voice got even smaller. "I wish I was that little again."

Dagger through my heart.

"Sure, being little's fun. But think about all the cool stuff you get to do now that you're a big kid."

"Like what?" She still wasn't that interested, but she was at least listening, which meant I had to immediately brainstorm all the ways being five was definitively and demonstrably better than being a toddler.

"Like what?" I repeated in playful-dad voice, buying myself two seconds while I searched for something. Anything. "Well . . . you don't have to . . . wear diapers . . . to go to the bathroom."

"That's not fun!"

"Yeah, I guess that is more of a win for Daddy. Oh, I got one: What about when we went to Six Flags this summer, and Klay wasn't big enough to go on that super scary roller coaster, but you were?"

Silence. Presumably because she was reliving the sheer terror of that 19-foot first drop.

"And then last week," I continued, "Klay didn't get to go to that movie with us. That was just you and me, right?"

Lulu sniffled. "And . . . and I get to go to the dentist next week."

Trying to predict how your child will react to any piece of information is a crapshoot at best, but even knowing that, I could in no way account for why she was excited about going to the dentist. I did know, however, that it was wise not to push too hard on that door and just agree with her.

"Uh . . . uh-huh. You get to go to the dentist. Good one."

Neither of us said anything after that as I piloted our van on its slow roll forward. Until that dinner with Tori and Brooke, I'd had no idea that school drop-off would work this way. My idealized mental picture of Lulu's first day had long involved me walking her to her classroom and hugging her goodbye and then her running in excitedly to have new adventures and me watching her go, wistful but content.

With less than one morning of experience, I could already tell how naive that had been.

The kids weren't supposed to get out of the cars until you were in the marked drop-off zone right outside the school's front door, and the adults weren't supposed to get out of the cars at all, let alone go into the school. There were teachers available to help, and Ms. Sandra had told us at orientation that for the first week or so, several extra would be out there specifically for the kindergarteners. But as the long line of cars made clear, not every student would be getting a personalized walk in. The staff would have to prioritize helping the ones who appeared to be coming apart at the seams.

Five minutes earlier, and that would've been us. As we neared the big moment, though, I wasn't so sure. Lulu's crying had gotten quieter. So much so that I found myself half hoping for another meltdown.

I realize how that sounds, and a lot of parents will tell you there's nothing worse than seeing your child upset. That's a pretty inexact statement, though.

It's all a question of motivation. For example, kid goes nuts in a restaurant or the grocery store, and it's almost guaranteed it's theatrical. When it's theatrical, we call it a meltdown. And meltdowns are many things—exhausting, embarrassing, frustrating—all of which inspire zero empathy, even (and sometimes especially) when it's your own flesh and blood.

That was what a small part of me was rooting for from the driver's seat that morning: a meltdown. Just to get a teacher over there and make that first long walk in a little easier.

But Lulu wasn't working on a meltdown as we pulled into the drop-off area. There was no embellishment. She was putting everything she had into a five-year-old's show of bravery, yet the sobs were still leaking out. It was the textbook definition of a *breakdown*.

And it was about to break me in half.

Because I knew it meant she was actually, legitimately, no-frills-attached scared. And because she got quiet when she got scared, I also knew the chances of a teacher spotting her and thinking she needed help were greatly diminished. So I had no choice.

I got out of the van.

A woman I recognized as one of the kindergarten teachers apparated at the passenger-side door like we were at Hogwarts.

"Good morning, I'm Ms. Alexa!" she said with a bright smile. "Do we need some help this morning?"

"Uh, yeah, thanks," I said, standing next to my open door. "My daughter, Lulu, is starting kindergarten today, and she's a little nervous." I glanced at her in the back seat. Her crying was still quiet, but it had gotten worse since I got out. She was almost shaking. It was awful.

"Well, I can definitely help with that," Ms. Alexa said, still beaming as she started for Lulu's door. "I do need to ask that you get back into the car, though, Dad. It just makes it easier all the way around."

I nodded even though there was nothing easy about any of this.

Ms. Alexa was opening the van's sliding door as I sat back down, my eyes on Lulu in her booster seat the whole time. She knew how to unbuckle her own seat belt but had made no effort to do so given the circumstances.

"Good morning, Lulu, I'm Ms. Alexa!" the teacher repeated when the door's automatic mechanism had slid it three-quarters of the way open. It was like the big reveal on a game show where the prize was your father sending you off to the unknown horror that is elementary school. "Can I help you get out of your seat?"

My daughter looked at me, panicked.

"Waaaaaaahhhhhhhhh!"

It was full-on meltdown screaming piled on top of her previous breakdown sobbing, generating the perfect storm of misery for both of us. I regretted having even considered that her throwing a fit would somehow make it easier. Clearly the lack of sleep was affecting my judgment.

I reached back to her and, while (mostly) dodging her flailing limbs, managed to unclick her seat belt. Lulu seemed genuinely shocked by this act of betrayal and locked her hands in a death grip on their respective armrests.

True to the dual horrors of the breakdown-meltdown, I felt crushed for my daughter and embarrassed in front of Ms. Alexa, whose unwavering smile throughout had gone from reassuring to a little unsettling.

"What?" I shouted over Lulu's screaming while trying to sound like I wasn't yelling at this woman who quite possibly had ceased to feel anything during these kinds of outbursts because she had seen so many.

"Can you sort of pry her fingers off the seat while I pull her out?" she hollered, as sunny as ever.

"Uh, sure, yeah," I fumbled back. I went to work pulling her little fingers off the cloth upholstery, convinced she would never trust me again. I wouldn't blame her.

"It's going to be okay, sweetie," I said, leaning in as close as I could. "I love you so much, and Klay and I will be back to get you soon. And then we'll go and get a treat, and you can tell us all about your day."

I couldn't tell how much, if any, of it got through to her—she was so loud, I had a hard time hearing the words myself—and then Ms. Alexa was lifting her twisting body out of her seat and setting her down on the sidewalk.

"I gotcha, Lulu," she said. She knelt down so she was on Lulu's eye level and took her hand. "I'm going to walk you all the way to your class. You don't have to do it by yourself. Okay?"

The screaming had stopped once Lulu was out of the van, and she gasped something resembling "okay" in response. I felt the tiniest surge of relief at having at least heard her talk again.

"Okay, good." The smile was back on Ms. Alexa's face, and it was safe to say I had never been more grateful for an act of kindness from someone I didn't know. "Now let's go. And don't forget to wave bye to Dad and your little brother."

Lulu looked right at me through the open door, her face red and covered in tears. She held her hand up in a wave whose sadness was rivaled only by its uncertainty. I felt like the cruelest human being on the planet. So much for relief.

The two of them walked away, and I hit the button to shut the sliding door. I wiped my eyes with my hand and, because I couldn't bring myself to watch them go, checked on Klay in the mirror.

"You doing okay, bud?"

"Lu *really* sad," he said.

For whatever reason, I laughed once through the catch in my throat. "Yeah, she is. She'll be okay, though." I said it as much for me as for him. Actually, it was all for me since he was onto trying to suck his foot.

I shook my head in appreciation of him and was about to drive away when I caught a glimpse of the car behind us. Chad's face was in profile behind the wheel.

He was driving a BMW SUV because of course he was. And he was turned around, one hand holding a travel mug of coffee (I had spilled mine everywhere on the way out of the house) and the other waving to Crispin, who had shut his door on his own and was now literally skipping down the sidewalk like he was on his way to Disney World. Chad wasn't even getting impatient that I hadn't started pulling forward yet. It appeared to be the most pleasant first-day-of-kindergarten farewell in the history of Willow Road Elementary, if not elementary schools everywhere.

I couldn't wait any longer, not even the time it would take for me to get coffee or get back to our house. I unlocked my phone, tapped Tori's name in my contacts, and put it on speaker while starting to drive.

"Jack?" she answered after the second ring.

"Hey," I said. "Sorry to call so early."

"Is everything all right? I didn't see your car there this morning. How did your drop-off go?"

"Oh, it was a waking nightmare."

"God, I'm sorry. That's pretty normal, though."

"Yeah, that's what I hear. Thanks. But that's not why I'm calling."

She didn't say anything, and I thought about how I wanted to approach this. After all, it's not every day you get to ask someone to be your campaign . . . whatever. What was the right word? Manager? Adviser? Strategist? I didn't even know.

Sticking with the basics seemed best.

"So I have this idea," I started.

CHAPTER 9

By the time Tori and I met at Coffee Brewers on Sunday afternoon, I had formally filled out the paperwork declaring my candidacy for president of the Active Alpaca Parent Board. And by "filled out the paperwork," I mean I had responded to the school-wide email from Ms. Weekler asking for the names of anyone planning to run.

Tori had immediately agreed to be my campaign manager and almost as immediately made me swear to never refer to her as such. She thought it would make us look like we were trying too hard, which was one of the main contrasts she wanted to draw between Chad and me.

"He wants it because he wants everyone to think he's dad of the year," she had said when we were still on the phone the first day of school. "You want it because it needs to get done."

Right then I had known I had asked the right person to be my campaign's nonmanager manager.

"Well, it's official," I said, setting my phone down as she joined me at the table with an oversize mug. "It's just me and Chad. No one else is running."

"Really? Not even Trish?" Trish Merletti was the mom of a third grader who, in Tori's words, had "never met a solution she couldn't complain about." Tori had been convinced she'd want in on this, especially if the only competition was two kindergarten *dads*.

"Nope. He and I just got an email from Ms. Weekler. Election's set for September twenty-third."

"Okay. So we've got just over a month. Good thing we've already gotten started."

She was being generous. I hadn't done anything beyond asking her to help me and responding to that email. I had been too preoccupied, dealing with the disaster that was Lulu's day one drop-off so I could get her to go back for day two. Kayla had told me not to stress so much about it, that Lulu would get used to everything in due time. But she wasn't there for the shrieking, she hadn't seen the look on our daughter's face, and I was going to do everything humanly possible to try to avoid repeat performances. Also: Homework in kindergarten? Apparently a thing now, and I didn't want Lulu to get off to a slow start because she was sad, so I was doing it with her.

I'll admit this doesn't sound like a scenario a grown man of almost 40 should be overwhelmed by, but by the end of the first week, I was wiped out on all things Willow Road Elementary—particularly troubling considering the first "week" consisted of only two days.

Then again, the promise of a new lovie had made Friday's drop-off marginally better than Thursday's, so as long as Kayla made enough for us to maintain an astronomical stuffed animal budget, we could look forward to mornings that were merely gut wrenching rather than outright torturous.

But while I was busy helping Lulu with sight words, Tori had been working every connection she had, especially among the third- and first-grade parents, to raise my profile online. I'd picked up something like 30 new followers from the school in just over two days. I get that this doesn't sound like much on its own, but in an election where it seemed reasonable to assume voter turnout would be somewhere only in the double digits—how many people could care about an elementary school parent board, really?—it did feel pretty significant.

"That's all thanks to you," I said and then paused. "Uh, any idea what we do next?"

"Mm, glad you asked," she said after finishing a sip of her latte and raising an index finger to acknowledge the question. She reached down into her bag and produced what looked to be a brand-new Moleskine. Back in my life as a director of corporate strategy, I had always used a notebook when everyone around me was on laptops or tablets. Janice had referred to it as my "spell book" because I was a "magician" when it came to coming up with solutions. I had secretly loved that.

"I'm assuming you've seen Chad's totally necessary campaign site," she began, "with its even more totally necessary campaign slogan."

"You mean 'Chad Henson: For the Kids'? Yeah, I may have stumbled across it and proceeded to get violently ill."

"Of course you did. You know it's terrible, and I know it's terrible. It's a three-word distillation of everything we hate about him."

It wasn't lost on me that she had used "we hate" as opposed to "you hate." Even if I didn't win the election, I'd feel like I had accomplished something if it cemented our friendship as something stronger than a couples' hang once every few months.

"So we need a slogan that's less revolting," I said.

"No—what we need is nothing."

I took a bite of my scone. "'Jack Parker: What We Need Is Nothing.' I've got to admit, it does have a nice ring to it, in an antiestablishment sort of way."

Tori laughed. "Yes, it does. But no one running for a parent board anywhere has ever needed a campaign slogan. And neither do we."

"So just to be clear, my campaign's nonmanager manager is suggesting our most prudent course of action is not to do anything."

"When it comes to a slogan and a website, yes. It just makes you look phony."

"One hundred percent. But that still leaves the question of what we should actually be, you know . . . doing."

"I'll tell you: we skip the hard sell and get other people to do our talking for us. Starting with Elena Choi."

I was confused. "Elena . . . didn't you tell me she and Ms. Weekler are tight?"

"I believe I said that as president, Elena was up her butt," Tori corrected, writing something down in her notebook. "So yeah, full disclosure: that was at least fifty percent snark because I've never been able to stomach the kind of person who runs for a parent board."

"But you're . . . helping me . . . run for a parent board?"

"Well, this is different. You're my friend, and Chad's a schmuck."

I smiled. Other than Kayla, I hadn't sat down one on one with another adult to talk about something besides our kids in God knows how long, and this was the first time Tori and I had done something just us, without Kayla and Brooke there as conversational insurance. It already felt like we were settling into a rhythm.

"Thanks," I said, a little embarrassed at how nice that felt. "But still: Why do you think she'd want to help me?"

"I didn't. Not until yesterday."

"Why? What happened yesterday?"

"I was talking to Liz Morrison. Do you know her?"

I shook my head.

"She's another parent on the board—who just happens to be Elena Choi's best friend. And she told me that Elena and Ms. Weekler had a falling-out last spring."

"About what?" I asked.

"I don't know. Something that happened during a district-wide meeting to review how the schools handled the flu outbreak last year.

Elena hadn't even been planning on running for another term as president, but she was so angry she changed her mind."

"That doesn't . . . I mean, why would that make her run again? Wouldn't she want to *stop* working with Ms. Weekler?"

"You would think. But at Willow Road, the president of the parent board sits on the committee that does the five-year reviews of the principal and vice principal. And guess who's up for her review?"

"Ms. Weekler," I muttered like the friend who takes a beat longer than everyone else to realize the plot twist.

"Ding, ding, ding," Tori said flatly. "And by all accounts, Elena was ready to make her life miserable."

That was a lot to digest, but the espresso machine kicked into high gear and made it pointless for me to respond for about 10 seconds, anyway. When it stopped, two things were clear.

"One," I said, "I respect anyone who runs for president of a parent board out of spite."

"That goes without saying."

"Two: this explains why Ms. Weekler is so set on discouraging other people from running and getting a toady like Chad in there. She wants to control as many votes on that committee as she can."

"Which means we have to be prepared for her to pull out all the stops to get him elected," Tori said. "The teachers get a representative on the review committee, too, and she's already fighting an uphill battle with them."

"She is?"

"Yeah. She pushed the school board for exterior upgrades to the school's building and grounds, most of which were of what I'd call 'questionable' utility, because she thought it would send a signal that Willow Road was 'an elite learning environment.' I don't know how she got them to agree, but she did."

"Hence the 'learning colonnade.'"

"Among other things. But when the construction went over budget, she went back to the board and, in a closed-door meeting, lobbied *against* bonuses for her own teachers to make up for it."

"Ugh," I said, pausing the scone midway to my mouth. Chad's Habitat for Humanity scheme came to mind, and I filled Tori in to let her know just how willing a participant Chad would be in whatever Ms. Weekler cooked up.

"Well, maybe she could've used his help," Tori said. "Because unfortunately for her, her backroom dealing got out. Like, to everybody."

I was so surprised I swallowed too fast and started to cough. Tori grinned.

"Pretty much. The board didn't go for it. But the teachers were justifiably livid. That's why she's so invested in the outcome of the election. So at the debate, you're going to push for each candidate to have a representative present when the votes are counted."

You ever notice how sometimes, you can feel yourself blink? This was one of those times.

"At the what?" I asked.

"The debate."

"There's a debate for president of the *Active Alpaca Parent Board*?"

Tori leaned back and smiled. "There's going to be now."

I could picture telling Kayla about this, but I could not picture how long it would take her to stop laughing.

"Because . . . ," I pressed.

"Because I want these parents to see he's all surface and that you've got substance. Not to mention it'll let us show you have a sense of humor about the whole Chocsplosion! thing."

One of the reasons I had avoided going back to work was not wanting to revisit the humiliation of how I'd lost my job in the confines of an interview. Now Tori was proposing I go up on a stage and get flambéed with it.

I was ready to launch into my counterargument—whose main point was going to be "No, seriously"—but Tori's eyes were suddenly pulled to a spot over my left shoulder, and I knew without her having to say anything that something in the room had shifted. A second or two later, she fixed her face into a fake smile.

"Ms. Weekler," she said firmly. By the time I looked, the principal was walking up to our table.

"Ms. St. James, Mr. Parker," she said. "What a pleasant surprise. I didn't realize that the two of you knew each other."

"Our wives work together," Tori said. "And as it turns out, Jack's a pretty good hang."

The look on Ms. Weekler's face suggested slang was not her strong suit. Tori, who took a sip of her drink, appeared to revel in that, but letting an awkward silence play out indefinitely was not *my* strong suit.

"I also asked Tori to help me with my campaign," I blurted out. Tori somehow shook her head without moving a muscle.

"Your . . . campaign," Ms. Weekler said, staring down at me while adjusting those tortoiseshell glasses. "I see. You know, Mr. Parker, being president of the Active Alpaca Parent Board isn't about drawing attention to yourself. It's a commitment. It's about making the school better. For the children."

"Oh, uh, of course. That's why I'm running."

"I'm glad to hear that. Because we already have a very qualified candidate in Mr. Henson, and I wouldn't want someone who doesn't plan to take this seriously to get in the way of that."

"Jack's just as qualified as Chad, if not more so," Tori said.

Ms. Weekler legit snorted. "I'm sorry, I don't mean any offense." Lie and lie. "But I find that hard to believe."

"And why is that?" Tori said, hovering over her cup. "What do you even know about Chad?"

"Well, I know that he owned his own business long enough to sell it rather than burn it down." The lack of emotion with which she said it took the condescension to a whole other level.

"That seems *super* relevant here," Tori said.

"And I didn't own it," I muttered. "I just, like, worked there." Good one, Jack.

"Medium Americano for Deidre," the barista called from the counter. Ms. Weekler smiled a satisfied smile.

"To be continued, I suppose."

She walked away in what would've been undisputed triumph if not for the piece of toilet paper clinging to the bottom of her boot. Tori pointed that out to me with a sideways glance to the floor.

"I don't know whether to laugh or to cry since she did do a pretty exquisite job of roasting me," I said when Ms. Weekler was gone.

"What're you talking about? That was perfect."

"Uh, did you sit through the same conversation I did? Because in case you missed it, my comeback to her about burning down my office was that no, Ms. Weekler, I wasn't in fact successful enough to own the business, I just worked there."

"I know. It was beautiful."

I'm not sure I could have defined *nonplussed* if I'd had to, but I do know it was the right word to describe me in that moment.

"Look," Tori explained, "she was going to fight us on doing a debate. But after that performance, she's way more likely to think you'll just wet the bed and help Chad win."

"That's a real confidence boost, thank you."

"That's what I'm here for. Plus you saw how she tried to throw the fire in your face. We take that away from them with a little humor, then anyone who brings it up just sounds like a jerk."

I had to concede that she had a point, even if I still wasn't crazy about the idea of a debate. On the other hand, maybe it would let me show the handful of people who would attend that my lasagna-reheating talents were in no way indicative of my overall skill set as a human being.

I had been a magician once. Maybe I could be one again. In a non-book-me-for-your-kid's-birthday-party way.

"All right, I'm in."

"Good," Tori said, returning to her notebook. "But we're getting ahead of ourselves, anyway. First things first: Elena Choi. I'm hosting a Labor Day slash going-away party for her at our house next Sunday. There'll be no Chad and no Ms. Weekler. That's when you're going to get Elena's endorsement."

I took a sip of coffee to clear away the scone remnants. "Why are you the one hosting her going-away party?"

"We're not, technically. Liz mentioned that she really wanted to do something for her but that her house is a mess because they're remodeling their kitchen."

"The struggle is real."

"Yeah, it was pretty obnoxious the way she slipped that in there. But it gave me the chance to volunteer our house. So Liz is hosting it there, and you and Kayla are invited because, obviously."

I was feeling like maybe Tori should be running herself, although I was pretty sure she would still choose food poisoning over the Active Alpaca presidency.

"You know," I said, setting my cup down, "if you ever get tired of marketing, I think you have a real future in parent-board politics."

"Thanks, but I'd rather give Brooke lifetime control over all our TV decisions." She tapped her pen on the page. "One more thing. Did you sign up to volunteer for anything at orientation?"

"There's a field trip for the kindergarteners pretty soon. I signed up to go on that."

"Good. The first bookfair's also in September, like, a week before the election. Volunteer for that too. The more parents we can get you talking to, the better."

"That sounds low-key awful."

"Hey, you signed up for it."

"I don't know what you're talking about," I said, only pretending to be nonplussed this time around. "I signed up to make the school better—for the children."

"If you ever say that again, I'm off the campaign."

CHAPTER 10

Of all the things I had worried about with Lulu starting school, the social dynamics were at the top of the list. Would the other kids be nice to her? Would she have someone to sit with at lunch? What about on the playground? Would she join in playing or be too freaked out to talk to anyone? Or would it be the opposite? Would she make friends but get along a little too well and get into trouble?

What kind of trouble a kindergartner could get mixed up in, I wasn't sure. Probably something to do with glue sticks.

So when I picked her up on the Wednesday of week two and she told me she had a new best friend and wouldn't be scared to go to school anymore, she quieted at least a few of my fears, even if she weirdly refused to tell me the kid's name and the next morning's drop-off was the worst of the week. But by Thursday afternoon, not only did she have the best friend, the best friend's dad had said she, Klay, and I could come over Friday after school.

"Can we, Daddy? Can we?"

My answer was a heartfelt "I mean, if you really want to."

Don't get me wrong: I was happy for Lulu. It's just that showing up at the house of someone you yourself aren't friends with—let alone a complete stranger—to watch your kids play together is one of the more odious social interactions humankind has dreamed up. Kind of the antithesis of starting a softball team with the people you work with as an excuse to get a beer after the games. And to make sure you look forward to going to that house even a little bit less, we call it a "playdate."

"Yay!" Lulu cheered.

"Can you tell me your friend's name now?"

"Best friend."

"Right. Can you tell me your *best* friend's name now?"

"Crispin. Crispin Henderson."

Could I be that lucky? Could there be two? No. No one's that lucky. This was what I got for making fun of that name. I breathed in one last second, clinging to the impossible, and then clarified, "You mean Crispin Henson?"

"That's what I said."

And that's what I got for insulting complete strangers.

I tried to think of a way to get out of it. Kayla tried to help me think of a way to get out of it. And by the time we were cleaning up the dishes after dinner, we thought we had it.

"That's what Mommy heard," I said. "All the toys at Target are on sale tomorrow."

We really needed to work on some nonretail sources of motivation for our kids.

"What's *on sale* mean?" Lulu asked, handing me her plate.

"It means the prices are lower, but only for a little while."

"Why?"

"Because the store makes money by selling things to people, and they don't make as much when the things cost less."

"Why?"

"Because that's how money works."

"Why?"

Kayla jumped in from her spot arm-deep in sink water. "Lulu, wouldn't it be so fun to go to the store after school tomorrow and get a new toy? Anything you want."

"Well, not *anything*," I said, and Kayla jabbed me with her elbow.

Lulu was thinking hard. "Could we go before we go to Crispin's house?"

"Uh, no," I said, "I don't think so. They invited us to come right after school, so it would be rude to ask to move it back. It might mess up their dinner or something."

"Could we go *after* on our way home?"

"That's a good question." I felt like a defendant starting to wither under cross-examination. "I'm not really sure. Maybe Mommy knows if that would work."

Kayla didn't turn around, and she didn't miss a beat. "You know, I think the sale ends during the time you're supposed to be at Crispin's. That's what the email I got said."

"But I want to go to Crispin's *and* I want to go to the sale!" Lulu said, her eyes filling with tears. "How do I choose?"

"You just have to pick one," I said. "And between you and me, I'd probably take the toy."

"But . . . ," she choked out in between what was now full-on crying, "I want . . . to go . . . to Crispin's!"

By the time Kayla was putting her to bed, we retreated to lying about our lie, telling Lulu that actually, there was no sale, we had mis-understood the email, and so we guessed that meant she, Klay, and I would go to Crispin's after all. Surviving small children requires these sorts of white lies; it's part of the parent code that's not in all the par-enting books. But if you know the code, you know the very next line is that once said lies start causing your child actual emotional anguish, you pull the plug. Otherwise, when they grow up, your kids are going to put you in a home the first chance they get.

Friday there were a few clipped texts between Chad and me (he had passed on his number through Crispin). There was also a text conver-sation with my mom where she asked if she could FaceTime with the kids in the afternoon, and I said Lulu had a playdate.

<Does Kayla have Klay?> she asked.
Odd question. <No, she's at work.>

So you're taking both of them?

Yeah.

That's a lot to handle, Jack.

I groaned at my screen. <Do it every day, Mom.>

I mean in someone else's house. Make sure to keep an eye on him.

Thanks for the tip.

Maybe my role in our family would sink in for her if I incorporated as an LLC. JP Stay-at-Home Dad Services. Lulu and Klay could pay me in fridge art.

And then, before I knew it, I was knocking on the front door of 530 Misty Tree Court (what precisely was a misty tree?) on the Friday of Labor Day weekend. I did so like it was any old house, not a way station on the precipice of hell itself.

Too much?

"The infamous Jack Parker," Cassie said when she opened the door, wearing a wide smile that somehow managed to be icy. We had never met, but Chad's incessant posting made it feel like we had, and I fought the urge to remark on how #blessed I felt that we were finally getting together.

"You must be Cassie," I said, sensing that my own smile resembled more of a grimace. "It's good to meet you. Thanks for having us over."

"Lulu!" came a high-pitched shout from inside. Crispin appeared at his mom's side a second later, and then he and Lulu hugged. As much as I wanted to hate every inch of every interaction between our families, I had to admit the two of them were pretty adorable.

"So I gotta ask," Cassie said as soon as Klay, who I was holding, and I had joined them in the house. I instantly forgot about the heartwarming moment I had just observed and steeled myself for a question about the parent board or high school or whatever else she thought might trip me up. "Can you take their shoes off? And yours too? We just had the floors stained."

I hesitated. "Oh. Sure."

Real talk: I was hanging on to more than a few pairs of socks with holes in them, and I couldn't remember what I was wearing. I was also overdue on clipping my toenails, which was part of the reason I had worn shoes rather than flip-flops in the first place. Obviously, clipping them would've been simpler than clicking around like a velociraptor. But every time I thought of it, I was either running late on getting a kid out the door or about to fall asleep at night—so, long story short, there was now about a one in three chance the Hensons were going to get acquainted to an alarming degree with what Kayla referred to as my "machete toes."

I closed my eyes as I slipped my shoes off and then reopened one halfway to sneak a peek. Thank God.

Klay was next, and I knelt down and set him on the floor to de-Velcro. "Lulu, can you get yours?" I asked, and she started fumbling with her laces. After all the mental energy I had expended willing my socks to darn (I think that's a word) themselves, I was painfully aware of Cassie standing above us, and once you're conscious of someone waiting on you to take off your shoes, you can't become unconscious of it. But after what felt like an hour, the three of us were in our socks, and Lulu and Crispin went tearing off into a playroom.

It was only then that I noticed Cassie had shoes on. Heeled boots, in fact.

"He can't stop talking about Lulu," she said while I tried to register this latest development. "And Crispin has always been *very* particular, so she should feel pretty special."

I grunted an "mmm" in response. Even her compliments felt like digs. It was easy to see why she and Chad had been drawn to one another.

"And this little guy must be Klay," she said in a way that sounded like AI trying to reflect genuine human warmth. I had picked him back up because he was clinging to my leg like their house was the last place in the world he wanted to be. I wouldn't say he was my favorite kid right then because that feels wrong. But he wasn't not my favorite.

"Klay, do you want to go play with your sister and Crispin?" Cassie asked, then looked at me. "We probably have some trains or something he'd like in there."

His head perked up. Then a toy dog started barking from inside the playroom, and he basically started clawing his way out of my arms.

Traitor.

"Chad's making you guys coffee," she said as she started leading me down the hallway.

"Are you joining us?" I asked, full-on befuddled by the thumping of her heels on their supposedly sensitive floors.

"Me? I was actually on my way back to the office. You know how it is there." She cringed unconvincingly. "Sorry."

"No, it's cool, I know I was fired." I could only deal with one Henson at a time, and I would need all my reserves for Chad. "Do you need me to move my car? I didn't know which side of the driveway to park on."

"No, you're good. Mine doesn't fit in the garage. It's out at the curb."

I had seen the hulking thing on the street in front of their house and assumed it was some sort of municipal services truck. It looked like it could consume Chad's SUV whole.

"That's yours?" I asked.

"Uh-huh," she said proudly. "And you want to know the best part? It only gets, like, ten miles a gallon."

"And that's . . . a good thing?"

"Oh yeah. It drives the tree huggers nuts."

Totally normal, that's what all this was. But at least I was feeling a little less guilty about the fuel economy of my minivan.

The hall gave way to a large, granite-countered kitchen where the afternoon sunlight streamed in seemingly from all angles. Chad was in the middle of it, busying himself with something at the center island, his back to us as if he hadn't heard Cassie and me coming.

"Jack and his kids are here," she announced. He put up an index finger without turning around, commanding us to wait. Amazingly, his wife appeared even less inclined to do so than I was.

"O-kay," she said under her breath. You could have cut the derision with a knife. "Nice meeting you, Jack."

She was walking back down the hall before she got to my name. Then the only sound was the kids in the playroom punctuated by her heels—seriously, had she just been messing with me?—as she headed toward the front door. She hollered a quick goodbye to Crispin, and I heard the door open. When it closed and Chad still had that finger up, like he was putting the finishing touches on the Declaration of Independence and didn't want to lose his train of thought, I'd had enough.

"Cassie seems nice," I said to his shoulders. He had shoes on too. "Where'd you two meet? A coal-fired power plant?"

He dropped the finger, finally, and turned to face me. I was expecting that self-satisfied grin of his, but something was different. He was different. He looked . . . tired.

"I can't keep doing this, Jack."

"Doing what?"

"The sarcasm. The thinly veiled jabs at each other. The rivalry. *Our* rivalry."

I grabbed one of the six chairs around their kitchen table. I didn't think I was going to fall over, but I was pretty staggered by what I'd heard and wasn't taking any chances. It was the first time in my memory that he had conceded, or at least implied, that *I* could get the better of *him* and not just the other way around.

He walked toward their farmhouse-style sink. It looked big enough to hold a week's worth of dishes, and I was a little more jealous of that than would be cool to admit. He pushed the button to warm up the Keurig and grabbed a mug out of the cabinet above, gesturing toward me. I nodded, and then he got a second out for himself. While he was doing all this, I noticed he'd left a piece of paper on the island.

"I know what you're thinking," he said, leaning back against the sink as the first cup started to brew. "It's my fault. I was awful to you all the way through high school, and then I showed up here unannounced, like, twenty years later and acted like you should just forget all that and be my friend."

I didn't say anything. A lifetime's worth of experience with him had not prepared me for this, and I still didn't trust where he was going with it.

"And here's the thing: You're right, Jack. It *is* my fault. And I didn't even realize it until Crispin came home from school crying every day."

"I saw him that first day. He seemed excited."

"He was. But then he got scared. Until all of a sudden he wasn't. Because of his new friend—Lulu."

Chad paused and moved to the refrigerator. "Do you want milk or sugar?" he asked.

"Just milk."

He pulled the carton out and topped off my drink. "That's good," I said, still from across the room. He put the milk down and walked the cup over, handing it to me with a smile that was, again, more tired than anything else. Then he headed back to make his coffee.

"This is going to sound corny," he said, stopping halfway there, "but something about seeing him struggle reminded me how hard growing up was even *without* someone messing with me. And not only that, but then it was the child of the person I had given a hard time . . . it was that very person's daughter, *your* daughter, actually being the one to help Crispin, all these years later." He started walking again. "I don't know. That probably doesn't make any sense."

No, what didn't make any sense was the possibility, remote as it may have been, that Chad wasn't irredeemable. And not only that, but that once upon a time, back before he was making my life miserable at Lakeside High—or maybe even *while* he was doing it—he was just struggling to get through like the rest of us. Could that be true?

"I get it," I said. "Something about watching them go off without you . . . it does something to you."

"Yeah," he said quietly. "I think on some level, it's why I looked to get involved at the school. To ease the transition." He pulled the Keurig's handle down, crunching it into the pod. For some reason, the sound took me back to the party in high school when he had offered a freshman 20 bucks if he could crush a beer can on his head. The kid did it but bloodied his forehead in the process, and Chad had just laughed. He'd never paid him.

Struggling or not, that was Chad. At least it had been.

"On top of that," he continued, "I don't know if you could tell, but my marriage isn't exactly in the happiest of places at the moment. This move has been . . . it's been rough. On all of us."

I had been going to take a sip of my coffee but drew the cup back down. My suspicions were immediately back on the rise, and I sensed that something imperceptible but real had changed. It had begun to feel like Chad (or his dog) having cancer all over again. Neither of us said anything for a minute or two. By the time he was done pouring milk in his coffee, I was convinced the next words out of his mouth were going to be asking me to drop out of the election because they "really need this right now."

"So about the parent board," he said. That alpaca-plotting, election-stealing mother—

"I wrote you this letter, Jack." He grabbed the piece of paper from the island and placed it on the table in front of me. "Pardon my stationery," he added with an embarrassed chuckle.

It was written longhand on a piece of white construction paper on which Crispin had scrawled his name across the top in red crayon. I would've found it a much more bizarre choice if I didn't also live in a house with a five-year-old and know that gently used construction paper was routinely the only kind of paper available.

However, the message itself was pretty unexpected:

> Dear Jack:
> I can't believe that all these years after we went to high school together, we're right back where we started, running against each other in a school election. My pledge to you is to be better this time around—to be kinder, to be constructive, and most of all, to keep things in perspective. I know either one of us would do a great job for the kids, and I also know I would like to be friends with you when this is all over.
> I'm sorry for all the times in the past when I made that impossible.
> Chad

I reread the words "I'm sorry" and then read them again.

"I . . . uh," I started. He'd burned me so many times that I don't think there would have been any way for me to totally accept what he'd written as true. That he'd put it in writing also felt fishy. But as we stood there in his kitchen, as two adult men, two dads, he seemed sincere. It was hard to act too cynical.

"I mean, thanks. I appreciate this."

He smiled, more wholly this time. "Good. I'm glad." Neither one of us was sure what to say next.

"I bet the kids could use some snacks," Chad said at last. "Does Lulu like apples?"

"She does." I felt my phone buzz in my pocket. "That would be great."

He returned to the island to grab two red ones from a fruit basket and got out a cutting board to slice them up. I checked my phone. It was a text from Kayla asking me how everything was going.

"Hey, you don't happen to have a phone charger I could use, do you?" I asked. "I didn't even realize it, but I'm down to, like, nine percent."

"Sure—right there on the counter, next to the butcher block."

"Great, thanks."

<Surprisingly well>, I typed back to Kayla after I'd plugged in. I knew the vagueness of that would intrigue her, so I decided to wait for a minute or two to see her response.

While I did, my eyes were drawn up from the screen by a framed photo, tucked back behind the knives. In it, Chad was posed like Buddha alongside a statue of Buddha, eyes closed as though he were accessing another spiritual plane—one where I guess you ask a photographer to take your picture so you can display it above your wine fridge?

There was the Chad I knew and loathed.

I found that oddly reassuring. Because I wasn't sure what to make of this reformed Chad. Like, was he even reformed? At best, he had matured from pure evil to run-of-the-mill pretentious. Whether that would make him easier or harder to beat was difficult to say. But at least there wouldn't be a repeat of the Jizz Parker incident.

"Daddy!" Lulu yelled, suddenly appearing with Crispin under the archway leading into the kitchen. "Klay climbed into Crispin's washing machine!"

I could almost feel my mother judging me from South Haven.

"Yeah, that's not good," I said, setting my phone down. "Lead the way, you two."

The three of us raced off together to rescue my toddler before he ran himself through the spin cycle.

CHAPTER 11

"All right, Daddy has to get his phone, and then it's going to be time to go, okay?" Lulu and Crispin were building some sort of racetrack, and Klay thought he was helping, so no one was listening to me.

"Well, I guess we can try to have this fight again in two minutes," I said, mainly for Chad's and my entertainment. "I'll be right back."

"We're good," he said, smiling. As I walked out of the playroom, he was asking the kids if he could take a picture of their track, and my hunch that they had been intentionally ignoring me was confirmed by how quickly they cheered the photo idea.

I didn't take it personally. Against all odds, it had been a good couple of hours inside the belly of the beast, which I was closer to being able to refer to simply as *Chad's house*. It helped that his kid really did seem to be a good egg; Klay started crying at one point when the dog toy got stuck under the train table, and Crispin immediately stopped what he was doing and crawled under there to get it for him. And when he and Lulu started arguing over what to draw on his whiteboard, it was Crispin who said sorry, unprompted, while I had to remind Lulu to do the same.

I was glad they were friends, and it did make me wonder even more if Chad had been anything like that before he became what he became.

Most of what happened in high school remained a conversational third rail, but he and I did briefly revisit the sophomore-year election and managed to laugh about his asinine answer to the optional-testing question. It was also the first time I had gotten past the trading of anecdotes and really talked with another dad about the challenges of staying home. It sounded like Chad hadn't anticipated jumping into that role and he was going through some of the same stuff I had over the years: figuring out your identity without work, questioning your worth if you're not earning, being self-conscious when you're the only dad on the playground.

One thing I didn't tell him was how game-planning with Tori had gotten my mind moving the way it had back at Scrub. It had felt good. But it had also triggered a degree of guilt. Like it would mean I didn't love my kids enough if being home with them wasn't my whole world. Becoming a dad had given me a sense of purpose when working had ceased to provide one. Acknowledging that any part of me missed that life felt almost . . . I don't know, disloyal.

As for Chad and me, we'd never be friends. We had too much of a past for that. And on some basic level, I couldn't relate to anyone raising a small child in a house filled with that much white furniture and so many off-white accents. A white couch? Really? Who has the energy?

But it was progress.

When I got to the kitchen, I realized the letter was still sitting on the counter, so I folded it up and took it with me. I didn't know what I was going to do with it, but it felt rude to leave it there.

The sun was lower and right in my eyes as I pulled the charger from the socket and then the cord from the bottom of the phone, which I saw was almost fully charged. And at the same time I saw that, I saw something else.

Something weird.

There was a text from Kayla from almost two hours before: <Don't leave me hangin'!> I had never checked my phone after retrieving Klay, and that message was clearly in reference to me telling her things were going unexpectedly well.

But then, 15 minutes before I picked my phone back up, she had texted, <Whoa what's going on> and followed that with a phone call when I didn't respond.

It sounded like she thought something had happened since we last talked. But that didn't make any sense, so I assumed she was just getting impatient about my original text. Except—would she have called about that?

<About to leave>, I typed out. <Everything's fine. I'll call when we get in the car.>

I headed down the hall to the playroom—past a Henson family beach portrait that was everything Brooke had predicted it would be that night at dinner—and was still trying to decipher what else Kayla could have been texting and calling about when I got there.

Chad stood to meet me. His gaze lingered, almost like he was studying me for some sort of reaction. When I just kind of shrugged, he smiled and showed me his phone.

"Hope you don't mind," he said, "but I couldn't resist."

He held it close enough for me to see the picture he'd posted while I was gone. It was one of Lulu and Crispin posing proudly with the track they'd built and holding a handwritten sign that read: "Chad Henson: For the Kids."

His comment below? "I approve this message."

I reread it, and then read it again, this time with my blood pressure rising.

"You put my kid in your campaign ad?" I said.

Chad laughed. "I'd hardly call it an ad, Jack. And besides, it's not like anyone knows she's your kid."

Never before had I been so relieved by something I found so insulting.

He pulled the phone back, and I tried to tell whether the kids were paying attention to us. They seemed even more engrossed in the track than before, so I took my chances on a direct confrontation.

"Don't you think it's a little weird? Especially after everything we talked about earlier?"

His hand went to his chin, and he started with the nod. A smile curled ever so slightly at the corners of his lips.

"All right, Lulu and Klay," I said, shaking my head and looking past him, "we gotta go. Say goodbye to Crispin."

"I'm not ready to go!" Lulu yelled.

"It's time," I said. "C'mon. Get your shoes."

She started whining loudly but got up and shuffled her way toward the front door, Crispin following behind her. Klay still wasn't moving, so I stepped around Chad and picked him up, and we fell in line behind the two bigger kids.

"I think you're overreacting, Jack. I didn't mean anything by it."

"Right."

Chad held his phone back up. "Look, I'm deleting it. See? It's gone. Seriously—I wouldn't ruin this for the sake of a cheap dig."

The only conversation while we put our shoes on was between Lulu and Crispin, who were already talking about wanting to play at our house. Was I overreacting? Was it really not that big of a deal? Was it possible Chad had been going for something cute and funny between our kids and just got it wrong?

No. It wasn't.

But how the letter fit into that, and why he'd voluntarily delete the post, was a mystery. This playdate had gone from encouraging to mind bending in the span of a few minutes.

"I appreciate you deleting the post," I said after I had stood back up, and I left it at that.

I looked at Crispin and made my voice upbeat. "Thanks for having us over, dude. I can see why Lulu likes playing with you so much." He looked down and smiled, and I turned to open the door.

"Lulu, you are welcome back here anytime," Chad said, all syrupy. "You all are."

"Terrific," I said with my back still toward him. "Let's hit it, you two."

Lulu and Crispin hugged each other one last time, and then we were out. I heard the door close behind us, and Klay held my hand while Lulu danced ahead excitedly, telling us all the things she and Crispin were going to play when he came over. I got them in their seats, discovering as I did so that Klay had swiped a train.

"Like trains," he said, showing it to me. I tried to care enough to walk it back up to the house, but that game was over before it started.

"That's one of Crispin's trains," Lulu said as I pulled her brother's shoulder straps tight. "Klay, that's stealing!"

"You can't really steal when you're two, Lulu," I said and pushed the button to shut the automatic door. "It's more like a property dispute."

"He has to give it back," she said when I got into my seat. "He can't just keep it."

I sighed. "You can take it to Crispin at school, okay? I'm sure the feds will let it slide as long as we give it back to him Tuesday."

"Who're the feds?"

"Never mind." I started the van's engine. "Just let me call your mom, and we'll get going." I still hadn't figured out why Kayla had called. I thought it might be because of Chad's since-deleted post, but the timing didn't line up.

I was about to unlock my phone—I really needed to resync my Bluetooth so I could stop doing this by hand—when it lit up with an incoming call. From Tori.

"Hello?" I said, switching her over to speakerphone and putting the van in reverse.

"Dude—what the hell?"

"Hey, I got the kids in here, and you're on speaker."

"Then take me off speaker."

"I'm driving."

"Then *pull over, Jack.*"

I had never heard Tori mad before; it was a little terrifying. So I drove around the corner from Chad's and parked on a leafy side street. Not knowing what was going on, I decided to play an audiobook CD of *The Lion King* that reliably managed to hold both of the kids' attentions and got out of the van to talk to her.

"Okay, we're good," I said after shutting the door. A woman was walking a dog on the sidewalk across from me, but otherwise, no one was in sight. "What's going on?"

"Why don't you tell me?" Tori replied, clearly exasperated.

"Uh, well, I've been off-line for a couple of hours, so I'm not sure. We had a playdate at Chad's."

"No kidding."

"Tori, really—I have no idea what you're talking about."

"Uh, *your post?*"

"My post? I didn't . . . hang on. I'm outta the car now, and I'm putting you back on speaker." I took the phone away from my ear and opened the app. There, staring back at me from my profile, was the reason my wife had checked on me the second time and why Tori sounded ready to sacrifice me to the god of the Clarendon photo filter:

A picture of what was presumably my middle finger flicking off Chad's letter. Which, in case you forgot, included his child's name innocently written across the top.

I read the caption below to myself while Tori did so out loud.

"'Playdate for the kids at Chad's,'" she quoted. "Barfy face emoji. 'He just gave me this letter.' *Two* barfy face emoji. 'And who names their kid Crispin?' *Three* barfy face emoji!"

I thought I might pass out.

"Jack? Hello? What were you thinking? This makes you look vindictive! And like a sociopath! A vindictive sociopath!"

"Tori, I swear to God I didn't do this."

"What do you mean, you didn't do this? Then who did?"

"I don't know, but . . ."

My stomach churned, and I felt for a second like I was about to channel one of those emoji all over the hood of my car.

"Son of a . . . ," I said through gritted teeth.

"Hold on." The anger was gone from Tori's voice now. "This really wasn't you?"

"Of course not!"

"Because it kind of *sounds* like something you might say."

"Sure, to you or to Kayla! Not to the internet!"

I heard a turn signal in the background. She was in the car, too, probably on the way to pick her kids up from their after-school program.

"Okay, fair point," she said. "So it was . . . Chad? But how?"

"It had to be when I left my phone in the kitchen to charge. I put it down to go get Klay out of the washing machine."

Still sounded bizarre, even then.

"You what?" Tori said.

"Forget it. But I must've set my phone down without locking it, and then he went in and posted from my account."

She mulled that over, and Lulu said something about Simba through the open back windows. The dog walker was gone, and the street seemed to be abandoned, except for us. I was replaying the entire afternoon, especially the time in the kitchen.

"So the letter—was that real?" she asked. "Like, did he actually give that to you?"

"Yeah. It was this whole heart-to-heart about how seeing Crispin struggle in school made him remember how he had struggled, how he had been a jerk to me, and now how his marriage isn't great . . . God, I'm an idiot. The whole thing was a setup."

"But how could he have known he'd be able to get in your phone?"

My heart felt like it was going to pound out of my chest. This whole situation was both too strange to be true and so authentically Chad that I couldn't believe I had bought it. I took a deep breath and tried to calm myself down.

"He didn't plan the phone piece," I said. "He couldn't have. He wrote that letter just to throw me off, to get me to let my guard down. Maybe he thought that if I didn't hate him anymore, I'd drop out of the election, like I did in high school."

"I guess."

"He even gave me this whole sob story about how the move's been hard on all of them and how getting involved at the school would ease the transition for both him and Crispin. And I listened to him, Tori! But it's an ego play, plain and simple."

"It still seems like a lot of effort to put into a pretty obvious Hail Mary," she said.

"Does it even matter? Because I gift wrapped something even better." I looked at the picture again before adding dryly: "But hey, at least no one's liked it, right?"

"Of course no one's *liked it.* You're basically declaring war on super-dad and his five-year-old." She stopped. "Wait, have you not deleted it yet?"

"Don't you think that could make me look worse? Like I'm not standing behind . . ."

"Delete the post, Jack."

"Deleting."

"Thank you."

For the first time since we had parked, a car turned onto the street. I watched it take a left into the driveway immediately ahead of us, the driver giving me, the stranger standing outside his minivan, the once-over as his Tesla silently rolled toward the garage.

"You know what's really crazy?" I said.

Tori laughed. "You mean crazier than the guy you're running against for president of the Active Alpaca Parent Board stealing your phone to impersonate you online and then trash himself?"

"Amazingly, yes. Right before we left, he posted a picture of Lulu and Crispin holding a 'Chad Henson: For the Kids' sign."

"What?"

"No, wait, it gets better. He then showed me the post, and when I called him out on it, he deleted it. Voluntarily. And told me he wouldn't ruin everything we had talked about for the sake of something like that."

She attempted to respond but got interrupted by her car doors flinging open and her daughters climbing in and launching into competing accounts of who had been the first to call the other one a baby while waiting for Tori to get there.

"Abby, Cecilia—quiet." She waited for their argument to die down to a murmur. "So what do you want to do?" she asked me. "I mean, we've got Elena's going-away party in two days, and this is bound to come up."

I stared at the stop sign at the end of the block, my haze of confusion and anger beginning to lift. I didn't have a perfect solution; perfect would've been inventing a time machine to go back and lock my phone.

But the situation didn't demand perfect. It just required not backing down like I had last time. Because this wasn't senior year, and the last thing my kid's school needed was a wannabe influencer having any real influence.

"I say if Chad wants the whole school to know he's always been like this," I said, "we have no choice but to oblige."

CHAPTER 12

My dad's conversational range covered golf, cigars, and the stock market, and most of our communication consisted of him sending me stories from the *Wall Street Journal* and me pretending I had a subscription to read them. With my mom, it was more of a running dialogue, conducted mainly via text, except for our Sunday phone call, which we did each week whether we had anything new to say or not. These calls were usually about 10 minutes long, so when I looked down and saw that we had passed 13, it was time.

"Well, I should probably get going," I said.

"All right, I'll let you go."

"What are you and Dad up to today?"

"He's golfing, and I've got to return a blender."

"Why? What's wrong with it?"

"I don't like the way it blends."

"What do you mean?" I asked, examining the blinds on our bedroom window. I really needed to dust more often than my current schedule, which was once every 8 to 12 months.

"What do you mean, what do I mean?" she said. "I blended something, and I didn't like it. It was too smooth."

My eyes moved from the blinds to a blank spot on the wall. Setting aside the notion that it was possible for an appliance designed to make things smooth to make them *too* smooth, I focused on the even more fundamental flaw in her hypothesis: "They're not going to let you return a used blender, Mom."

"Sure they will. I cleaned it."

"Okay, well, good luck with that," I said before offering a silent prayer for the poor soul working that customer service desk.

"So do you and Kayla and the kids have any plans?"

"Uh," I stumbled, like I was struggling to remember what we were doing when I was in reality struggling with how much to directly lie about and/or omit. She hadn't forwarded me a job post in a couple of months—"You can work from *anywhere* now, Jack"—but talking about the parent board would bring a quick end to that streak.

"Oh, right," I said. "We're going to this, uh . . . this Labor Day party."

"That sounds nice. Where at?"

"Some good friends of ours," I said. "A couple we met through Kayla's work." And then, because I didn't want to accidentally stumble into something about Elena Choi's going-away or Chad or the parent board, I added: "Tori and Brooke—I think I've mentioned them before."

To be honest, I didn't know how my mom felt about two women getting married. What I did know for sure was that she wouldn't know how to talk about it or how to react to me telling her the couple hosting said Labor Day party was made up of two women. She would then proceed to get awkward, thus allowing us to say goodbye without me sharing any more personal details.

"Well, that's all . . . very good . . . for them," I heard at last.

If only my conversation with Elena could've been so predictable. I had assumed Tori would make the introduction, but after she greeted us at her front door and directed Kayla and the kids to Brooke, she pulled me aside and let me know she wanted me to fly solo. She thought the interaction between Elena and me needed to be more organic, especially since the two of them didn't have the type of relationship where one would walk up to the other and go, "Hey, here's someone you should meet." So she pointed Elena out to me near the sectional sofa, reminded me of what we had talked about ahead of the party, and wished me luck.

A circle of well-wishers surrounded our outgoing president. As I was looking for any excuse to procrastinate, I made a move to take the four kids for grilled cheese at the build-your-own panini station—a Liz Morrison hosting flair that Brooke had accurately described as "absurd yet delicious." But both my wife and campaign manager were onto me and interceded, leaving me to post up alone near the dip table, waiting for an opportunity to introduce myself to Elena.

That wait could've gone one of two ways: I could've stood quietly in the corner and avoided making small talk with the other parents—the preferable choice for obvious reasons—or I could've warmed up for the big conversation by mingling with potential voters.

I made the mature decision. Mainly because within 30 seconds of parking myself by the french onion, I got recognized, and there was no turning back.

"Wait," a guy with wire-rimmed glasses said to me. "Aren't you . . . Chocsplosion!?"

I sort of winced. "Uh, yeah."

"I use that gif of you all the time," he said.

"The one where I try to say 'What's what?' with my mouth full, or the one with the caramel?"

"The caramel. You know, I read somewhere it's one of the fifty most popular memes of all time?"

I was going to tell my parents that the next time they asked about my résumé.

In the time it took for there to be an opening with the guest of honor, I spoke with no fewer than five parents, none of whom I had met before and none of whom had seen my fresh internet fiasco featuring Chad's letter. Or at least none of them mentioned it. That, coupled with

how normal each of these conversations was, left me cautiously optimistic that my alleged overuse of barfy face emoji hadn't penetrated the
Willow Road Elementary zeitgeist to the degree Tori and I had feared.

I embarked on the walk over to the couch with a renewed confidence. As I went, I felt the letter, folded into quarters, in the back
pocket of my khakis. Tori thought bringing it with me was overkill, and
now I doubted that it would even come up. That was okay. I liked the
comfort of having the physical evidence with me.

"Excuse me, Elena?" I said, doing that head-tilt thing that's supposed
to act as a preemptive apology when you approach someone cold—especially when they're looking down at their phone, which she was.

"Uh-huh?"

"Hi, I'm Jack Parker."

A blank stare quickly followed by a hopeful glimmer of dawning
recognition. I had seen that glimmer a hundred times since the fire,
up to and including 15 minutes earlier, with the guy at the dip. It gave
me nightmares that Chocsplosion! would one day find its way into my
obituary.

"Jack Parker—you're the letter guy, right?"

I stood corrected. And hey, at least it was a new embarrassment.

I smiled. "I was hoping you hadn't seen that."

She locked her phone but kept it in her hand. "I guess I didn't, not
technically. You had deleted it by the time I went to look. But Liz had
screenshotted it."

Friggin' internet.

"Well, first off," I said, wishing I had brought a drink with me to
build in some natural pauses in which to formulate my responses, "I
want to let you know that that wasn't me. I mean, it was my account,
but I didn't post it. I got, like, hacked."

Her eyebrows arched over her glass of white wine. "Hacked?" she
said after she'd swallowed. Someone in the kitchen cackled loudly at

that precise moment, and while the laugh had nothing to do with our conversation, it matched Elena's expression perfectly.

"I know how that sounds," I admitted. "But I promise you I would not post something like that. Not in a million years."

"Actually, I believe that," she said. "Kind of."

"Wait—you do? I mean, kind of?"

"Yeah, kind of. I *wanted* it to be real because it was such a train wreck. Like with a capital *T*. But it also seemed a little too good to be true. Especially since you're running for the AAPB."

Elena had been skeptical of the post's origins from the start—that was good. So was the news I could get by referring to the Active Alpaca Parent Board by its reassuringly bland acronym. Now provided everyone approached what they encountered on the internet with the same informed, critical eye she did, I would be home free.

I entertained excusing myself to scream into a throw pillow.

"So if it wasn't you, what happened?" Elena asked. There was a directness to the way she was engaging me now, and I couldn't tell if it was interest in the story or impatience with me for bothering her with it.

"Uh, well . . ." Everything I was about to say was true, and yet the cringeworthiness of the accusation still made my cheeks go red. "It was actually Chad. Chad Henson. The guy who gave me the letter."

Longer sip of her wine this time. Man, I wanted a drink. I counted the framed photos on Tori and Brooke's fireplace instead.

"I met Chad this week," Elena said eventually. "He seemed nice enough—and then almost too nice. Then I found out he's 'Deidre's guy,' and that's a recipe for . . ." She trailed off and bit her lower lip, almost as if she was physically preventing herself from saying something more. It gave me a second to (re)connect "Deidre" and "Ms. Weekler" as the same person.

"The point is," she continued when she had collected herself again, "you're both running, you have some sort of history with each other, and so I could see him trying to sabotage you. She *definitely* would to get what she wants. Or who she wants. So it's not like I'm saying it's not possible. But not this way."

"I don't understand," I said.

"Men don't write letters like that. People like the two of them"—here I took her to be referring to both Chad and Ms. Weekler for some reason—"they especially don't write letters like that. They can't stomach looking vulnerable. And you're saying that he not only gave that letter to you but then had a change of heart, broke into your account, and turned it against you?"

"It's a little more complicated than that. But yeah, basically."

"That feels a little too conspiracy theory–ish."

I wanted to tell her she was right: it was a conspiracy, one two decades in the making. Instead, I went with what I could prove.

"So you don't think Chad wrote it?" I said, unable to control a nervous grin. "Like, I wrote the letter myself?"

"I mean, no offense." She didn't seem that worried about offending me. "But yeah, I guess so."

"But why would I do that and then delete it?"

"I don't know. Maybe you got cold feet after you posted it." She paused and then raised her glass to me. "Maybe you were drunk."

"I can promise you, I wasn't," I said, registering a mental "I told you so" for Tori as I produced the letter from my pocket—along with another piece of paper folded inside it. And this time I could tell for sure: Elena was intrigued.

She put her phone away and set her wine on an end table to take the two sheets from me.

"I recognize the letter," she said. "What's this other thing?"

"A copy of a page from Chad's and my senior-year yearbook," I said. "Specifically, his 'Farewell from the President.' Every year before this, the senior class president's letter had been typed out like everything else. But Chad insisted his letter be published exactly the way he had submitted it—*handwritten*."

He'd devoted the first paragraph to explaining he'd done it this way so we'd all know it was really from him. As opposed to who? The professional speechwriting apparatus supporting high school class presidents everywhere?

Elena studied both pieces of paper for a solid 60 seconds. I got out my phone and pretended to read something while I waited. I checked I had locked it when I was done. And then checked it again.

"So he really did write the letter," she said, not looking up. "I'll even give you that he probably did it insincerely. That still doesn't prove he posted it, though."

"But you said you believed that part wasn't me, that I wasn't the one who posted it."

"No, I said I *kind of* believed it wasn't you. Maybe he did give it to you, and you just decided to trash him for it."

Tori had reminded me how all of this would sound to someone who didn't know my history with Chad and that I couldn't blame Elena for challenging me on it. I didn't. But I was afraid my frustration was beginning to show.

"All right," I said. "Say that's true. It's not, but say it is. Aren't you at least a little bit curious about what would compel him to write something like this, what 'all the times' he made it impossible for me to like him actually were? What he actually did back then?"

Elena gave the papers one last glance and handed them back to me. She didn't say anything, but she was listening. So I told her.

I told her about the clown costume and the phone numbers. About Maria Flores and the prom. About the disappearing cancer diagnosis and me "being too nice to ever win anything."

About Jizz Parker.

This—not showing her the letter and the yearbook page, but this—this was the plan I had hashed out with Tori after our phone call, to present Elena with the full scope of who Chad had been, of who I knew he still was, of everything he was apologizing for with that letter. Because while the sentiment behind it had been fake, it had been effective because the stuff it referred to was as real as it gets.

"So believe me when I tell you," I said, "he's a bully who punches both down and around, and he doesn't care who he hits or what lies he tells. And somehow, this is a person I'm supposed to trust to act in the best interest of our kids?"

"They were going behind your back?" she asked when I had finished. "For two months?"

"Uh, yeah," I said. I had gotten pretty animated during my little moral stand, and I was thrown that Maria was the part of the story she had homed in on. "It was . . . it sucked."

Elena nodded her head, lost in thought for a moment, and then retrieved her glass from the table.

"So why tell me all of this? It's not like I get to pick my successor. I don't even get to vote in the election. Deidre made that very clear."

I took a deep breath. "I know. But I was hoping you might be willing to, like, endorse me."

She pursed her lips. She looked surprised. And pleased.

"I think I can do that," she said when another round of laughter from the kitchen had died down. "To be clear, though, it's not because I believe Chad was behind all this."

"You don't?"

"No. But I don't not believe it either. I don't know what to believe. What I *do* know is that I don't care. Because if even half of what you said about Chad is true, he's exactly the kind of person Deidre Weekler wants for the job. And after what she's put me through—let's just say it's more than enough for me to support you."

"Well, hopefully you won't phrase your endorsement that way." Angling for a laugh, I managed to elicit a smile from her.

"That letter," she said. "If you really aren't the one who posted it, I'm glad someone did. He's even skeezier than I thought."

"You have no idea. And seriously, thank you. I think this will go a long way with a lot of the parents."

"I guess we'll see," she said. "Now, if you'll excuse me, I should probably keep making the rounds. It is my party, after all."

"Oh, yeah, of course." I hung there for a second, debating one last question, concluding that I shouldn't ask but knowing I wouldn't be able to resist.

"Hey, can I ask you something? I mean, one more thing?"

"Sure," she said, noncommittal.

"What happened between you and Ms. Weekler, anyway? Is it something that I need to worry about?"

This time she did laugh, but silently, emptily, to herself. She hesitated, looking first to the ground, then out the window, and finally to the last sip of wine in the bottom of her glass. After she took her drink, she lifted her eyes. They were suddenly swollen from holding back tears.

"Not unless you're afraid your husband's going to cheat on you with her too."

CHAPTER 13

Everything had blown up back in the spring around the time of the school board meeting, just like Tori had said. But while she had heard it was a fight during the meeting, nothing had happened until later that night, after Steven Choi gave Ms. Weekler a ride home because her car wouldn't start.

"Or so she claimed," Elena said, her eyes red.

Apparently he'd come crying to Elena the next morning, swearing up and down it was a onetime mistake that would never happen again.

This situation wasn't quite as unfathomable as it might first have sounded. I didn't know a thing about Steven Choi, and referring to an elementary school principal 10 to 15 years your senior as *Ms. Weekler* over and over again wasn't quite a siren call to imagine her as a sexual being—matronly, maybe, but not sexual.

But matronly Deidre Weekler was not.

"No!" Kayla gasped in disbelief when I told her the story that night, after the party. We were lying in bed, my arm around her, and this was big enough news that her head popped up above my shoulder. "Way to bury the lede, by the way," she said, looking down at me and softly batting my chest. She was backlit by a unicorn nightlight Lulu had insisted we put in our room two years before and that we had never gotten around to unplugging.

"Hey," I said, "if you ever cheated on me with our child's principal and then I told another parent about it, I'd hope that person would have the decency to ease into the retelling of the story by starting with the Active Alpaca Parent Board news."

I didn't break during my little soliloquy, which made her laugh.

"Aah, what are our lives right now?" she sighed, putting her head back down on me.

"If it's any consolation, not telling you right away at the party was one of the hardest things I've ever had to do."

"So why didn't you?"

"This just feels like one that should stay between us, you know? I mean, it blew their whole life up. That's the real reason they're moving to Boston. They're both from there, both of their parents are still there, and, most importantly, Ms. Weekler is not. Elena said she thought she could stick it out and get her revenge by being on that principal-review committee, but after the satisfaction of winning again wore off, it was too much. This whole thing with her here and him there is basically a trial separation to figure out what she wants."

"Why do you think she told you all this? I mean, you just met."

"I asked her the same thing. She said it felt good to tell someone, and it was easier than telling someone she knew well. Like there was an anonymity to it."

We lay there listening to the crickets through the open window. After a while, Kayla squeezed me.

"I'm real thankful for you, Jack Parker." I kissed her on her forehead, and she burrowed in a little closer.

"I gotta say, though, I can kind of see it," she added. "Knowing absolutely zero about him and their marriage, of course."

"Oh, thank God," I said. "I was worried it was just typical man goggles. But Ms. Weekler is . . ."

"Uh, yeah."

"Wait," I said, crinkling my nose. "How do you know what she looks like? You weren't at the orientation."

"Spinning. I've been in the same class with her a few times, but I never knew her name until this week. Then I realized who she was but forgot to tell you."

There was a pause, and then Kayla started to kiss my neck, followed by her hand going up the inside of my T-shirt. Discussing the principal's sexual escapades will have this effect.

We didn't talk a whole lot after that.

The next morning, my eyes opened when I heard the kids, and I rolled over and looked at Kayla. This was the last day of the three-day weekend, and I had sort of assumed she would be the one to get up with them since I had taken them on both Saturday and Sunday, and she had a trip coming up Wednesday. But she was sleeping so soundly and we were in such a good place from the night before—thanks in part to her suggesting we "do that thing we almost never do"—that I didn't want to disturb her. It also helped that Lulu and Klay had waited until almost 7:15 to wake up, which in little-kid time is the equivalent of staying in bed all day to sleep off a hangover.

My screen-time principles always became more relaxed in direct proportion to our proximity to dawn, so when we went downstairs, I got them started with breakfast and a show. Groggy but awake, I decided to get a jump on the laundry I had been putting off all weekend. It wasn't like Kayla thought doing laundry was my job, but it also wasn't the kind of thing she'd think to start on her own. Pair that with being home all the time and the simple reality that I had more hours in which to do it, and it was a task that clung to me like the stains it was my charge to remove.

Man, I needed to do toilets too.

I was the guy who had devised the strategy that got Scrub toothbrushes into every Walmart in five states. I never missed that guy more than when *scrub* was instead an item on my to-do list involving the bathroom.

As for the laundry room, it's right off the kitchen, and Lulu and Klay were too zoned out to care, so I didn't bother telling them where I was going.

"Daddy!" Klay yelled before I had gotten half the load in.

"What?" I yelled back.

"Daddy!"

"Hold on." I dumped the rest of the clothes in, measured out the detergent, and hit start (which for some reason was fashioned as a play button, like that made the process of laundering your entire family's clothes somehow fun).

I reemerged into the kitchen to see my son jiggling his sippy cup like a business traveler in a hotel bar signaling for another martini. I briefly considered giving him the whole "Klay Parker, you bring that cup out here yourself" spiel. But him getting to me likely would've taken between two minutes and the rest of the day, with the way he moves when the TV's on, so I settled for implicitly endorsing his less-than-desirable behavior and just judged my lack of parenting while refilling his cup.

"Daddy's going to the bathroom," I said, delivering the milk and deciding this time to announce my departure. "I'll be back in a few minutes."

Not 30 seconds later, Lulu was in the doorway. (Closing the door when it's just you and them is for people who have never been projectile vomited on.)

"I want to play Guess Who?" she said. I'd been missing being able to play board games with her whenever we wanted. Pre-8:00 a.m. was not ever when I wanted, however.

"I thought you were watching."

"I got bored."

"Well, I'm going to the bathroom."

"Pee or poop?"

"What does it look like, Lulu?"

"Aah, that will take forever!"

Look, I get that I'm making all this sound tedious and belittling, and that's because it was. And I consider myself one of the lucky ones: I can speak up and not get judged too harshly. At worst, I'm the comically overwhelmed dad, the incompetent fish out of water. Women, on the other hand, have been expected to just suffer through this stuff without complaint since the beginning of time. So allow me to use the ludicrous privilege I've been given simply by virtue of possessing a Y chromosome to underscore this simple truth on behalf of all parents, and especially the moms, who feel they can't:

Having kids is amazing—but it can also suck. Full stop.

And being a stay-at-home parent? That takes it to another level due to the sheer amount of exposure we get to the kids' tyranny. This in turn can lead to tension with the non-stay-at-home parent. He or she will take the kids for an hour and innocently greet you with something like "Wow, that was rough" when you walk in the door—usually after you've done something exciting like go to the grocery store on your own—to which you'll want to respond, "Really? Was that hour rough? That *one hour*? I couldn't tell because you only texted me seven times."

But you don't say that. Because it's not intentional on their part. The feeling doesn't just evaporate into thin air, though. It can't. Which is why when I had asked Kayla the week before if she could work from home the morning of the bookfair to watch Klay and she said no, we had gotten into an argument.

"So, all that stuff about having my back on this . . ." I'd said.

"I do! I said I'd get home on time when you needed me to. But I can't miss the Monday meeting."

"Even with two weeks' notice?"

"Yes, even with two weeks' notice."

"Why can't you just call in, then?"

"It looks weird if I'm not there."

"Kayla, you're a senior partner."

"Exactly—I'm a senior partner. You used to know how this stuff worked."

"Oh, so if I had a job, I'd understand you better?"

"That's not what I said."

"But it's what you meant, right?"

I had directed this at Kayla, but I might as well have been asking myself if I believed I was giving her what she needed. It would've been more productive, anyway. The problem was it had been simpler for both of us to paper over the argument with apologies and for me to figure out the bookfair on my own without us really resolving anything.

So you can understand why when Kayla came downstairs a little after ten o'clock that Labor Day morning, two and a half more hours of random requests and irrational reactions and thankless tasks stacked on top of me like a Jenga tower, and told me she needed to "jump on email for a few minutes," part of me was still smarting from the last fight. And that part of me wanted nothing more than to ask her, "Are you serious right now?"

I didn't, though, because with her going out of town again in two days, I didn't want hard. I wanted easy.

So instead, we talked idly for a few minutes while she made herself a cup of coffee. Or we tried to. Every 30 seconds, either Lulu or Klay would reappear in the kitchen with an "emergency," such as the loose thread on her stuffed koala that absolutely required immediate trimming or his extreme displeasure over . . . something.

"Klay, Daddy can't understand you. What're you saying?"

"He's mad I took the train," Lulu chimed in from the other room.

"Lulu, give him his train," I hollered back.

"It's Crispin's train!" Walked right into that one.

I sighed, and Kayla looked at me apologetically before giving me a peck on the cheek. "I'll be as quick as I can," she said.

She disappeared around the corner en route to her office, and I turned my attention back to the train thieves, calling Lulu to the kitchen and reassuring her that she could return the stolen property to its rightful owner the next day at school.

"Fine," Lulu said. "I'm hungry."

"Cool," I said, walking over to where Klay had already tossed aside Crispin's train so he could play with magnets on the refrigerator. Resting on its wheels on our tiled floor, it was a slipping hazard as well as a poignant reminder that I was dealing with emotional terrorists. "Why don't I make you a snack while you do a couple of pages from your homework packet?"

"Ugh. Why do I have to do *homework*?"

"I'm gonna level with you, Lulu: I don't know why you have homework in kindergarten, either, but you do, so let's get to it." She had homework. I couldn't get over that. Sometimes I caught myself still thinking of her as the four-month-old in the motorized swing staring at me and blowing spit bubbles as I read her board book after board book. But those days had long since gone, even for her little brother. Did it make sense for me to keep staying home? Or was that just a fiction I'd crafted for myself to justify not having a job? On the one hand, I couldn't imagine not being home with Klay or there to pick Lulu up from school. But did daydreaming about that Walmart deal mean I wanted something other than to be a referee in a dispute over a toy locomotive? Was that what I thought Kayla wanted and why I had gotten so defensive about the bookfair?

I looked at five-year-old Lulu, hoping I'd see an answer in her face. What I got was a disapproving pout as she slumped her way over to a chair and pulled it to the kitchen table, the dragging of its feet sending a clatter throughout the house.

We then proceeded to pass an uncharacteristically quiet several minutes, Kayla emailing, Lulu working, Klay magneting, and me loading the dishwasher, refilling the paper towel dispenser, scrubbing a stain off the floor, and mixing Lulu's Greek yogurt. She was finishing it when Kayla came back into the room.

"Boom—fifteen minutes," she announced. "I told you I'd be fast." It was faster than I thought she'd be. But that still didn't make it so I was the one who got to sleep in. If thinking that made me petty, then I was petty.

"Mama!" Klay shouted, running toward her like he was greeting her at baggage claim. She scooped him up.

"Hey, baby! Have I got something fun for you."

"Just Klay?" Lulu asked, suddenly registering Kayla's presence.

"No, all of us." Her eyes moved from Klay to Lulu to me as she built the suspense, which made me skeptical about how much fun I'd be having. "Who wants to go to the carnival with Cecilia and Abby and their mommies?"

"Yay!" Lulu and Klay cheered together. My reaction was less enthusiastic.

"The one in the parking lot at the mall? It's going to be, like, a hundred degrees on that blacktop."

"That's the one," she said with a knowing smile as she put Klay down. He and Lulu started running celebratory laps around the kitchen table.

"Could we maybe have talked about this first?" I asked, lowering my voice so the two of them wouldn't hear. Tori and I had been texting about getting the families together since everyone had the day off, but this was not at all what I had in mind. "Chasing the kids around out there is going to be exhausting, and I've been up since, like, dawn."

I was poking. I couldn't help it. But whether Kayla felt guilty about sleeping in, didn't want to argue in front of the kids, or was in a benevolent mood from being so well rested, she let it slide.

"I know. But Brooke seems into it, and I didn't know how to say no. I'll buy you all the churros you can eat."

The woman knew my weaknesses.

"Wow, big week, Lulu," I said over her and her brother's giggling. "Mall parking lot carnival and rampant OSHA violations today, and if we survive, your first field trip on Thursday."

"I don't have a field trip," she said without stopping.

"Yes, my mistake—your Beginning-of-Year Bonding and Nature Day."

Kayla pivoted on her bare foot to look right at me. "Shut up—it is not called that."

"You think I could make something like that up?"

"Shh, hold on a sec." She appeared to be mouthing letters to herself, her face morphing into a mixture of disbelief, disdain, and delight the longer she went.

"Oh my God, it is!" she exclaimed.

"It is what?"

"Spell Beginning-of-Year Bonding and Nature Day out like an acronym."

My face began contorting like hers had, and by the time I got to the *and*, I knew where this was going.

"BOYBAND? Our daughter is going on a BOYBAND?"

"Ha ha—yes! To repeat: What are our lives right now?"

She meant it as a joke. But if she'd asked me for real, I wouldn't have known what to say.

CHAPTER 14

Fun fact about that carnival: none of the adults had wanted to go.

Tori had mentioned our text conversation to Brooke, who in turn texted Kayla to say how great it was their spouses were becoming BFFs (which, I'm not ashamed to say, made me blush a little). In the course of that conversation, Brooke had suggested the carnival as a joke. Kayla had written back, <haha ok>, to which Brooke responded, <Wait did you think I was serious?>—but not until several minutes after Kayla had told our kids we were going.

So we had no choice. But Brooke and Tori did. And yet there they were, waiting for us with their daughters at the entrance, which was really just the space between two bike racks that weren't pushed all the way together. I didn't have to be an expert on adult friendship to know that showing up to a traveling carnival called "Karnival," hastily assembled on the blacktop outside a food court, meant my friendship with Tori was the real deal. It all but wiped out my annoyance that our plans to meet up had resulted in a trip to a parking lot.

Brooke greeted us with a huge smile. "It may be ungodly hot, but that's nothing that eighty-eight percent relative humidity can't fix." Her arms, fully exposed in an Obama '08 tank top, were already glistening with sweat.

"Hey, if the Tilt-A-Whirl operator hasn't taken his shirt off, it's not a real carnival," I said.

She winked at me. "Fingers crossed."

The four of us hugged even though we had seen each other just the night before for Elena's party, and Lulu immediately gravitated toward Cecilia and Abby, who were making plans to ride that swinging pirate ship thing they were thankfully not tall enough to go on.

"I got an email from Ms. Weekler late last night," Tori said as I transferred Klay over to Kayla so I could fish out my credit card to pay for our family to get in. It was $40. To go to the Karnival. When you subtracted their operating expenses, that had to be at least $37 in profit.

"Oh yeah?" I asked.

"Yeah. She agreed to the debate. It's happening."

Kayla couldn't have looked more thrilled. "Can I get my ticket now, or . . ."

"Easy there," I said. "Someone's gotta stay home with the kids."

"Stupid motherhood," she said and walked over to Brooke and the girls.

A kid in a hut the size of a porta potty took my credit card, which gave me a moment to let it sink in: I was going to debate Chad Henson. Again.

"When is it?" I asked Tori.

"Five days before the election. September eighteenth. Six o'clock at the school."

"And any idea why Ms. Weekler agreed to it?"

"I told you: she thinks it's a sure thing. From her perspective, there's no reason not to. She thinks Chad's going to wipe the floor with you."

I laughed. "I don't know what would give her that impression." My credit card was handed back to me without a word, and we rejoined our wives and kids.

"Mark it down," I said to Kayla. She was in a squat, putting sunscreen on Lulu and Klay, a task we had flipped for before leaving the house. "September eighteenth. Six o'clock. You're on kid duty. Because I've got a score to settle. Or something." Our normal babysitter had gone off to college, and we'd yet to find a new one we trusted could handle the kids' bedtimes, Klay's in particular. His attitude toward sleep was like my dad's toward a colonoscopy: He didn't need it, so why did everyone keep pushing it?

"I'm there," she said, standing up. She had her hair in a ponytail and these oversize sunglasses on, with a white T-shirt showing just a touch of cleavage, and for the next 30 seconds, anyway, I didn't mind the heat so much. "Although I'm pretty bummed I won't get to see you in action."

"Don't worry—I'm sure Chad will post about it from all his accounts. And mine."

"I'm hungry," Abby announced, reminding the grown-ups that we weren't there to chitchat or otherwise socialize in a manner that didn't directly involve our children.

"Me too," Lulu added.

"Food's a good idea," Kayla said. "I did promise Daddy churros, after all."

We spent the next 40 minutes waiting in line, eating at a picnic table partially shaded by a ring toss game at the end of the midway, and then, while the kids happily zigzagged around a series of trash cans, strategizing how to avoid getting dragged onto the roller coaster. According to the handwritten sign we had passed, it had been closed for 15 minutes "for repairs," and the consensus among the adults was that anything that required repairing on a roller coaster could not take less time than the line for elephant ears.

"Okay, so don't look," Kayla said when my head was bent down scrounging for crumbs. Hey, it wasn't like I could leave any behind. It was a churro, for God's sake.

"What?" Tori asked. She and Brooke were facing away from the midway and couldn't see what Kayla had seen either.

My wife dropped her voice to a whisper. "I think Ms. Weekler just walked by."

I swallowed. "Was she with anyone?"

"No." We all looked at each other, and then Kayla was jumping up from the table. "I'm going to follow her."

"What? Why?" I asked.

"No one goes to a carnival by themselves," she said, stepping over her seat and dodging Klay, then Abby. "She's obviously up to something. And I'm the only one of us she won't recognize."

"What about your spin class?" I said.

She waved me off. "We've never even made eye contact. It's fine."

She was already five steps away when I hollered "Meet us at the carousel" at her back.

Tori, Brooke, and I sat there, assessing what had just happened. I agreed with Kayla that Ms. Weekler was probably doing something shady, but that didn't mean it had anything to do with me or the election. Maybe Steven Choi was back in town and they needed a discreet place to meet.

"I wonder what she was wearing," Brooke said. I laughed loudly, and Tori massaged her left temple like she was annoyed, but she was smiling.

"Look, I'm not saying I like the woman," Brooke clarified. "But we can all agree that she has . . ." She paused, working through the same dilemma Kayla and I had faced the night before when talking about this in bed.

"Aged well?" I tried.

"Yes," she said. "I was just going to say she has a nice ass, but yours is classier."

"All right, you two," Tori said, shaking her head as she got up. "Kids, who wants to go ride the carousel?"

There was a chorus of "Me!" and Brooke and I rose with the remnants of lunch and dumped them in the trash. Klay wanted to be carried again, so the three girls walked a few feet ahead, with him and the adults trailing behind. Tori and Brooke then broke off into a side conversation about a text one of them had gotten from one of their sisters. Rather than focus on how disgusting it felt to be lugging around a two-year-old in the heat, I revisited whether there would be any circumstance wherein I would be justified telling the two of them about Steven cheating on Elena with Ms. Weekler. Our discussion of Ms. Weekler at the table had raised the threat level on my likelihood-to-gossip scale from "can probably do the right thing" to "burning a hole in my insides and needs to come out." But somehow, I managed to shove it back down. I didn't know Elena well, but she had entrusted me with something personal, and I wanted to respect that.

After the party, Elena, Tori, and I had agreed Elena would endorse me by posting a short video that Wednesday, the day before the field trip. Tori and I had debated the risk of doing it too far before the election, which was still almost three weeks away, but Chad definitely had the higher profile at that point, and we needed to catch up.

Elena's endorsement also figured to help mitigate the effects of Barfy-Face-Emojigate. There was a comment on Chad's most recent post about "Learning to Love Your Child's Cry Language" that referred to me as "classless" and another that didn't mention me by name but offered, "At least we have one adult running." All things considered, it wasn't awful, but I was looking forward to getting a different message out there from someone as respected as the outgoing president of the board.

Tori and I had plans for my own social media too. I would make some jokes about how spectacularly off the rails parenting could go. Nothing too harsh—unless I was being self-effacing—just things we knew other parents were thinking and feeling, even if they weren't saying it.

"Let him be superdad," Tori said. "You be real dad."

Kayla figuring out the BOYBAND acronym had led to a post that picked up its 41st like while Tori and I were on the carousel with the kids. It wasn't a Chocsplosion! viral sensation, but it was six more than Chad had gotten on anything he'd posted since the start of the campaign.

Yes, I knew the number.

The ride ended, and we reunited with Brooke. We were deciding whether Lulu wanted to venture into the fun house with the older girls when Kayla reappeared, looking like she had solved the Kennedy assassination.

"I told you!" she exclaimed when she was still 10 feet away. Brooke took over wrangling the kids, and Tori and I waited for Kayla to continue, which she did as soon as the thwack-thwack of her flip-flops came to a stop in front of us.

"I told you she was up to something," she repeated with a triumphant smile.

"Are you going to tell us what it is?" I asked.

"Chad! She was meeting Chad!"

I had wanted to believe she was there for a covert meeting between them because it would be so satisfying to have a reason to hate them even more, but I had pushed it out of my mind as too improbable. But there was my wonderful, beautiful, sleuthing wife confirming that my nemesis and his patroness were legitimately in cahoots, and I couldn't have loved her more for it.

"How were they together?" Tori asked. "Like, what was the interaction like?"

"She kept touching his arm. It was gross."

"That's probably not all he'd let her touch," said Brooke, who was somehow listening over the ruckus of our collective offspring. Kayla and I exchanged glances, but she stuck to what she had seen—or, more relevantly, heard.

"I couldn't make out a lot of what they were saying because they were standing so close to the bumper cars, and it was loud," she explained. "But I did clearly hear her say the word *debate*, and he did not look happy about it."

"Why?" I asked. "What did he do?"

"He did one of these"—she pulled her head back from us—"and started shaking his head no. That was the first time she reached for his arm."

"So he's scared," Tori said.

Kayla nodded. "That's how I took it."

"Then what?" I asked.

"Once she calmed him down, she got out her phone. She was showing him something on there for a long time—like two or three minutes. Their heads were almost touching, and it looked like she kept pointing at stuff."

"Well, that could be anything," I said. "They could've been looking at my posts, at his website . . ."

"The questions for the debate," Tori suggested.

"Yeah, you're right." Then I thought about what she was saying. "Wait, why would she have them?"

Tori looked at Kayla to reassure herself she wasn't the only one getting this. "Um, because she's the moderator?"

"Ms. Weekler?" I asked, the sweat on my forehead adding to my exasperated vibe. "She's the moderator?"

"You think she would've agreed to it any other way?"

Now I looked to Kayla, like she could somehow solve this for me. Kayla shrugged. "I just assumed it would be her."

"Awesome," I said. What better way to make sure everyone remembered I was the dummy in the Chocsplosion! video than Ms. Weekler and Chad coordinating the attack ahead of time. I'd avoided anything too terrible in the wake of the fake post with the letter, but now we were doubling down on the potential for disaster with the debate. "If

I go missing in the fun house, it's because I've run away and become a karny with a *k*."

They both laughed, and I went to walk over to Brooke and the kids, who were moving in four different directions. But Kayla hadn't budged and, apparently sensing it, neither had Tori.

"Don't tell me there's more," I said, freezing in my tracks.

"I don't want to," Kayla said. "But there was one other thing."

I braced myself. "What?"

"It was after they were done with the phone. She put it in her purse, and when she looked back up at him, he said something to her."

She stopped, still unsure whether she should break the news to me even though we all knew she had no choice.

"What was it, babe? I gotta know now."

"Not what he said—who he said."

My eyebrows raised in expectation.

"Sidney Edmonds."

CHAPTER 15

I spent two days racking my brain about how the man who had fired me—at least in part over a candy bar—was going to insert himself into the parent-board election at my daughter's elementary school some six years later. Just knowing Sidney knew I was running raised him like a specter from my memory, his fury the day of the fire confronting me all over again, as if to say, "How *dare* you think you're capable of doing this."

But beyond my own mental torment, I had no idea what he could be up to. As such, I was left with checking Chad's posts every 10 minutes, waiting for I didn't know what to drop. I couldn't even enjoy Elena's endorsement video, which was lovely, especially considering she hardly knew me.

I did get another reminder about how this was bigger than Chad and me, though. Because while there was nothing Sidney related, Chad did announce that as president, he would push to have the school eliminate the technology fee everyone paid at the beginning of the year.

"We all have computers and tablets at home," he had written. "Any family that wants to should be able to opt out of this technology tax."

First there was the blatant mischaracterization that every family already owned what the kids would need. Then there was the technology fee itself. I hadn't even realized we'd paid one, so I did a little research now that he was taking aim at it. Designed to supplement the technology budget the school received from the district, it made it so all the kids, regardless of family income level, would have access to a tablet they could use throughout the year.

The cost? Twenty-five dollars per student.

But Chad got away with not mentioning the dollar amount, thus turning a $25 charge into the bogeyman, because when the technology fee had been instituted a few years earlier, it had just been folded into the materials fee families paid, raising that from $50 to $75. The 10 percent or so of students who qualified for free or reduced-price school lunches had the entire materials fee, including the technology component, waived automatically, and spreading the cost out over the majority of the school population was what made it work.

Railing against it as a technology "tax" let Chad position himself as a defender of the school's families against bureaucratic overreach. In reality, allowing people who absolutely could afford it—say, a parent-board presidential candidate driving a BMW—to opt out of the technology fee would undermine the whole program and hurt people who actually needed the help.

It was the senior-year trip to Chicago all over again.

Between the fee and Sidney, I'd gotten myself so worked up that I'd broken down and bought that pack of cigarettes I had contemplated before Lulu started school. Still hadn't smoked any of them, but they were on standby. In the meantime, my coffee intake was up to the levels it had been when the kids never slept all night. Which meant all the caffeine was disrupting my own sleep.

To get my mind off the election, Kayla suggested I start using Klay's naps and my nightly TV viewing to throw myself into a show. By Wednesday, I was six episodes deep into *Desperate Housewives*.

"I'll confess this wasn't a show I would've guessed you'd pick," she said from her hotel room via FaceTime. We did this sometimes when she traveled, chatting intermittently while I watched TV or read and she worked.

I laughed. "Me neither. Although I do have some strong Lynette Scavo energy." There's a scene in the pilot where she runs into an old coworker from her past life as a professional, and she feels pressured to say parenting is "the best job" she's ever had even as her kids trash the grocery store and her sanity in the background. From that moment onward, Lynette and I—we had an understanding.

"I hope it's not that bad, Jack."

"It's not. Except when it unequivocally is."

Kayla looked away from her laptop and straight into my screen, slipping her glasses up onto her hair. She only wore them at night if her contacts were out and she had work to do.

"I'm being serious," she said.

I hit pause.

"Today at Target Klay screamed at me because I wouldn't buy him fruit snacks and then threw a thing of blueberries out of the cart. While I was on my hands and knees picking them up, Lulu ran away and hid in the peanut butter aisle, where some old guy was waiting to tell me that if I couldn't control my kids, I really shouldn't bring them to the store. Our daughter then thought that was the right moment to ask me to take her to get a milkshake, and when I said no, she spent the subsequent ten minutes crying that it was, quote, the worst day ever."

Kayla waited to respond—maybe to see if I was done, maybe to weigh her words before she did. Maybe both.

"Is there anything good about it?" she asked at last, frowning, a little hurt in her voice. That made me feel terrible.

"Hey. I'm sorry. I was just trying to be funny. Of course there is. An hour later, we built a killer blanket fort, and they both piled on me and told me I was the best dad ever."

She smiled. "Lots of absolutes in your day today."

"Yes, there were," I said, smiling back. "We're raising two amazing little people. It's just . . . okay. Remember how I told you when you had to work from home at the beginning of COVID and the entire world was terrifying, there was this part of me that was actually less stressed? Because you were here every day?"

"Well, it helped that I wasn't losing my job, either. Plus I was working—you still had to do most of the stuff with the kids yourself." Even if her words were downplaying it, I could tell she was happy I'd brought this up.

"I mean, it wasn't a vacation. Global pandemics rarely are. But you were here. And you're, like, my person, you know?"

"Now you're just trying to get in my pants."

"That would be quite the feat, given our current setup."

"Speaking of," she said, "lest you be misled, it's not all glitz and glamour out here on the road. While our children were busy adoring you—and they do adore you, Jack—I was dining out of a plastic box from the hotel gift shop before settling in for a cozy night with my Excel sheets. It's a great consolation prize for giving up all those nights of bedtime stories and tucking people in."

Kayla loved her job. Or she had. So I wasn't ready for this.

"Do you ever . . . I mean, would you want to do something different?"

"That's funny—I was going to ask you the same thing."

"What?"

"Have you thought any more about maybe going back to work?" she said, studying me as much as she could over our broadband connection.

"You mean when Klay goes to school, right?"

"Or sooner. There is an entire industry built around childcare, you know. And I'm worried you're getting bored. *Desperate Housewives* is a little too on the nose."

Even her just putting out the possibility of me not being there with Klay made me panic. But while I felt like I fit more at home than I did at a job, neither one was exactly, 100 percent right. I kept thinking about that Walmart deal. I had been really good at what I did, but the fire had obscured the memory of that for a long time. Then along came this election, and I had started to use my mind to think strategy again, and the old Jack didn't feel so distant anymore. I liked that feeling—and it scared me because I didn't want to be away from my kids.

I should've told Kayla that. Or something like that. But not being sure what, if anything, I wanted to change, I fell into getting defensive (and yes, a little dramatic) about the choices that we'd already made. That *I'd* already made.

"I'm not leaving him, Kayla," I said, my pulse quickening.

"Okay, relax—it was just a suggestion."

"You don't need to tell me to relax. And honestly, it seems like *you're* the one who wants me to go back to work."

"If you wanted to, yeah, I'd support that."

"Because of the money?"

"No, I . . . look, two incomes wouldn't be a bad thing, right? But this isn't about that. I just feel like you're getting kind of restless around the house. But if you don't want to work right now, you don't need to."

"Why'd you say 'right now'? What if I don't ever want to work again? Can you be okay with that?"

"God, Jack, stop trying to parse my words for hidden meaning. I don't even know what we're arguing about. I'm just saying it's your call, okay?"

We sat there in our respective quiets. Having an argument over the phone had always been awkward, and the addition of screens hadn't made it any less so.

"I gotta go," Kayla said finally. "I've got some things I need to get done before bed."

"Okay. Sorry for . . . this."

"Yeah, me too. We'll figure it out."

"Yeah. All right. Bye."

"Bye."

I unpaused the show but didn't take any of it in. She'd said not to parse her words, but how could I not? Maybe she regretted taking the last promotion and wouldn't have done it if she weren't our lone source of income. Or did she just think I wasn't motivated anymore and wasting my potential? Okay, that was more likely to be my parents than my wife. But maybe not. Then again, it could really be just what she said: my call. The problem was I didn't know what call to make.

After 15 minutes of thinking in circles, I didn't want to think anymore that night, so of course there was no chance I'd stop. But I was tired, and at least I could lie down, close my eyes, and ruminate in bed. Turning the TV off, I remembered I still needed to pack Lulu's lunch. I should've done it right then, before my brain had a chance to register the urge to put it off. Because not even three weeks into my first child going to kindergarten, I had discovered just how disproportionately tedious it was to make school lunch, especially when there was regularly no other adult around to divvy it up with.

Single parents really are the closest thing we have to superheroes.

Plus Klay was coming with me on the field trip, so instead of the normal one lunch, I had to do two. Ugh. I felt the bed drawing me closer and decided I could make them in the morning. And then I snoozed one time too many, and Lulu didn't want to get dressed, and Klay didn't want to stop playing, and poof, there we were, scrambling out the door late with precisely zero lunches.

Hello, whatever I could find in the display case at Coffee Brewers.

"What're you thinking, bud?" I asked Klay as we sized up their offerings.

"Cookies!"

"Cookies?" I repeated back to him jokily. "You can't have cookies for lunch!"

He started giggling, and that made me smile because he's got the best laugh.

"Is that Klay?" came Sammi's voice from behind the counter. "What're you doing inside, dude? I'm used to seeing you in the drive-through!" This made him laugh even harder.

"Aww, so cute!" she said. "What can I get you two today?"

"Well, we're headed on Lulu's *first-ever* field trip, and Dad didn't get around to making lunches before we went sprinting out the door, so I think the box with the cheddar and fruit for her, a couple of applesauce pouches for him, and a large iced coffee for me." I thought about it for a second. "And two chocolate chip cookies."

"Yay, cookies!" Klay celebrated.

"Sounds good to me—fourteen fifty-seven," she said. "And that's funny about the field trip. I think the guy in the drive-through said he's going on the same one."

I looked over to the window. Chad. My face apparently said it all.

"Not a fan?" Sammi asked as she handed back my credit card.

"You could say that." I considered how I wanted to phrase it. "We have a bit of a history."

"Ha, us too. He insists we remake his drink at least three times a week." She lowered her eyes and her voice. "We've started screwing it up on purpose now just to tweak him."

I had been going for a one in my wallet, but that now felt woefully inadequate. "And that's five dollars from me into the tip jar today."

She laughed and thanked me and then went to get our order. Because the coffee was prebrewed and none of our food needed to be heated, she came back quickly, Chad still waiting at the window.

"I really hope I beat him back to the school," I said. "One day we got there only seventeen minutes before the tardy bell instead of twenty, and Lulu felt rushed, so she made me promise our car would be the first one in line today." Getting ready for this field trip had been the most connected I'd felt to her as a kindergartner, since I'd actually get to see her interacting with the other kids and the teachers. So I, too, was probably overinvested in this going exactly the way she and I had discussed.

Sammi's flurry of activity behind the counter came to an abrupt halt. "Well, what are the chances?" she said, straight faced. "We just dropped his drink and have to start over. Oops."

"You all are the best," I said, drawing out the last word and grabbing our lunch supplies and coffee with one hand and Klay's hand with the other. "Let's do this, little man."

I hustled us out, hitting the fob to open the van door before we had even left the shop. "Me do it, me do it!" Klay yelled as I went to lower him into his seat. He had chosen a hell of a moment to decide he was ready to start handling this himself.

"Buddy, Daddy's kind of in a hurry. Just let me do it, okay?"

"Noooooooo!" It sounded like someone falling off a cliff in an action movie.

"All right," I sighed. "Go ahead."

To my son's credit, he was focused. He was determined. And when he plopped down in that little bucket seat and announced with a smile that he was ready for me to buckle him in, he was proud. It was cool to see his sense of accomplishment and share in that with him.

He was also so slow that if you had told me enough time had passed for Chad to already be at the zoo making up alpaca facts, I would've believed it.

"Okay," I said, working the straps as fast as I could. "Here we go, here we go, Klay and Daddy, here we go. Going to the zoo. Aaand . . . done."

I hit the button to close his door and was already in my seat, turning the ignition, by the time it shut. I put the van into reverse while clicking my seat belt into place, only to hear my dashboard beeping at me. The backup assist. A car was going by behind us.

More specifically, a BMW SUV.

"Dammit," I said a little too loudly, but Klay was too busy gnawing on a Berenstain Bears book to care.

I waited for Chad to pass and then rolled back. The Coffee Brewers lot had a one-way entrance and a one-way exit, each of which was big enough only for one car at a time. Chad was already headed toward the exit, and there was a stream of a few cars turning in at the entrance, dispelling any fleeting notions I had of going rogue and escaping that way. That meant my only choice was to follow him.

The light at the corner had just gone red, and there was a semitruck coming up in the right lane. This wasn't so bad. We'd both be stuck behind it and go from there.

But Chad's driving was a distillation of his entire personality. Instead of waiting his turn, he gunned it out of the parking lot, blatantly cutting off the truck in the process. The driver shouted at him from inside his cab, which I appreciated, but it was small consolation.

Because this was it. This was where Chad was going to lose me. He would show up at the school first, leaving Lulu devastated when she walked out and our car wasn't at the front of the line, ahead of all the others. Plus, I had told Ms. Sandra I'd be there early in case they needed help getting the kids organized. Now they'd be looking for me, thinking, "I get the sense that Chad's taking all this a little more seriously than that Jake guy. And isn't that Jake's daughter screaming bloody murder? I just don't think Jake's up for being president, you know?"

Yes, I did know, hypothetical parent/teacher who didn't know my name and who I had conjured from my insecurities.

But what was I going to do? With the 18-wheeler behind Chad, I was sealed in.

Then I noticed the center lane.

It had been completely empty before Chad pulled out, and no one had come along since. I scanned the ground outside my window.

Sidewalk. Huh.

I thought through my options and looked up to my rearview mirror. "I think I can make it, Klay."

"Daddy make it!" he said before returning to chewing the corner of the book.

There was no one behind us in the driveway, so I backed up a few feet, then shifted back into drive and cut the wheel hard to the left.

"Wheeee!" Klay cheered as we bumped up onto the concrete of the sidewalk. This got the attention of a Prius driver, who looked startled. I smiled nervously, totally betraying my chance to play it off as something I did every day.

"You're doing this for Lulu," I said under my breath, like it was a mantra. And also like it had nothing to do with my own stress over wanting her first field trip and my first real interaction with the teachers to go perfectly.

I checked the center lane one last time and, seeing it was still clear, lightly pressed the gas. Our front wheels touched down, followed shortly by the sound of the curb gouging something on our underside. I winced.

"That wasn't good," Klay said. I didn't know whether to defend my driving or be excited he had spoken in a grammatically correct sentence.

Whatever had made that sound wasn't enough to deter us, but I was pretty sure I'd be looking up our deductible when we got home. That was a problem for later, though. We were out of the driveway, onto the street, and the light was still red. I gave the woman in the Prius a sheepish wave, rolled past the tractor trailer, and pulled up next to Chad, the first two in our respective lanes. I sat there, heart pumping, waiting for him to look over, but as the left-turn arrow went yellow and we were about to get the green, he still hadn't. No problem.

I just revved my engine. Like I was Vin Diesel.

CHAPTER 16

In hindsight, I probably should've taken advantage of Chad being distracted and used that to get to the school first. Because no matter how satisfying it was to pump that gas pedal once to get him to look over, and then again when he did, there was no getting around the fact that he was in a BMW and I was in a vehicle that was at least 17 percent discarded Cheerios and french fries.

The worst part was that he didn't even have to gun it, like he did with the truck. He just smoothly accelerated to 50, caught the next light at the yellow, and left me and my wounded pride rolling to a stop at the intersection of State and First, his vanity license plate taunting me as it went:

HENSOME.

I could only assume that was a play on his last name and the word *handsome*, which made me want to go back and give Sammi $50 to come up with something a lot worse to do to his coffee.

When I got to the school, he was already out of his car, surrounded by a circle of parents laughing about who knows what. It looked like they were filming a campaign spot. It also meant I hadn't just failed to get there before Chad; I hadn't gotten there before anyone, even though I had pulled up with close to 10 minutes to spare.

I threw the van into park. No sign of the kids yet. Maybe if I met Lulu right away when she came out, she wouldn't be upset about how far back our car was in the line, and I could still try to help the teachers. There was time to rally.

I got Klay out of his seat and had put him on the ground when the gaggle of kids started streaming out of Door D.

"All kindergartners, on the bus," Ms. Sandra hollered. "Grown-ups, we will see you there."

I forgot all about making a good impression on the teachers and focused exclusively on finding Lulu. We had gone over how I'd be the one driving her maybe five times. The teacher I remembered as being Ms. Brianne was the closest to me, so I picked Klay back up and flagged her down as nonaggressively as possible.

"Excuse me, Ms. Brianne? Hi, I'm Jack Parker."

"Oh, sure!" she said. "So great you can come with us today!"

"Yeah, happy to do it. Anyway, I . . . uh . . . I told my daughter I'd be driving her to the zoo?"

"Actually, all the kiddos ride the bus together."

"Yeah, I know," I said. "I mean, I heard. I'm afraid she's going to get upset since this wasn't what she was expecting."

"Who's your daughter?" she asked, breaking away from the pack and coming over to talk with me.

"Lulu. Lulu Parker." I scanned the masses for the multicolored long-sleeved peacock shirt she had insisted on wearing that morning. I had finally given in about it, but only because I was going to be there and could bring something short-sleeved for her to change into when it got too hot, which felt like it would be in about 10 minutes.

"There she is!" Ms. Brianne said, pointing about two-thirds of the way up. How did teachers learn names so fast? Lulu wasn't even in her class.

"Aah, yes. In the totally understated peacock shirt, as you can see."

Ms. Brianne laughed. "And she does seem to be having fun."

She was right. Lulu was talking animatedly with Crispin (who else?) as they waited their turn to get on the bus. I was happy because she was happy and clearly adjusting to the whole school thing better than I had thought she was, but I was also kinda sad. I told myself it was because Chad's kid was involved, and that probably was a piece of it. Mostly, though, I think I was just bummed she didn't need me at least a little bit. It would take years, but our gradual separation was beginning, and I'd watch it keep unfolding right before my eyes. At some point along the way, I'd need to figure out what I wanted to do when *dad* would no longer be my primary job description.

"Well, is there anything I can help with?" I asked. "I told Ms. Sandra I'd be around if you all needed anything."

"Oh, right, she did mention that! Nope, I think we're all set for now."

"It's almost like you teachers know *exactly* what you're doing," I joked, even as my brain begged me to ask, So we met at the school because . . . why?

"I'm glad at least one of the candidates thinks so," she said with a knowing smile. She started to head back to the kids. "See you at the zoo!"

Well, that was interesting. The technology fee had been proposed by the teachers. Was that what she was referring to? Were they upset about Chad's post too? I filed this away to tell Tori.

Klay and I got back to the car, and soon we were all caravanning to a zoo you wouldn't have expected to find in a town of our size. It wasn't like the one in San Diego, but there were tigers and lions and even giraffes, and it was accredited by whatever national organization accredited the big zoos, so you didn't feel like a jerk for being there.

"This is cute," I heard Chad say to a mom in the parking lot as I was getting Klay out of his seat; he did it in that way that leaves no doubt that *cute* is the last word you'd use to pay anything a compliment.

"Nothing like the San Diego Zoo, of course. We went there at least three times a year. A-mazing."

San Diego promptly dropped in my power ranking of famous zoos I had never visited.

The teachers took the 65 kindergartners through a special prepaid entrance for large groups while the 15 "special friends"—9 moms, Chad and me, someone's grandma, and 3 younger siblings, including Klay—split up between the two regular admission lines.

By the time we were all in, the kids were raring to go, and I showed Klay where Lulu was. He and I both waved, and the look on her face when she waved back more than made up for the fact that she was still standing side by side with Crispin.

"Boys and girls, boys and girls, let's quiet down for one more minute," Ms. Sandra said in a surprisingly effective effort to restore order. "We've gone over the zoo rules and our school rules. The last thing we need to do is thank all of our special friends for coming with us to the zoo today. Can you say thank you?"

"Thank you!" they all yelled at once in a tsunami of adorableness.

"Now remember how I said we're going to break up into groups," she continued. "There are three teachers plus twelve other grown-ups. That makes fifteen. And the fifteen of us are going to split into five groups of three grown-ups each, with thirteen of you kindergartners in each of those groups. We've already divided you up."

I was glad she understood what she was saying because the only thing I heard was there was a chance Chad and I would be coparenting our way through the walkable rolling pasture of the Australia exhibit with 13 children in tow.

However, these teachers were once again several steps ahead of me. As Ms. Sandra started to read off group numbers and the names of the adults leading them, it became clear she had put us in alphabetical order. So when "Mr. Henson" was announced as the last chaperone for group two, I knew Mr. Parker was home free in group three, four, or five.

How they had assigned which kids went with whom was a little more nebulous, other than if a student had a grown-up on the trip, they got to be in the same group. That meant Lulu and Crispin were being split up. He looked pained when he had to walk over to the group led by his dad—which, understandable—while she came sprinting over to Klay and me when Ms. Sandra read her name. That got some chuckles and *aws* from the moms and, in addition to making me smile, would have been worth at least a couple of points in the polls, if polls for president of the Active Alpaca Parent Board had existed.

I was leading with two moms I hadn't met before: Tracy Jarvis (maybe Jervis?), who I found out was on her third kid at Willow Road, and Lana Ordoñez, who was on her second. Lana knew I was running for president but didn't seem to know about the barfy emoji, and Tracy didn't seem to know there was a parent board or had chosen to block it out. I worked in that I had been endorsed by Elena as casually as I could, but it was hard to tell how much that resonated with them. Neither sounded like they cared very much for Ms. Weekler, though.

In other words, my people.

Our job was simple enough: see as many of the animals as possible, get the kids to the picnic area at 11:00 a.m. for lunch, and make sure we didn't lose anyone in the bathroom or the reptile house along the way. The only wild card was who was going to read the questions the teachers had given for each exhibit, the goal being to get the kids to pay attention to more than which animal made the biggest poop.

None of us were jumping at the opportunity, and I thought about suggesting we take turns, but then I remembered I was supposed to be convincing other parents of my ability to lead and of my overall good-naturedness.

"If you two can help me a little with this guy," I said, pulling Klay away from his attempt to scale the fence around the tortoise enclosure, "I'd be happy to do it."

They traded looks. "Works for me," Lana said while Tracy nodded in agreement.

"Hey, 'Works for me': that should be my campaign slogan," I said, which made them smile and offered the perfect window to add, "How ridiculous would that be? A campaign slogan—for parent board?"

That got a laugh, and so began my stint as a pretend tour guide. And *pretend* was the operative word because after failed attempts to get the 13 of them excited over the diet of the American bison and the tunneling capabilities of prairie dogs, I decided to go off book when we got to the lions.

"Do you all see Mr. Henson over there?" I pointed him out on the other side of a little man-made lake, near this ox-looking creature we hadn't visited yet. "Did you know he and I went to school together when we were kids"—a few ohs started to bounce around the little faces staring at me—"but that instead of the alpacas, our school was called *the lions?*"

"Did your school have a real lion?" some kid asked me in wonder while simultaneously picking his nose.

"Only on Tuesdays," I said, a line both Tracy and Lana enjoyed.

"Did you play together?" Tracy's daughter asked.

"Who, me and Mr. Henson? Well, we played soccer together, but it wasn't nearly as fun as it sounds."

On the way to the anteater, Lana remarked how random it was Chad and I had known each other in high school. So, twist my arm, I told them about Maria and the prom.

Tracy made a yikes face, and Lana just said, "Wow."

"Yeah," I said to the two of them, then looked back down to the kids. "All right—who wants to see the alligator?"

That suggestion proved popular, as did me asking them when we got to the alligator whether they thought it ever brushed all those teeth or had Doritos breath 24-7.

"Mr. Parker, alligators don't eat Doritos!" one of the girls yelled over the laughter.

"He's just being funny," Lulu said, half-amused and half-mortified by her father for the first of what I guessed would be roughly a billion times.

I looked back over the wooden railing down into the gator's faux swamp.

"Am I?" I asked leadingly, and then they all, my daughter included, appeared to start questioning everything they thought they knew about alligators. We arrived at the picnic tables for lunch with several of them debating whether that 800-pound killing machine would prefer Cool Ranch or nacho cheese. Turns out I gave pretty entertaining tours.

Our young charges reunited with their lunch boxes, Tracy, Lana, and I chatted for a minute, and I felt pretty good about the chances of them voting for me. They hadn't heard of the technology fee before, either, and they both responded well to what I had to say about its importance in giving all the kids access to the same resources and the idea of using the parent board to promote equity more generally—something that had been on my mind ever since Chad started talking cuts.

But then I discovered I should've been allowed only to talk to parents whose last names were immediately adjacent to mine alphabetically.

"*You* do this?" It was a mom two tables over, and the awe in her voice was unmistakable. "Like, every day?"

"Well, maybe not the homemade granola every day," Chad chuckled. "But yes, I make his lunch." Pause for effect. "Every day."

"That's so great," a different mom added.

"Oh, it's not that big of a deal," he said, reveling in the attention. "Finding things he'll eat—that's the bigger challenge. I really have to be purposeful with my shopping."

Several other mothers were listening by now and appeared to be sexually aroused.

"You do the *grocery shopping* too?" the original one asked.

"Guilty as charged," Chad quipped.

"I can't even get my husband to load the dishwasher," number two said.

"I actually handwash everything," he said. "I find it relaxing."

Oh. My. *God.*

"Maybe we should give you your own holiday," I mumbled, making sure it was loud enough for him to hear through the multitude of conversations the kids were having.

"What was that, Jack?"

"I'm just saying," I said, not looking at him or any of the moms in particular, "you make your kid's lunch. Great. So does everyone else here. And you don't see anyone giving them credit for it."

If I thought I was going to become a feminist icon among the moms at Willow Road Elementary by acknowledging that Chad was seeking praise for something all the women there did with no fanfare, I couldn't have been more wrong. One with fire engine–red nails began a very exaggerated crunching of her water bottle, and another angrily pulled her hair back into a ponytail, presumably so it wouldn't get in her way while she kicked me in the groin.

I was so busy watching their reactions I didn't even realize my more fundamental error.

"And what did you make for Lulu's lunch today?" Chad asked.

Crap buckets.

"Uh, well, last night kinda got away from me a little, so . . ."

He raised his eyebrows, pressing me to go on. I felt the blood rushing to my face as I fumbled for the good excuse that would get me out of this. I wasn't going to tell them I'd gotten into a fight with my wife and had just gone to bed. So that left only one option.

"It was . . . uh . . . a *Desperate Housewives* marathon. And I forgot to make it." The guilt emanated off me. "So I picked something up on the way in this morning."

The mom who had first asked him about making lunch rolled her eyes. Water Bottle stifled a laugh. Thank God Lulu was distracted by trying to get Klay to do his cow impression for one of her friends. I didn't want her to see her dad looking like a moron.

"I really believe it's a parent's job to be their child's advocate when it comes to their diet," Chad said, smarmy as ever. "That's why I think we should have a gourmet-snacks bar in the cafeteria. It would cost more than a standard school lunch, but aren't our kids worth it?"

"Forget how many of them couldn't afford it, right?" I shot back, reminding myself that he was the moron.

"Jack, I don't think this is the time or place, do you?"

It wasn't, but I didn't care. I was a candidate for president of the Active Alpaca Parent Board, and I didn't need to wait for the debate. I was ready to hit back, starting with that technology fee.

But I didn't get the chance.

"Excuse me, Mr. Parker?" Ms. Sandra asked, tapping me on the shoulder. "Did you tell the children it was okay to feed the alligator Doritos?"

CHAPTER 17

A double-barreled bedtime is where the delusion that you have any degree of control over your life goes to die.

It's both kids—at least one of whom is guaranteed to be a devout sleep atheist—versus you and your inability to be in two places at once. (Parents with three or more kids? Sure, they exist, but based on what I've seen at bedtime, that existence is a logical impossibility.)

"Why do you have to do my bedtime?" Lulu said, more an accusation than a question. We were sitting on the floor in Kayla's and my bathroom, me blow-drying her hair after her shower. "I want Mommy."

"Mommy has to work late tonight, remember? So I'm doing both of your bedtimes." Klay, who had been playing with a tub of blocks I had explicitly told him not to drag out of his room, immediately burst into tears.

"Ugh, again?" Lulu groaned, backing up her brother. "That's three nights in a row!"

Did she think I didn't know that? I knew that. If knowing that were an Olympic sport, I'd have more gold medals than Michael Phelps. If knowing that were Scrabble, I'd be *quixotic* on a triple word score. If knowing that were the X-Men, I'd be . . . a good one?

Comic books were never my thing.

It wasn't like I was choosing to torture them. Kayla had hardly ever missed bedtime before her last promotion, but just like the travel, it had become increasingly common in the months since then, such that her getting home at a normal time was starting to feel more like the exception than the rule.

"I know you want Mommy," I said, moving the aim of the hair dryer from Lulu's hair to the right leg of my shorts, which were still wet from Klay's bath. "Mommy wishes she could be here. She just has a lot to do this week."

I thought about debate night, a little over a week away. Kayla had shown me the entry for it on her calendar when she got home from her trip, but the circumstances I found myself in on that bathroom floor still made me nervous something would go wrong. If work got crazy at the last minute and she couldn't get home, I didn't know what I'd do. I could ask Tori to watch the kids, but I was really counting on her to be there in the gym for support. A mad dash to get out the door that night also wouldn't put me in the best mindset to face Chad. Neither would dragging my children along as the clock ticked down toward bedtime and they transformed into full-on gremlins.

My shorts now more damp than wet, I flipped the hair dryer off and stood up. "All right, team: let's do this. Klay, you're up first. Lulu, you can play or read in your room."

"Aww," he whined. "Lu go first."

"Really? You want Lulu to go first? You're two. What're you going to do? Work on your macramé?"

"What's macramé?" Lulu asked.

"You ask a lot of questions," I said.

"He could watch," she suggested. That was true. I had already let them watch more TV than I liked while making dinner, but these were battle conditions. And in battle conditions, anything went.

"Okay, Klay, do you want to watch something while Daddy does Lulu's bedtime?"

"That's not fair!" she yelled.

I narrowed my gaze on her. "Excuse me—what?"

"Why do I have to go first?"

"I thought you wanted to go first."

"Just because I said he could watch doesn't mean I want to go first! And I shouldn't have to go first! I'm older!"

"Uh, you don't have to go first!" I said, wishing some other adult was around to stand witness to this Ferris wheel of logic she had dragged me on. "That was the whole point!"

She cheered and ran off to her room, and I looked at Klay, who had left his toys behind for a far more interesting activity: trying to solve the baby lock on the cabinet under the sink.

"Let's go, little dude."

That set off a fresh round of crying, wherein he defiantly held on to the cabinet like it was a buoy saving him from washing out to sea. I pried him off and then, due to his sudden thrashing, tucked him under my right arm to carry him down the hall to his room.

The first few minutes in his bed were touch and go. But the under-rated thing about shrieking is that it expends a lot of energy, which meant he faded fast.

"You're here already?" Lulu said when I got to her room, making no effort to mask her disappointment.

"Hey, I'll give you another twenty minutes if you want to put yourself to bed."

She stopped rocking her yellow rocking chair. "By myself?"

"Yup."

"No, thanks." She jumped off the chair and ran to her bed, her book still under her arm. Once she was in, I switched off her light and climbed in next to her.

"What are we reading tonight?" I asked. She was on a real Curious George kick, so when I turned on my phone's flashlight, there was the Man in the Yellow Hat once again deciding the wild animal he'd chosen to raise as a child could be left unattended without triggering disastrous consequences.

She started to drift off while we were still reading, and there were no further arguments when I closed the book and turned off the light. I checked a post I'd done earlier in the day, a screenshot from my notes app of a list titled "Seven Signs You're Running for Your Kid's School's Parent Board":

1. You're maybe a little too opinionated about the shape of the cafeteria's chicken nuggets. (Why would they ever *not* be dinosaurs?!)

2. You've yet to experience the horrors of an e-learning day.

3. You're hoping that this somehow gets you out of the candy sale.

4. You tell yourself it has nothing to do with your daughter going to kindergarten and your subsequent existential crisis as a stay-at-home parent. *chokes back tears* Excuse me.

5. You support the technology fee.

6. Seriously, that last one's not a joke.

7. It was developed by the teachers and ensures the kids have equal access to technology. It's a good thing.

I was at 19 likes and 3 fire emoji. I then peeked at Chad's most recent dispatch from the front lines of douchedom, a link to a how-to video of him making bread. Twenty-four likes. Apparently the zoo lunch crew weren't the only ones buying what he was selling.

A text from Tori popped up.

Where's Kayla?

<Just got home.> I'd heard the garage door open while I was checking Chad's feed. <Why?>

You need to be at Target in 20 minutes.

I looked at my phone skeptically before replying:

???

It took her a minute to type her answer, during which I crossed my fingers that Lulu had fallen asleep and sneaked out of her room. Risky, yes, but if her sleeping didn't stick, I could now call in Kayla for reinforcements, which changed the whole dynamic of the night.

As I pulled the door shut behind me, Tori's message came through. Apparently Kathy Francis had some information she had to give me, and she was willing to do so only under the cover of the home-goods section.

<Okay, stupid question>, I typed back. <Who's Kathy Francis again?>

MS. WEEKLER'S ASSISTANT!!!

I stopped in the middle of the stairs, Kayla looking up at me from the bottom.

"I gotta go to Target," I said, still processing what this development could possibly mean.

"At eight thirty? On a Wednesday?"

"Kathy Francis is ready to talk." I put it out there with confidence, like it made all the sense in the world.

"Who's Kathy Francis?"

"Uh, Ms. Weekler's assistant? Like, *everybody* knows that."

"Did *you* know that?" Kayla asked.

"Obviously not."

"And what, she just texted you out of nowhere and told you to meet her at Target?"

I stopped next to her. "Hi, by the way," I said, kissing her on the cheek. The argument from when she was on the road hadn't come up again. We hadn't gotten into another fight, but we also hadn't settled anything. "No, she texted Tori and told Tori to tell me to meet her at Target in, let's see, seventeen minutes now. Duh."

"Sure, sure, sure," Kayla said, following me down the hall to the kitchen. "Seems like pretty standard behavior."

"Hey, we all knew what I was signing up for when I entered the high-stakes world of elementary school politics." I bent down to slip on my shoes. "Speaking of, if I'm not back in an hour, call the authorities and tell them to look for my body in the freezer aisle."

"Ooh, can you get some ice cream?"

I frowned. "You moved on from my grisly murder pretty quick there."

"What do you think the ice cream is for? I have to cope with my grief somehow, Jack."

"Good save," I said, grabbing the knob of the door to the garage. "Wish me luck."

"And not something boring, like chocolate or vanilla." Her head was in the refrigerator, so I could see only the bottom half of her legs. "Like a real flavor. Love you!"

"Uh-huh."

At that time of day, the drive to Target took under 10 minutes, but that was more than long enough to imagine the movie these events were bound to inspire—sort of an *All the President's Men* but for Lifetime.

"I wonder what Pacey from *Dawson's Creek* is up to these days," I said to myself, making my first casting decision as the automatic doors slid open to welcome me in. They had the air conditioner going full blast, and the wave of cold that hit me caused the hairs on my arms to stand up. Because I still had a few minutes to kill, I decided to hang a right away from all the cold and frozen stuff in groceries and take the long way around to home goods. I realized as I did that I didn't know what Kathy Francis looked like, and I never got enough of a phone signal in Target to try to look it up. I hoped she would be easy to spot.

Alas, I needn't have been worried.

True, I didn't know for sure that the only person in sight, the one pretending to carefully examine the craftsmanship of the woven storage baskets, was indeed Kathy Francis. But the sunglasses and black hoodie paired with the work slacks and sensible shoes removed most doubt.

I approached her slowly, leaning toward the shelves to try to catch her eye in her peripheral vision.

"Uh, Kathy?"

"Shh!" she said without looking toward me. "And don't use my real name."

"Okay," I said more quietly than before but refusing to drop all the way to a whisper. "What should I call you, then?"

She thought for a second and then smiled. "Call me Deep Throat."

"Yeah, I'm not gonna do that. For a variety of reasons." I mean, I appreciated the Watergate esprit de corps. But no.

"Whatever. It doesn't matter. You don't need to call me anything. Because this is the one and only time we're meeting, and this meeting never happened."

"Well, I should tell you I am going to buy some ice cream after this, so, you know—paper trail."

"Look, do you want my help or not?" Her voice had assumed its normal volume, and I recognized it from the day I had called the school office about Lulu's dentist appointment.

"Sorry. I'm just a little confused. Like, why didn't you text me yourself? The school has my number."

She exhaled. She was getting impatient. "Like I said, I didn't want there to be any kind of record between me and you about meeting here tonight." She paused to fish something out of her purse. "Or of me giving you this."

Kathy handed me a yellow-gold interoffice delivery envelope wound shut on the back with a figure eight of red thread. I got another chill, but this time not from the AC.

"What's in here?"

"Something I overheard Deidre giving to Chad. Something to help his campaign. And I know for a fact he's using it, so I thought you should have it too."

I went to start unwinding the thread, but she put her hand up.

"Don't look at it here. Take it home."

I stopped and switched the envelope to my side. "Why are you doing this?"

"Because she thinks she can have whatever she wants, and it's wrong. And because Elena Choi is my friend."

So it seemed at least one other person had heard what had gone on that night in the spring.

"Fair enough," I said. "And thank you."

She gave a single nod of acknowledgment. "Remember, this never happened."

"Right." It was clear she wanted me to leave first, so I did.

"One more thing," she said when I was about out of the aisle. I turned to face her again, but she was back to staring at the shelf.

"Yeah?" I asked.

"There's a two-for-one on ice cream in the Target app."

CHAPTER 18

"Please tell me that's a box of wine."

"Oh, you know it's a box of wine, Jack Parker."

It was Saturday night, three days after I had met up with Kathy, and an Uber had just dropped Tori and Brooke off for a night of alcohol-infused debate prep. Brooke, who insisted on squaring off against me in the role of Chad, handed me three liters of red as she walked through the door.

"I hope you're ready for the full Henson," she said. "Because I'm going method."

"So you swore a blood oath to your hair gel on the way over?"

She rubbed her chin, nodded, and infused her voice with two tablespoons of pompousness. "That's a really interesting question, Jack."

"This hasn't gotten obnoxious at all," Tori said, pushing past us into the house.

While "debate prep" was in a lot of ways an excuse for the four of us to hang out without the kids—ours were already in bed, and theirs were with Tori's mom—Tori had suggested an added strategy session once we figured out what Chad was up to with the information Ms. Weekler had slipped him.

It hadn't appeared especially scandalous when I opened the envelope while sitting in the van in the Target parking lot: just the names, email addresses, and phone numbers of every parent at Willow Road. However, on the drive home, it dawned on me that the school didn't share contact information with anyone, not even among parents with kids in the same class. All communication came either from the all-school email list, which was controlled by Ms. Weekler's office, or from the teachers, via an app. Outside of social media, the only way for one parent to contact another was to ask for their info directly.

Unless your name was Chad Henson.

When I got home that night, I gave Kayla her two gallons of rocky road and cookie dough, called Tori, and put the phone on speaker to tell them both at the same time. Tori then fired off a few texts and made a couple of calls to parents she knew well, and within the hour, we knew that Chad was sending people messages introducing himself as the president-elect and inviting them to contact him if they had any concerns about the school. That neither Tori nor Brooke had gotten a text led us to conclude he knew enough not to send them to everyone.

I was fuming. "That lying piece of garbage. He thinks this is going to get him votes?"

"It probably will," Tori said. "People will see his name on the ballot and assume they're supposed to vote for him or something."

"I think it's more than that," Kayla added. We had the phone perched on the armrest of the couch, and her feet were on my lap. "I think he thinks this will confuse people into *not* voting. Like, 'If this guy's already the president-elect, is that thing I thought I heard about there being an election really even true?' How many people would even care enough to find out? He's basically gaslighting them."

"But Elena did that post . . . ," I said, my voice trailing off in anticipation of what Kayla was going to say.

"Yeah, but how many people saw that? Fifty? Sixty? And even the ones who did see it, how many of them are now just going to assume they missed the election? It's not like the average parent is going to start checking around with other parents, most of whom they don't even know, about the veracity of text messages from the school."

"People not voting could hurt both of us, though."

Tori jumped back in. "No, Kayla's right. Chad's banking on his core support being stronger and therefore more likely to show up and vote, no matter what. And with Ms. Weekler behind him, I don't know that he's wrong. Higher turnout hurts him, so he's trying to keep the numbers low."

Clearly the actions of someone who was running purely "for the kids."

We felt pretty confident we knew what their endgame was. In the three days since we had pieced it all together, though, we hadn't settled on the right way to use it against him, or whether we even should. We had briefly considered the idea of me using the list of numbers to contradict his lies, but both Tori and I had felt so gross about it that we ruled it out. No matter what, the debate had taken on added significance as a public, officially sanctioned way to show the other parents the election was still very much up for grabs—and that their votes mattered.

Chad wasn't just a liar; he was proposing a change that would actually hurt families at the school. I had asked Ms. Sandra via the app if I was right in thinking that the teachers still supported the technology fee. She confirmed they did and that a lot of them thought Chad's plan was ill conceived but they couldn't risk saying so publicly and getting on the wrong side of the parents if he won.

"I'm leaning toward just letting the texting thing go," I said when Brooke, Tori, Kayla, and I were seated around our kitchen table with glasses of wine and a spread of pretzels, tortilla chips and guac, and Ruffles and french onion dip (we were classy like that). "As much as I want to nail him on it, I don't think it makes sense. I need to focus on the debate."

"For God's sake, Jack," Brooke said through a mouthful of chips. "Chad's right."

"Excuse me?"

"You *are* too nice."

"Okay—how do you suggest I do it, then?"

The pleasure that spread across her face was unmistakable. "You already said it: the debate."

"The debate? How am I supposed to prove this at a debate?"

"Proof? Since when have debates been about proving anything?" She took another scoop of the french onion and looked at Tori and me. "I mean, really. You two are lucky you have me."

"I think it's time you put your money where your mouth is," Tori said as she refilled her glass. "Who's ready to do this?"

"Best Saturday night ever," Kayla said, clapping her hands in excitement before standing up and walking to the other side of the kitchen.

"Where are you going?" I asked. She and Tori had decided they would co-moderate, but I didn't know why that would entail a trip to the junk drawer.

"Oh, I wrote out questions," she said upon pulling them out. *"On index cards."*

"Oooh," Brooke said.

Tori turned back to her wife and me. "Lady, gentleman—or should I say Mr. Henson, Mr. Parker—if you would please take your places at opposite ends of the mantel."

Brooke put her empty glass on the table and headed for the spot to the left of the fireplace, where our vacuum cleaner would stand in as her podium. "You can call me Chad," she called over her shoulder as she went, signaling Tori had filled her in on his routine at orientation. "Mr. Henson is my dad!"

"I'm never sleeping with you again," Tori said, she and Kayla taking their places on the couch.

"That's a lie," Brooke shot back with a wink.

Tori tried not to smile but couldn't help it. She paused a few beats in an effort to inject a level of realism into the proceedings and then launched into her opening.

"Good evening, everyone, and welcome to the debate between the candidates for president of the Active Alpaca Parent Board, Chad Henson and Jack Parker. My name is Tori St. James, and to my left is my colleague Kayla Parker. Kayla, I believe you have the first question."

Kayla had slipped her glasses on and was all business. And because she's my wife, I can tell you: she looked hot.

"Yes, thank you, Tori." Kayla turned from Tori to Brooke. "Mr. Henson, early in this campaign, you were the target of a particularly pointed social media attack from Mr. Parker. What did you take away from that experience?"

"Objection," I said, despite being even more turned on by her than before. Is that weird?

"It's not a trial, Jack," Tori interjected. "You can't object."

"Yeah, but that's a ridiculous question. You know I didn't do that."

"You don't think Ms. Weekler is gonna go there? This isn't about making you feel good. It's about getting you ready."

I couldn't argue with that—especially not while standing behind a stack of empty diaper boxes—so I waved my hand in a mix of acknowledgment and acquiescence.

"Mr. Henson?" Kayla said.

"Well, if you're going to insist on calling me Mr. Henson, I guess I can't stop you," Brooke said with a syrupy laugh. She was creepily good at this. "As for Mr. Parker, all I can say is we've known each other for a long time, and I thought that when my family and I moved here, he and I could let bygones be bygones. Call me an optimist, I don't know.

But I guess he just isn't ready to move on and focus on the kids. That's his prerogative. It is regrettable that he attacked my son, though."

"Mr. Parker, your response?" Kayla asked, betraying zero hint of the marital vows we had taken to each other.

"Okay, for one, it wasn't an attack on your son; it was an attack on your son's *name*, which you gave him and is ridiculous." Kayla didn't break character, but Tori was shaking her head no. I closed my eyes and reset.

"Uh, what I meant to say was that I agree that that post was out of line. I know I have no way of proving this to all of you, but it wasn't actually me who made it. Nevertheless, it came from my account, so I take responsibility for it, and I'm especially sorry that Crispin got dragged into it."

Better, Tori mouthed at me, and I nodded in agreement. This time, Kayla was looking at me approvingly—until she reached into her pocket to grab her phone. The look faded as she studied the screen.

"Sorry, I gotta take this," she said, leaving the couch. They were down a couple of people at the office and trying to close a new account, so her work calls had been more frequent on the weekends, just like the later nights during the week.

"You want us to wait?" I asked.

"No, no, you keep going. I'll be right back." Some of the air went out of the room for me. I got it: she was being considerate. But I'd wanted her to say yes because it felt like that would mean this meant as much to her as it was coming to mean to me.

"Mr. Parker," Tori said, not giving me a chance to wallow, "the next question is for you. You were formerly an employee of Mouth Inc., where you rather infamously burned down one of the company's buildings and were fired as a result. What makes you think you'll be up to the *responsibility* of leading the Active Alpaca Parent Board?"

I was waiting for her to pull off her Tori mask and reveal herself to be Ms. Weekler, Scooby-Doo–style, because this was brutal. But she was right. I had to be prepared to answer. The way I handled this issue could go a long way in determining who would win. And the school would work so much better if the families and teachers were on the same page—not just with respect to the technology fee but also if we, as parents, made more of a habit of seeking out the expertise of those who were actually in the classrooms.

"Well, it wasn't the *whole* building," I said with a forced chuckle, "and as I'm sure most of you know from the video, technically, my firing had more to do with my choice of candy bar, not the fire. Incidentally, that should inspire a lot of faith in Mouth Inc.'s leadership, which, if I'm not mistaken, includes my opponent's wife."

"Careful," Tori said as Brooke raised her hand, exuding Chad-like impatience.

"But as for your question," I said, "before Mouth bought it out, I was director of corporate strategy for a company called Scrub. You all remember Scrub, right? That electric toothbrush that no one, including Mouth, could compete with? Anyway, it's been several years now—years I've been home raising our two kids, Lulu and Klay—but I'm confident my experience as a director of corporate strategy and as a stay-at-home dad make me the right candidate to lead the AAPB."

I stopped. That was the answer I had been rehearsing in my head, I had delivered it more or less how I had envisioned, and aside from the dig at Cassie, Tori seemed pretty impressed with it. I began steeling myself for Brooke's response, knowing she was ready to let loose with the most devastating attack about the fire she could come up with because that was surely what Chad would do.

But then I remembered her advice, and I realized I might not have to give him that opening.

"First of all, Jack—" she started.

"Hold on, my time isn't up yet." Brooke looked genuinely taken aback. "And as long as we're on the subject of responsibility," I said, turning from her to my imaginary audience and gripping the sides of the Huggies box, "I think the relevant question is whether *Mr. Henson* is responsible enough to be entrusted with a leadership role in the Willow Road community."

"What's that supposed to mean?" Brooke asked.

I faced her and pictured him. "For one, it means I want to hear you explain to all these parents how cutting the technology 'tax,' as you call it, will disproportionately hurt kids whose families have lower incomes, all so you can save a few bucks."

"Well, I don't think that's what I—"

"It also means I'd love to know how you got the names and phone numbers of all the parents in this school so you could text them, claiming to be the president-elect, when the very fact that we're standing on this stage tonight proves that that's a lie."

Ironically, although Brooke had devised this strategy, she didn't seem to have game-planned Chad's response to it. Maybe that was because there wasn't a good answer.

"I don't know what you're talking about," she finally said.

"You don't? No problem." I felt so locked in it was almost like he was standing there in our living room. I gestured toward the oven in the distance. "Show of hands: How many people here tonight got a text from Mr. Henson introducing himself as the president-elect? Wow. Looks like more than half of you. And didn't you wonder, How did he get my number in the first place?"

"I, uh . . . I got them from the school directory. Obviously."

"Nope. There is no all-school directory. I called and asked Ms. Weekler's office to be sure. I mean, her office *does* have all our numbers. But there's no *publicly* available list."

"Just what are you implying, Mr. Parker?" Tori said. She was trying to muster Ms. Weekler's indignation but couldn't because of how much she was loving this.

"I'm not implying anything. I simply want to know how Mr. Henson got his hands on information that only the principal's office is supposed to have access to."

Silence fell over the living room. I noticed for the first time that my heart was pounding even though my voice had stayed relatively even. Tori beamed up at me like a proud mom.

"That's what I'm talking about!" Brooke yelled with a fist pump, abandoning her alter ego. "And forget the boxed wine! We need real drinks! Where do you keep your scotch, Jack?"

"I think we have some hard seltzer."

"Close enough!" she said and headed toward the fridge.

"Whoa, hard seltzer," Kayla said, reappearing from around the corner. "What are we celebrating?"

"Our boy Jack taking my advice and burying that poser!" Brooke shouted from the kitchen.

"It was pretty great," Tori agreed.

"That's awesome, babe," Kayla said. She looked conflicted as she said it, though, and I knew something wasn't right.

"What's wrong?" I asked.

Brooke closed the refrigerator, and Tori stopped typing a text. We all waited on Kayla to answer.

"So the debate is still this coming Thursday, right?" Her voice was quiet.

"Yeah," I said, my stomach sinking. "The eighteenth. Why?"

"Ugh. That's what I thought." She looked down at the floor. "I think we need to ask if your mom can come to stay with the kids."

"Why?" I repeated, even though I already knew the answer.

"Work. I have to go to Minneapolis."

CHAPTER 19

What came next was drinking. Lots of drinking. By me especially. Not college or mid-20s levels of inebriation, but for someone in the vicinity of 40, it was a solid effort. And a matter of self-preservation. We had friends over, and I didn't want Kayla and me to get into it again in front of them. Having always been a happy drunk, I knew my buzz would keep me from dwelling on Minneapolis. But even then it was hard.

This was all about a potential new client. Did the presentation to them have to be in person, or did Kayla just *feel* like it had to be in person? They were an Illinois company, so why Minneapolis? Had she even said she had a conflict? Because this was exactly what I'd feared would happen. She had made a production of showing me the debate on her calendar—like I was being this paranoid, clingy spouse about the whole thing—and the thought of that only stoked my frustration more.

True, she did apologize. A few times. But all I wanted to hear was that I'd been right. And maybe for her to say that she wouldn't go if I really needed her there (even if we both knew there would be no good way for her to back out).

On top of that: the no-sitter thing. Now that Kayla wouldn't even be in the same state, I wanted the reassurance of Tori being with me at the debate even more. That left only one option:

I'd have to call in my mom last minute from four hours away.

I was sure she'd agree, after first finding a way to let me know it was a lot to ask without ever resorting to saying it. That wasn't a big deal. It was just part of the transaction with her. The real problem, of course, was that I'd need to fill my parents in on the "I'm running for parent board" thing after all. I wouldn't be surprised if she showed up with a brochure about MBA programs in hand.

Translation: more wine, please.

Kayla volunteered to be the one to keep her wits about her, which felt like the least she could do and completely unnecessary since we had no intention of leaving the house. However, that changed around midnight, when the need for a designated driver emerged after Tori—not Brooke, but Tori!—came up with what was, in my drunken estimation, "the best idea since the dawn of space-time."

"We should totally go prank him," she said.

"I got two cans of spray paint out back," I offered after the aforementioned praising of her brilliance.

"Mmm, how about something less criminal?" Kayla suggested. "And also: out back where?"

"We could doorbell ditch him," Tori said.

"What are we, in high school?" Brooke asked.

"Let's see," Kayla said. "We've spent the night preparing Jack for his rematch with Chad and are now actively considering driving to his house at twelve oh seven in the morning to prank him. So, yes?"

"The period for consideration has ended," I announced, ever so slurrily. "To the Jackmobile!"

"Jack, I wasn't serious," Tori said.

"Whew, you are drunk," Kayla added as I began slow-motion jogging toward the garage. "And if I'm driving you, what are we doing about our kids?"

"I got you," Brooke said. "This whole thing is too PG for my taste, anyway."

"Ladies, you heard the lady," I said, tossing my keys to my wife and missing by about three feet. "We ride."

Kayla looked from me to the spot on the floor where they had landed. "Nice arm," she said before stepping forward to pick them up. "We'll take my car. Chad doesn't know what it looks like." She pretended to get serious. "You know, in case things start to go down."

My eyes ballooned. I pulled out my phone and started searching my music, bouncing on the balls of my feet as I did. I was in a better mood now, but not so much better that I was going to let Kayla eye roll her way through this sans consequences. She instantly recognized what was happening.

"Jack," she pleaded. "Not the Yung Joc."

"Oh, meet me in the club, baby, because *it's goin' down*," I said, pretending I hadn't heard and thinking back to the first time I had laid eyes on Kayla. The party was at the house of a coworker who was dating one of Kayla's friends. I had been sneaking glances at her all night but was too nervous to go talk to her and was about to leave, knowing full well I was going to regret it. And then: the song. It had come on and was like my own personal hype squad.

I cranked it as loud as the speaker on my phone would allow. "It's our song, Kayla."

"No, it's *your* song." Sly smile. "I didn't need any help to take you home that night."

She and Brooke laughed a little too hard. I didn't want a fight, but I also wasn't here for the playful jabs. "You needed more help than you knew. Your twenty-minute dissertation about how Kelly Clarkson isn't grateful enough to *American Idol* was positively riveting."

Brooke found this even funnier than what Kayla had said, but my wife's laughter faded into a pinched smile. Tori sensed the change.

"All right, let's just agree you were both a little easy that night and move on. Are we really doing this?"

"Yes!" I said, recommitting to the plan. "Let's go ring this ding-dong's doorbell! Woo!"

It was goin' down on repeat all the way to Chad's house. I was the only one bobbing along when we pulled out of our driveway, but by the third time through, everyone's window was down and it was a car-wide endeavor, right up until we turned onto Chad's street. I wasn't surprised when Tori instinctively turned the music off, but I was when Kayla killed the headlights at the same time.

"Mrs. Parker," I said, leaning forward from the back seat, the music having melted away some of the tension I'd felt before we left, "I do believe this isn't your first doorbell ditching."

"Something like that. Which house is his?"

"The one with the tactical assault vehicle parked out front."

"Aah, perfect." She pulled up right next to it, leaving just enough room to open the doors on that side. We were completely hidden from their house, and the street was so dead that double-parking for as long as this would take didn't seem likely to cause a stir.

This was it. Game time.

Tori and I opened our doors and got out, but Kayla didn't follow.

I leaned down to the open passenger-side window. "You're not coming?"

"A good wheelman never leaves the car, Jack."

She said it straight faced, but even in my semicompromised state, I could tell we were each trying to keep the peace in our own way.

"To repeat: I think you've done this times prior," I said. She shooed us on our way.

Tori and I emerged from around the rear bumper of Cassie's truck-SUV love child and crossed through the outer edges of a circle of streetlight on the other side of the driveway, walking with purpose (and perhaps weaving a touch) toward the Hensons' front door. Chad's BMW was outside instead of in the garage, a fact I didn't pay much mind to until I realized Tori hadn't made it with me to the walkway that led up to the porch.

"What're you doing?" I whispered.

"Shh!" I didn't know why she was shushing; our voices sounded like they were at identical volumes to me. "There's something on his dashboard. Just do it, and then meet me behind his car."

"Okay!"

"Shh!"

I turned onto the path of cobblestones that would deposit me at their front door and went over my plan one more time:

Ring the doorbell, run like hell.

It was late enough for the house to be completely dark, so a sprinting getaway was probably unnecessary, as no one would answer the door that quickly. The last several feet before I reached my target, the relative pointlessness of this particular prank also grew more and more evident, not to mention there was a distinct possibility I might succeed only in waking up Crispin. Wine buzz or not, that thought didn't feel so hot.

So when I stepped up onto the porch, I hesitated. Was this worth it? Was standing there and ringing Chad's doorbell at 12:25 a.m. really going to accomplish anything?

"What happened?" Tori asked when I squatted down next to her at the BMW's tailgate. "I didn't hear anything."

"We've established that I'm marginally intoxicated, yes?" I held up my hand and made a tiny space between my thumb and index finger to emphasize just how marginally.

"Yes, marginally."

"So when a plan starts to feel dumb even when you're *marginally* intoxicated, it seems like a good idea to call it off. Even if he does have a 'Dance Like Nobody's Watching' welcome mat."

"Look at you, Jack Parker. That is some real emotional growth, my friend."

I felt my face form into a big goofy grin. "We are friends, aren't we?"

She laughed soundlessly. "Yes, I'd say we are."

"That makes me happy." It was a humid night, and I teetered a little in my crouch. "Even if this outing was a waste of time otherwise."

"Not entirely. The thing on the dash—it's something."

"Something how?"

"It was a folder. And one of the papers slipped out. Look." She showed me a picture on her phone.

"What is that?" I squelched a burp while zooming in. "A parent roster?"

"Yes. But look at the next column. They're, like . . . notes. Some kind of details about each of them."

I turned this over a little more slowly than usual before reading out loud: "'Propositioned me for a threesome with him and his wife'?"

"Wait. It does not say *that*." I handed the phone back to her so she could see for herself. "Oh my God, Jack. This is . . ."

She was interrupted by floodlights in our eyes.

We both froze. They weren't coming from Chad's house but from the garage across the street. A first-floor light in that house flipped on next. Maybe it was all the boxed wine, but I was almost certain I saw a silhouette of a person moving behind the window. It appeared that Tori and I shutting the doors on Kayla's car when we got there and then me talking louder than I realized had given us away.

"We've been made!" I said to Tori—because again, wine—but she was already taking off toward Kayla's car. However, she had gone only a few steps when she spun back to look at me.

"Jack!" she whispered as loud as she could. "What're you waiting for? Let's go!"

It was only then that I registered I hadn't moved. Like I thought if I just stayed still, no one would see me.

"Mary Alice!" I blurted, scrambling after her and apparently using the *Desperate Housewives* narrator . . . as an expletive?

I rounded Cassie's monster truck and saw Tori getting into our Camry. A hybrid, it was on and in EV mode, ready to whisk me away in perfect silence. I had made it.

Making my attempt to dive in through the open back window all the more puzzling.

"Dude!" Kayla exclaimed.

"I'm in! Just drive!"

I felt the car start to roll forward and, soon thereafter, the breeze blowing through my leg hair.

"A little help?" I said to Tori, who swiveled to her right and helped pull me in by the arm. After a fair amount of sweaty shuffling and shifting, I settled into my seat. I could tell the two of them were waiting for me to say something.

"I really have to pee."

They started laughing, and I did, too, the adrenaline of the last five minutes escaping into the night. Jeez—was that all it had been? Five minutes?

"Well, that got good at the end," Kayla said.

"Not only that," Tori said, "but we got another piece of intel."

"Oh yeah?"

"Yeah," Tori said, studying her phone a little longer before handing it back to me over the shoulder of her seat.

"What is it?" Kayla asked.

"I think it's . . . it's Ms. Weekler's Burn Book," I said.

"What do you mean? Like *Mean Girls*?"

"Uh-huh. I mean, it's not all insulting stuff. Like, for one of them, it just says, 'Really passionate about standardized test scores.'"

"Ha—sounds like an insult to me," Kayla said.

"Not once you hear some of the others," Tori said. "Jack, read what she has for Trish Merletti."

"Uh . . . here it is: 'Complains about everything, so just pretend not to ignore her.'"

"That's fantastic," Tori said, closing her eyes to savor it.

"Big fan of ol' Trish, huh?" Kayla asked.

"Seriously, this woman, Kayla—I despise Ms. Weekler, but she just distilled the experience of every third-grade parent into one sentence."

I went over the rest of the list as well as I could, which wasn't perfectly since I was still drunk enough for my vision to periodically be outwitted by the size of the text on the screen. But considering she had taken the photo looking down through the windshield, Tori had snapped a pretty clear picture of the paper, which consisted mainly of last names starting with *M*.

From what I could tell, more than half of the entries were the mundane (if not always flattering) stuff: "Only cares about parking," "Wants gym to be five days a week," and so on. But other notes were of a more . . . memorable variety.

"Who are Jenny and Jay Maldonado?" I asked.

Tori's eyes narrowed. "They have a fourth grader? I think?"

I was zoomed in so tight I had to scroll across the photo. "Apparently they gave a fifty-thousand-dollar donation for the library on the condition that it be renamed the Mr. Cotton Memorial Library because they, quote, had an unhealthy relationship with their bichon frise."

If laughing about Crispin's name hadn't succeeded in stamping our passports to hell, surely the amount of time we spent gasping for air over this dead bichon did the trick.

"That's awful," Tori said, the first one of us able to breathe again.

"Why would Ms. Weekler do this?" Kayla asked when we were stopped at a traffic light. "I mean, I get she's nefarious and whatnot. But why memorialize all this on an Excel sheet?"

"That's a good . . . ," I started before getting distracted by the header of the column with all the notes. I hadn't noticed it before.

"Tori, did you see this?"

"What?" she said as I handed the phone back to her.

"The label at the top of that column: 'Things You Should Know.'"

"The *you* being . . ."

"Chad!" I said. "It has to be! She's giving him CliffsNotes on all the parents!"

"That would explain why it was in his car," Kayla observed.

"And can you imagine if all the parents knew she was talking about them like this?" Tori said. "If they knew *she and Chad* were talking about them like this?"

"Too bad there's no way to tell them," Kayla said. "I mean, without people asking how you got it."

That's when I remembered just how much I love *Mean Girls*.

CHAPTER 20

Monday, September 15. Day one of the bookfair. Three days until the debate. And still no sign of my old boss.

Kayla's impending trip had added another variable to the Sidney equation. There obviously wasn't anything she could do to stop Chad and Ms. Weekler from using him to revisit my past failures. I just felt more exposed when she wasn't around.

The day before—which was the day after the abandoned doorbell ditching—I'd asked Kayla, in what I'd thought was an even tone, what time she needed to leave on Thursday. She'd responded by telling me she didn't know why I was acting like this Minneapolis thing was her fault. It was in the course of this conversation that I also found out she wouldn't be back in time for the election itself.

"So much for that one vote I could count on, huh?"

"I said I was sorry, Jack. I don't know what else you want me to do."

"Nothing. I don't want you to do anything." Like she could, anyway. "I was just asking about your schedule before I called my mom to ask her to come. You know, to watch our kids."

That last bit of snark had ensured we spent the next couple of hours steering clear of each other.

As for the call with my mom, that had somehow managed to go worse than expected. There was the exchange around "This Thursday?"

"Where's she going?" and "Why Minneapolis?" followed by the obligatory checking of the calendar, which hadn't had anything but her book club on it for about five years. Once that was out of the way and she had confirmed she could indeed be at our house Thursday after school, she told me how glad she was I was going out with the guys—guys that, who knows, might even know somewhere looking to hire a former director of corporate strategy?

"I didn't say I was going out with anyone."

"Scott says networking is key."

"I'm sure he does. He also has no kids and lives in New York."

"Well, Lulu's in school now, so it might be a good time to start thinking about your career again."

"I'm not so sure about that," I said.

"You were just so good at it, Jack."

"Yeah, thanks."

"So what are you doing, then?"

I closed my eyes. "I'm running for president of the parent board at Lulu's school, and Thursday night's the debate."

"Oh—well, that's . . . good too. Although it might make it hard to go back to work."

"Mom, the sooner you and Dad can accept I'm not going back to work, the happier we're all going to be."

"Ever, or right now?"

"I don't . . . stop trying to parse my words for hidden meaning, Mom. Please."

I was glad Kayla wasn't there to hear me rip off her line, which once again brought an abrupt end to a conversation, introducing a new level of stress to my mom's visit in a few days.

Even the school itself was getting to me that Monday morning. All visitors, parents and guardians included, had to be buzzed in. I had been grateful for that buzzer from the first time I saw it at orientation, as I knew it was a precaution designed to keep the school and my daughter safe. I would've been upset if there weren't one.

But as I heard the door click open to let me in for the bookfair, it filled me with sadness too. I had never had to be locked into any of my schools because nobody had reason back then to believe someone might decide to shoot them up. And then when it dawned on me that gun violence, of course, wasn't new but had always been a problem, just not where I'd lived, there was a wave of guilt too.

Because it shouldn't take having a kid of your own to get you to think about how prevalent this stuff is. But there we were.

The Active Alpaca Parent Board couldn't fix whatever was going on with me and Kayla. It couldn't convince my parents I didn't have to have a big job to be successful. And it certainly couldn't solve gun violence. But it could do some good, if given the chance.

Enter Operation *Mean Girls*.

Kayla was right: I couldn't just post the photo Tori had taken without raising questions about how I'd gotten it. And it wasn't like I could walk around the school, stuffing printouts of anonymous origin into kids' backpacks to be opened at home by their parents.

But the bookfair presented the perfect opportunity. Tori had told me it was traditionally the most overvolunteered event of the year due to how close it happened to the start of school, when everyone's enthusiasm hadn't yet flamed out, and the fact that it was basically an excuse to sit around gossiping and drinking coffee. Lots of parents meant both widespread distribution and that no one would be watching me too closely.

On Sunday, I printed the photo of Ms. Weekler's sheet, used a black Sharpie to redact all the names—but not the heading at the top of the page that bullishly declared "Willow Road Elementary Parent Roster (Principal's Office—Confidential)"—and made 50 copies. Those copies were stowed in the laptop bag I carried into the school. Once the gym was good and full of volunteers, I did a quick check to make sure they were all otherwise engaged, dropped the papers on an empty table nearby, and waited about five seconds before picking them back up and calling:

"Hey, Liz, what should I do with these?"

That Liz was Liz Morrison, Elena's best friend, AAPB board member, and the bookfair's organizer, who, thanks to the Burn Book, I now knew was a "stay-at-home mom who volunteers for everything (even when we ask her not to)."

"What are they?" she called back from the cashier stand.

"I don't know. There was a stack of them sitting here." I took a quick, puzzled glance at what was in my hand. "Looks like . . . oh. Something from the principal's office? That's weird."

She put down her clipboard and walked over.

"The principal's office?" she asked.

"Yeah, take a look. It says it's a parent roster, but all the names are, like, blacked out. It's . . ."

"A threesome?"

Her jaw dropped, and it showed no signs of going back up. I wondered if she could pick out the comment about her. I guessed not because, while insulting, it was vague enough that any number of moms—especially the subset currently at the school to volunteer—could've taken it as being aimed at them. The whole redaction-via-Sharpie thing had grown out of me not being savage enough to go full *Mean Girls* and publish the insults with the names still attached, but it occurred to me that this decision would also make it possible for everyone to read into just about everything. That was an absolute benefit for me because no one could be sure Ms. Weekler wasn't talking about them personally.

For all they knew, she thought *they* were the ones who never stopped complaining or unnecessarily inserted themselves at the school. Any one of the husbands could've been the one who proposed a sex party with the principal. And what kind of dog did that couple they met at orientation say they had? Wasn't it a bichon?

The first group of students was still 10 minutes away from coming in. Without another word, Liz took the whole pile from me and started handing them out to the other parents.

All that was left for me to do was sit back and watch.

"Did someone really threaten to sue if the school wouldn't recognize a ferret as a therapy animal?"

"Who do you think the third one from the bottom is about?"

"These are all copies of the same page. Does she have pages for all of us?"

"Elena told me what a troll she was."

"How did this even get in here?"

My eyes darted among them to see who'd asked that. I thought it might come up, and I had an idea of how I'd answer, but I was hoping to minimize lying to the voters, even if doing so here would be in the service of what I believed to be the greater good.

"Forget who took the picture or how it got here," Liz said, filling me with gratitude. "I want to know who the 'you' is in 'Things You Should Know.' Who's she doing this for?"

This was my chance.

"You all may not know this, but ever since I said I was going to run for president of the AAPB, I haven't exactly been Ms. Weekler's favorite. I think I'm the last person she'd want to pass information to." Liz and a couple of others nodded in recognition right as the heavens parted and sent Chad through the open gym doors with two to-go boxes of coffee.

"On the other hand," I said.

"Hey, everyone, sorry I'm a little late, but I brought . . . ," he started. "Whoa, I sense a little tension in here. What did Jack do this time?"

He laughed. No one joined him.

Liz walked over and handed him one of the copies. "We were just enjoying some reading material courtesy of your campaign manager, Ms. Weekler."

Chad put the coffee down and took it from her. He looked like he didn't have a care in the world—then looked like he was going to hurl all over Liz's Tory Burch flats. I waited for his eyes to search out mine.

"Pretty messed up, isn't it?" I said.

"Totally," he replied. It sounded like he was trying to unstick his tongue from the roof of his mouth.

"Oh, please," Liz practically spit at him. "Do you really expect us to believe you don't know anything about this?"

A line of moms had formed in front of him.

"Or maybe you'd be willing to confront Ms. Weekler about it?" said one I recognized from our day at the zoo. "Maybe in front of us?"

I looked at Chad. He did something I'd never seen him do before. He stumbled.

"I . . . uh . . . well, I don't . . ."

It wasn't an admission of anything, but it wasn't a denial either. The only thing that saved him was the growing sound of kids' voices closing in on the gym.

"All right, everybody, battle stations," Liz said with a disgusted shake of her head toward Chad, and we all fanned out to attend to our assigned duties. Some of us had posts at specific locations—I got a display devoted to this popular series of picture books called *Dogs Can't Go to the . . .* [fill in the blank]—while others were supposed to circulate and help the kids find what they were looking for. Chad composed himself quickly but couldn't get Liz to acknowledge him again and finally settled for loitering around the cash register with his two boxes of coffee no one seemed to want.

What a pity.

The bookfair was a two-day event, and when I had signed up to volunteer, I didn't know that the older kids went first. So instead of seeing Lulu, I was working the third- through fifth-grade day. I had been disappointed when I found out, but the execution of my covert op made up for a lot of that.

I had loved the bookfair when I was a kid, and this one was much like the ones I'd known. There were all these books you could normally find only in hardcover that were available as paperbacks for a much lower price; for the *Dogs* books, for instance, all but the most recent one were being sold that way. But even then, and even in a school where the average family was relatively comfortable financially, I still saw some kids buying six or seven books while others had one or none. Maybe the latter weren't big readers. Maybe the parents had forgotten to give them money. Or maybe they were the same kids relying on that technology fee to have access to a tablet.

One third grader stood there for at least five minutes, flipping through and laughing at multiple books at my stand. A few kids came by and grabbed copies of the hardcover as he did. But when he was done, he put them back on the shelf and left empty handed.

"Already got all those?" I asked after him hopefully. He smiled a little and shook his head.

One thing I did not expect from the bookfair was to feel all the feelings.

"There's *Dogs Can't Go to the Zoo!*" a cheery voice announced. I looked over to see the woman from the field trip leading a little girl in my direction. While she picked out her book, the woman offered me her hand.

"Hey, I'm Molly Andrews. I think my daughter, Chloe, is in Lulu's class?"

"Oh, hey—how's it going? Jack. Jack Parker."

The girl ran off with both a hardcover and a paperback. If this bookfair was about moving product, I was proving myself an all-star volunteer.

"I just wanted to let you know I was on the zoo field trip," Molly said, "and I saw what went on at lunch. You know, with those moms and what's-his-face."

"Ha, yeah. Chad."

"Right. Chad. Anyway, not all of us are like that. We can see through fake feminism. The way he was soaking up attention just for parenting—you were right to say something."

"Uh, I actually can't tell you how much I appreciate you saying that. Thank you."

"No problem. Watch yourself on that *Desperate Housewives*, though. It gets pretty weird."

"Thanks. I'm in the process of doing some reevaluating."

Molly hung around with me for a few more minutes, most of which we spent discussing how, even being new to the school, we weren't all that surprised that Ms. Weekler kept a log of what she hated about the parents.

"Her performance at orientation was all I needed to see," Molly said. "Because that's what it seemed like: a performance. Especially the way she gushed over Chad. She made it abundantly clear she wanted him to win."

We both stood there watching the last few third graders make their way through the checkout line. I was glad to have met her, and it was clear we were like-minded, but we had reached that moment where we both were ready to end the conversation without either of us knowing how. Or I thought we had.

"I do wonder how those sheets ended up in here, though," she said.

My nerves flared again. I had been ready for that question initially, but this was the thread that I didn't want anyone pulling at too hard.

"Yeah, it's a . . . I mean, the whole situation is strange, right? Starting with her helping him in the first place. Which probably means he'd be in her hip pocket."

"Oh, for sure." I braced myself for a follow-up, but thankfully, the fourth graders busted through the doors like it was Black Friday, and she said goodbye so she could go back to helping out on the floor.

Despite all my newfound success in picture-book sales, I expected my traffic would slow down as the kids got older and aged out of my target demo. I took the opportunity that provided to text Tori about my interaction with Molly, mainly because I was too excited about the phrase *fake feminism* to keep it to myself. (The report on Operation *Mean Girls* would have to wait until we could actually talk because, like Kathy Francis in a Target aisle, I had embraced an irrational fear of putting anything about it in writing.)

After I hit send, I noticed Chad's search for a sympathetic ear had ended; it was another mom from the zoo field trip, the one who had crushed the water bottle in what I could only assume was a substitute for my face. She appeared to be just as enamored with him here as she had been in the picnic area. I still felt like I had won the day, but the war was nowhere near over.

Tori responded to me with the Obama mic-drop gif, and I wanted to tell her she didn't even know the half of what had been happening. But I remained committed to my paranoia, so I waited and let her know I would be calling when we were done.

"Anything else you need from me before I head out?" I asked Liz as she locked up the cashbox. I'd had only a few fourth-grade shoppers and no fifth graders, making the last hour of my shift feel like twice that.

"Just for you to demolish Chad on Thursday night. I'd always planned on going, but I heard a few of the other moms say they are now too."

"I'll do my best. My debate prep has been intense, as you would expect from any event organized around a box of wine."

She smiled. "Well, I have to return this to the principal's office."

"Are you going to ask her about the . . . you know."

"Can't. I saw Kathy before the fair this morning, and she told me Ms. Weekler is at a conference in Champaign for a few days."

"Lucky her."

"I know. So I'm just going to slip a few into a folder and tell Kathy I found something that belonged to Ms. Weekler in the gym."

I hadn't expected such a calculated move from the architect of the build-your-own panini station at Elena's going-away party, but it seemed I had underestimated her.

The walk back to my van was a long one, reminding me that Ed Mims (the parent from the sheet who only cared about parking) had his reasons. The options if you needed to be at the school for more than 10 minutes could be described as inconvenient at best. But on that day, anyway, it didn't bother me too much.

The heat had broken, at least temporarily, as if to announce the beginning of fall. Other than the birds and the low hum of road noise in the distance, the only sound came from the soles of my shoes gripping the concrete of the sidewalk. And Liz, Molly, and the others had just left Chad a fragile husk of a human being.

It was a real victory cigar of a morning, despite all the baggage with Kayla and my mom that I had carried into it.

I opened my door, got into the driver's seat, and rolled down the window before hitting Tori's number.

"Sounds like that went well," she said by way of a greeting.

"You could say that."

I proceeded to recount in great detail the flawless execution of Operation *Mean Girls*—making sure to refer to it that way at least five more times after she told me, "You really need to stop calling it that"— and the well-deserved damage done to both Ms. Weekler's and Chad's reputations. We talked about the resulting buzz generated around the debate too.

"Wow," she said at the end of it. "Good work. Although this does make my news rather pedestrian in comparison."

"You found me a babysitter for the debate? If so, I can tell my parents I no longer need my mom's help because I've come to my senses, dropped out of the race, and decided to run for governor instead."

"Nothing quite that exciting. But it is about Chad."

I switched from casual gazing out the window to staring straight ahead through the windshield.

"I'm listening."

"I found out he's been lying."

"That's not exactly news, Tori."

"No, this is about his company. The one he had in Malibu. Except it *wasn't* in Malibu. And he didn't sell it for a big profit."

"Then what happened?" I asked.

"He destroyed it."

CHAPTER 21

That summer day he showed up out of nowhere at the playground, I had gone home and stress-googled *Chad Henson Malibu* to see if I could find anything about just how obnoxiously successful he had been. When nothing had turned up and I'd seen only personal stuff on his timeline, I'd counted my blessings and let it go.

Fast forward to Tori agreeing to be my campaign manager. We'd tried again: *Chad Henson startup, Chad Henson sale, Chad Henson million, Chad Henson tech, Chad Henson Antichrist.* All empty.

While I was at the bookfair, though, Tori had noticed something in the background of one of his posts: a poster-size photo of him posing with someone she thought looked like one of the Real Housewives. So she'd zoomed in. She hadn't been able to tell for sure who the woman was, but they were standing in front of something called Sunset Smoothies—the logo of which was, curiously, also on his bright-yellow polo shirt.

And this time, Google had not disappointed. Not even with a misspelled last name.

As soon as we hung up, I called Kayla. I knew she'd be busy, and neither of us had acknowledged, let alone apologized for, sniping at each other about Minneapolis, but I had to read her the two blurbs Tori had texted me from something called *Kern County Business Monthly*.

Sunset Smoothies to open first location in Bakersfield

Sunset Smoothies, which got its start in Stan and Maura Delfino's Long Beach kitchen in 1984, will open its first store in Bakersfield June 17. It will be the popular smoothie chain's 31st location across the state.

"We've succeeded everywhere we've gone by focusing on one thing: smoothies," Stan Delfino said.

To date, all Sunset Smoothies have been owned and operated by the Delfinos themselves. The new location marks a departure from that model, albeit a small one, as the couple's daughter and son-in-law, Cassie and Chad Hanson of Bakersfield, are the owners of the store.

"We look forward to serving the people of Bakersfield, our neighbors, for years to come," said Chad Hanson, a former insurance agent. "I'm especially excited about innovating on the classic Sunset Smoothies experience."

"You're sure it's him?" Kayla asked. "Even with the Hanson thing?"

"Yup—there's a picture with the story."

"Okay." I could hear the clicking of her keyboard. "So he owned a smoothie place, not a startup?"

"Not only that, but they're from Bakersfield. Bakersfield, Kayla! I don't know anything about California, but I do know that sure as hell isn't Malibu."

"Agreed."

"But wait—it gets better. This is from less than a year later."

Bakersfield Sunset Smoothies closes

The Bakersfield location of the popular Sunset Smoothies chain closed abruptly last month.

No reason was given for the closure, and the store's owner, Chad Henson, declined to be interviewed for this story.

"Hey, they got his name right this time," Kayla said.
"Huh? Yeah, I guess . . ."
"Sorry, never mind. Not the point."

. . . declined to be interviewed for this story.

However, some of the store's now former employees spoke to *Kern County Business Monthly* and cited a lack of leadership at the location.

"The owner didn't want to pay for managers or even to fix anything," Kimmi V., one of the employees, said. "All he cared about was that stupid drone delivery service."

Advertised as Sky Smoothie 2000, the service promised delivery of "handcrafted smoothies to your front door" at no additional charge. Kimmi, who asked that we not use her last name, and several others close to the situation said they quickly started referring to it as "Dumpster Fire Deliveries" after Henson destroyed multiple drones in rapid succession, including by flying one carrying three Mucho Mango Madnesses into the literal dumpster behind the store.

"The guy gets his drone license and all of a sudden thinks he's *Top Gun*," Kimmi said. "When he dropped a Berry Banana Bounty on the mayor for the *second* time, we knew it was over."

Former employees claim that between the cost of replacing the drones—"at least 25 of them," one estimated—and reimbursing property owners for damage done, not to mention the lost sales and customers, the location was soon hemorrhaging cash.

In its last days, the store rolled out a Buy-One, Get-Three-Free Promotion in what Kimmi referred to as ownership's "Hail Mary" to draw new customers. She said they were losing money on every sale and closed for good two weeks later.

"He [Henson] was always saying things like 'Great leadership starts with great ideas,'" she added. "We never saw either from him. It was just excuses. He blamed us. He blamed the cost of produce. He blamed the market and people not wanting to eat healthy anymore."

As of this writing, the 30 other Sunset Smoothies locations across the state are all still operational.

"So . . . he's really bad at smoothies?" Kayla asked.

"Bad at smoothies, reviled by his employees, incompetent at business—I mean, drones! He thought he could deliver smoothies with *drones*!"

"I don't . . ." More typing. "You're right, that is crazy."

"You sound pretty unfazed, actually."

"Sorry. Someone came into my office while you were reading."

"Never mind. It's not important."

"No, what was that promotion thing he tried again? The Buy One, Get One?"

"Buy One, Get *Three* Free!" I said, the energy coming back into my voice, knowing I had her attention again. "What even is that? BOGO . . . GOGO?"

I could hear her talking quietly to someone while acting like she wasn't.

"Or how about that his is literally the only location that's ever closed? His whole backstory is a lie." I waited. "Kayla?"

"I'm sorry, babe," she said. "It's nuts in here right now because of Minneapolis. But yes, I am glad to know we can keep right on hating him."

There's nothing quite so deflating as sharing exciting news with someone who doesn't share that excitement. Especially when it's because they're distracted by something you've been fighting about. And especially when that someone is your someone. I didn't even get to the bookfair.

"All right, I'll let you go," I said.

"Hey, I really am sorry, Jack. Just not a good time, you know?"

"Yeah, I know."

The next couple of days leading up to the debate passed in relative silence. By that I mean figurative, political silence. I knew that news of Ms. Weekler's school-wide diss track on behalf of Chad was making the gossip rounds among a subset of the parents, but I was hearing about that secondhand, mainly through Tori. I worked to keep up amid the chaos that was our house, my children sensing my compromised emotional state with Kayla at the office late every night and using it to test how firm my grip on sanity truly was.

"Daddy, I have a question," Lulu said to me when we got home from school on Wednesday.

"Uh-huh," I grunted as I worked on getting Klay out of his car seat. I'd glanced at a text from my mom while turning the van off and was now distracted by when I was going to squeeze in a grocery run to get her store-brand mayonnaise. Because Hellmann's was "too mayonnaisey."

"I'm hungry," Lulu said.

"That's not a question."

"But I am."

I lifted Klay up. "All right, Lulu, what would you like?"

"I don't know."

"Well, maybe let's, you know, *get in the house first*, and then we'll figure it out."

We settled on fruit—none of which had been washed, of course. I discovered the strainer wasn't in the lazy Susan, which meant it was in the dishwasher, which meant it was still dirty, which meant I was going to pick off the dried pieces of macaroni and use it anyway. I walked over to the couch, where Lulu took the bowl of fresh grapes, blueberries, and strawberries without breaking eye contact with the TV—when had they turned that on?—or in any other way acknowledging my existence. I supposed it was better than being told the blueberries were "too blueberry-y," although that might've explained why she ate only half of them.

Tori and I continued to talk, text, and email. The more I missed Kayla, the more I leaned on Tori. Talking with her could, of course, never replace talking with my wife. But having someone who had the bandwidth to discuss the debate Thursday night or who was going to watch Klay on election day itself—God, I still couldn't believe Kayla was going to be gone for that, too—was going a long way in keeping things together for me. I just hoped that once this was all over, we would have formed enough of a friendship that we wouldn't go back to being people who interacted only when our wives did. I didn't need a lot of friends if I had one like her.

When it came to the debate, we knew we wanted to do everything we could to drive home the image of Chad as Ms. Weekler's handpicked lackey, particularly after the bookfair. We also spent a lot of time on Sunset Smoothies and whether to bring it up. It wasn't like we had a focus group to tell us whether it would come across as a low blow.

One thing we were sure of was that the conversation would turn to Mouth and Chocsplosion! at some point. Not only would Ms. Weekler be running the show, but we also knew Sidney had given them something to use against me. Maybe it was the HR complaint from the one employee I'd had to fire back when we were still Scrub. His name was Dylan, and he had been coming in an hour to an hour and a half late for the better part of a month when I'd asked if everything was okay. When he said that it was, I'd reminded him that the office opened at 8:00 a.m. and that he needed to get in earlier. He said that he would, and the interaction ended pleasantly enough. Or I thought that it did until I received notification of a complaint that I had "verbally attacked" him in front of "several coworkers." The only person who had been around was Philip, no doubt on his way to reheat some fish, whose entire statement to HR had been, "Dylan's an idiot."

Ah, Philip. I couldn't believe I'd ever thought about laying him off.

Not surprisingly, Dylan hadn't lasted much longer. But Tori and I knew the Henson campaign hadn't enlisted the help of the man who had fired me to paint me in a good light—a man who, conveniently enough, was also Chad's wife's boss.

By the time Thursday morning rolled around, I felt like I used to when I'd studied as much as I could for a test but was still unsure whether I was prepared. I was, however, ready for a fight.

Possibly more than one.

"Got everything?" I asked Kayla, sitting down on the bed next to her suitcase. She had come with us to do drop-off before leaving for the airport. That turned out to be a mistake because it messed up Lulu's routine by reminding her Kayla wouldn't be home again until Tuesday. Cue all the tears and everyone generally feeling like garbage.

"I think so," she said. "Oh, wait, can I grab a few condoms? You know, in case I meet someone?"

She joked like this when she got nervous, and I knew she was, as she was running point on the presentation to the potential client. Even so, I didn't laugh, not with how hungover I felt after spending half the night up with Klay, who had chosen 2:00 a.m. to decide he was afraid of his closet.

"Jeez, Jack, lighten up. If I ever cheated on you, you know it would be with Ms. Weekler, right?"

"Hilarious."

She zipped the suitcase shut. "What's going on with you?"

"Nothing's going on with me."

"Look, I have to leave in, like, five minutes, so if you need to talk about something, now's the time."

Klay started yelling for me from his room, where he was playing. "Don't worry about it," I said. "Duty calls."

I got up to leave, but she put her hand on my arm. "Please don't do this right now."

I stopped, my head drooping as I did. "You said you'd be here."

"I know."

"When I needed you for this parent-board stuff, you said you'd be here. Now you're not even going to get to vote for me."

She took a step back and started putting on her shoes. She had worn the same pair of white low-top Chuck Taylors when she flew for as long as I had known her.

"I know," she repeated. "And as I've said, I'm sorry about that. This is just such a big opportunity. It could open up so much new business for us."

"Great. So you can be gone even more."

That did it.

"Really?" she said. "We're doing this over the *Active Alpaca Parent Board*? Because you don't even want to win. You know that, right? You just don't want to lose to Chad."

"Wow, Kayla—you know, you might be right. It's amazing how big of an expert you are on what I want and don't want, considering you're hardly ever around. You do know it's possible to have a job and *not* travel all the time, right? I did it for years."

"Yes, you *did*. And now you *don't*. And I'm the reason you get to make that choice. Me being out there means you don't have to be."

"How many times are you gonna throw that in my face?"

"I'm not throwing any . . ." Her tongue pushed out her lower lip, and she grabbed her bag from the bed before looking at me again. "Everything's not about you, Jack. Stop blaming me for this midlife crisis or whatever it is you're going through."

"Is my 'midlife crisis' the reason you couldn't be bothered to listen for two minutes while I read you those articles about Chad?"

"You knew what a bad time it was before you called. And you're welcome, by the way, for coming up with time I didn't have to write those questions for your debate prep. Not that you acknowledged that."

"You mean the debate prep you bailed on to take a phone call and then tell me you were going out of town when you said you'd be here? That debate prep?"

"You sound like a petulant child."

"You sure it's not my 'midlife crisis'?"

She took a breath, and when she spoke, it was quieter than before.

"Listen to me, and listen closely, Jack. You think it doesn't go both ways? Do you know how often people, other women, give me that look that says, 'Why aren't you at home?' They don't have to say it; I know they're thinking it. And no matter how much I love my job or how good I am at it—and I'm *really damn good* at it—I'm always supposed to feel guilty about not 'picking my kids.' *Always*. And the most infuriating part is that sometimes I do. But if I do say I have to miss a meeting to get home for something, then it means I'm not taking my career seriously enough. No man has to carry that around."

It sounded so obvious now that she'd put it out there that I was ashamed I could've had such a blind spot when it came to what she was saying.

We stood there, not making eye contact, for the next 30 seconds, maybe longer. It started to feel like we each wanted a redo of the last couple of minutes, like we each knew we could've done better. But I also knew she had to go, and we were both angry, and neither of us could apologize that fast and possibly mean it.

"I have to leave," she said, softly but firmly.

"I know. Let me know when you land."

"Okay."

I listened to her go down the hall and love on Klay and tell him she'd miss him. He didn't seem to acknowledge her, and I wasn't sure what would suck worse if I were the one going out of town: my child going into hysterics over it or deciding to completely ignore me.

Kayla had experienced both in the course of an hour.

I sat back down on the bed and tried to clear my head. I lost track of how long I was there, but the garage door had opened and closed and Kayla had left, and I still hadn't moved. We were past apologies. That much was clear. Or at least it was clear to me. I was scared Kayla didn't see it. But my confusion about what I wanted, paired with her unrelenting schedule—we'd have to fix it soon, and the only way to do that was to fix it together. What that would look like, I still didn't know. But it couldn't happen while she was in Minneapolis.

So I made a deal with myself: focus on smoking Chad. Because the last thing I wanted to tell Kayla was that we'd gone through this election for nothing.

CHAPTER 22

My mom arrived an hour after we got home from school, as expected. I heard her knock while Klay was yelling, "Daddy! Elmo potty! Elmo potty!"

To clarify: that meant his stuffed Elmo was *in* the potty, not that he wanted an Elmo potty seat on which to go potty. We had one of those too. But after finding poop on the friggin' *ceiling* one day, we had decided to press pause on his potty training.

"I've been knocking for a few minutes," she said when I opened the door.

"Yeah, sorry about that. I was in the middle of a search and rescue mission. In related news, Elmo's going to take a spin through the wash."

I left her hugging the kids and went to get that started. The questions began as soon as I returned from the laundry room.

"What time do they need to go to bed?" "Do they go to bed at the same time or different times?" "Are they allowed to watch TV?" "How much TV?" "Did you get the mayo?" "Can they have a treat?" "Do you consider fruit snacks a treat?" "Did they take a bath?" "When was the last time they took a bath?" "She's taking showers now?"

This was not unusual when my mom visited, and I was always struck by the irony of her seeking my guidance on every possible decision since she simultaneously operated within a worldview where I was to know little more than my kids' names. In that sense, these Q&As could almost feel flattering—in a weird, exhausting sort of way.

Once they got settled in together—she and Lulu liked to play Connect 4, with Klay acting as official disk distributor—I went upstairs to get ready for the debate. I had already washed my hair that morning, and it was early enough that I had some extra time, so I decided to indulge in a rare luxury and take a bath myself. I turned the bathroom fan on to drown out the rest of the house and tried to zone out as much as I could, with mixed results.

Kayla had landed safely in Minneapolis by then, and we had exchanged a short string of *good luck / you too* texts. It was . . . fine. Some people might not even have considered our fight particularly dire—or even a fight, period. But it was the biggest one *we'd* had. And now she was two states away.

"Daddy, can we have mac and cheese for dinner?" Lulu asked, busting through the door.

"Sure, Lulu."

"Yay!"

She didn't leave the doorway. "Was that all?"

"Daddy, Grandma can't reach the mac and cheese."

I looked at the clock on my phone. Fourteen minutes. That was longer than I usually got.

"I'll be right there."

She slammed the door, and I got out to towel off. I still didn't feel the need to rush downstairs, figuring I would get dressed then and leave for school a little early, after getting dinner started. I returned to the kitchen just in time to hear Lulu laughing through her retelling of how

Klay had spit Children's Motrin all over me shortly before Grandma's arrival.

I didn't remember my mom being overly concerned about getting sick when I was growing up, but ever since we'd had kids, she'd seemed paranoid about catching something from them. This had only gotten worse since COVID and was yet another reason I tried to avoid asking her to babysit. Like, I wanted her to see them, but I also wanted to respect her feelings, and there was no avoiding the fact that children are germ magnets.

So I had weighed whether or not to tell her about the Klay thing and ultimately deemed it unnecessary—mainly because he seemed fine but also because it hadn't happened until she was almost in our driveway. There wasn't anything I could do. I still felt a little guilty about it, though, so I supposed the ensuing conversation was my penance.

"What's wrong?" she asked me gravely. "Is he sick?"

"Oh, no. Just a tiny fever. You know how toddlers are. I actually think he's getting a tooth. He told me his mouth hurt."

"Do you think it's strep?"

"No. Like I said, I think he's just getting a tooth."

"When should he take it again? The Motrin?"

"I don't think he's going to need it again."

"But when *would* he need it again?"

I pulled the box of mac and cheese down from the cupboard above the refrigerator. "Not until nine. I'll be home way before that. And seriously, Mom, he's okay. Don't worry."

"I'm not worried. I'm just asking."

Did I say her questioning was flattering? It was more like a quiz.

The three of them kept playing Connect 4 while I got the kids' dinner going, my mom's attention now split between placing her disks and scanning Klay's face for signs of the apocalypse. Sometime before the water started to boil, he got up from the table and started running laps around the couch with a bucket on his head.

"Okay," I said after dumping the noodles in. "Those should be ready in seven and a half minutes. Just make sure to stir them a few times."

My mom left Lulu and walked over to the stove, the loosey-goosey nature of my stirring instructions not computing.

"How many other candidates are there?" she asked.

"Huh?"

"At the debate. How many people are running for the PTA?"

"It's not a PTA exactly. At least I don't think it is. There aren't any teachers. Damn. I should know this."

"Don't curse in front of your mother."

"Sorry. There's just one other one. Actually, I don't know if you'd remember him or not, but it's a guy I went to high school with. Chad Henson."

Her face looked like after you find a sippy cup somewhere other than the fridge and open it to sniff and see if the milk is still good, only to discover it's more chunks than liquid.

"Really? That weasel? I never liked him."

It was one of the nicest things she'd ever said to me.

I didn't have an "I love you" kind of relationship with either of my parents, but I told her anyway. Then I kissed the kids on the tops of their heads, explained to them again where I was going when they asked for the fourth time that day, and got out of there before any more questions, from them or her, were thrown my way.

I went to start the engine as soon as I sat down in the van. But I stopped short. It occurred to me to take a moment for myself, to try to regroup and refocus once more.

The last time I had met Chad on a debate stage, I had driven to school in a green Ford Tempo with 175,000 miles and one beige door on it. Now I would be rolling up in a red minivan with four red doors and two car seats plus a distinctive rattle that I had settled into ignoring, post-off-road adventure. So that was different. So, too, were the circumstances around the two debates. But the objective remained the same: convince a roomful of my peers I was the right guy for the job and he wasn't.

I didn't know if I'd succeed. But for the first time since the fire, I knew that I was.

CHAPTER 23

In a certain sense, any political debate, from elementary school parent board to president of the United States, is just for show. So many of the people you're talking to already have their minds made up and are only there looking for ways to score points on the other side.

And yet this one felt meaningful. Not just because of the simple fact that it taking place proved Chad had been lying when sending texts to all those parents. It was also because I was sure that, in the event of a Chad presidency, there would be people who'd be inclined to push back against him on something like cutting the technology fee—but first, they needed to know it wasn't just some random expense they were being asked to pay.

The debate was my chance to tell them.

Tori was waiting for me near the front doors of the school, sitting on top of a little brick wall off to the side of the wide concrete entry walkway.

"Hey," I said.

"Hey." She was staring.

"What?" I asked.

"How do I put this delicately?"

My mind raced. It could've been anything. Maybe Ms. Weekler had canceled the debate and declared Chad the winner of the election. Was that possible? I didn't think so. But I also didn't see who could stop her. Or what if she had found out about the Kathy Francis meeting and was waiting to spring it on me? What good that would do, I wasn't sure. Then again, if anyone could figure out how to use it, it was her. Or how about this: Chad had found Maria Flores and was going to have her call in during the debate to tell everyone all the reasons she had dumped me for him in high school, including but not limited to my dancing having been compared to a crossing guard with a severe case of gastrointestinal distress.

Another Tripp Zelich original.

"Your fly's open," Tori said.

I looked down. "Oh thank God."

"You all right?"

"Yeah, just a little scattered. Negotiating the handoff with my mom is always an adventure."

"Based on everything you've told us about her, I'm kind of shocked she didn't notice. Your pants, I mean."

"I know. I think she was too busy trying to social distance from my kids. She did remember Chad, though. She called him a weasel."

"All right, Mom. I like her more already."

We started walking toward the doors. The debate wouldn't start for half an hour, and we were the only ones out there at the moment.

"Did Kayla get to Minneapolis okay?"

"Yeah."

I thought about whether to bring up the fight. It probably wasn't where my mind needed to be as we were about to cross the threshold into the school. But the appeal of talking to someone about it—and to Tori specifically, I realized—was too strong.

"We had a whole thing this morning before she left."

"Was it about how much she's been working?"

I nodded. "That was a big part of it, yeah." Unpacking my conflicted emotions about my own future would take longer than we had.

"Brooke and I got into it about the same thing the other night. It's like, I'm thankful business is so good, but . . ."

"It gets rough being the one on the other end. I just wish it wouldn't have happened right as she was leaving."

"Well, if it helps, you two are as solid as anyone I know. It sucks to feel like it's hanging out there, but I'm sure you'll fix it as soon as she gets home."

"Thanks." I appreciated the reassurance, even if it seemed a little misplaced. Kayla and I were in sync in so many ways, this really was uncharted territory for us.

I hit the button that rang through to the front office. As tempting as it was to announce us as "Jack Parker and Tori St. James of the Parker campaign," I stuck with "We're here for the debate" to ensure I didn't lose my campaign manager right before I went onstage.

"Ugh, what is that smell?" Tori asked as we approached the gym.

"Lulu said they had something called sea nuggets in the cafeteria today."

"It smells like the time I walked in on my grandparents having sex."

If I'd had a drink, I would've done a spit take.

"I needed that. Thank you."

"You wouldn't be thanking me if you'd seen it. But you're welcome."

Outside the gym, there was a table that hadn't been there during the bookfair. On it was a sampling of assorted Chad Henson paraphernalia, with a life-size cardboard cutout standing next to it instructing you to check under your seat for your very own bag!

"Chad swag," Tori said. "Unbelievable. How much do you think he spent on this?"

"I don't know. But if I ever see a parent with a 'For the Kids' iced-coffee tumbler, I think I have a moral obligation to throw their cold brew in their face."

"Looks great, doesn't it?"

I didn't know why it surprised me to hear him stride up behind us like that; we were there to debate each other and would soon be sharing a stage. He was like an 8:00 a.m. class in college: no matter how many times you had suffered through it, it never got any easier.

"Deid . . . I mean, Ms. Weekler told me it would be okay to set it up out here," he said.

"Subtle touch there," Tori said, pointing to his dark-blue T-shirt emblazoned with *Vote Chad* in large white block letters.

"If there's one thing I learned in the startup world, it's always be closing," he replied, flashing what appeared to be some freshly whitened teeth.

"I was sorry to see there was no 'For the Kids' hair product," I said. "Seems like a missed opportunity."

He acted confused. "I'm not sure I know what you mean, Jack."

"Oh, I think you do, Chad."

"Let's save it for the debate," Tori said to me. "Okay?"

She was right. It was too early to be that on edge. We had talked about not pressing and letting the opportunities come to me. This was the time to take a page out of his book and be all smiles.

"Sorry," I said. "Hey, may the best graduate of Lakeside High win."

"You said it, Jizz." He laughed and went into the gym. I tried to bore a hole into the back of his head with the sheer force of my loathing.

"Tell me again why I'm not leading with 'disgraced drone operator from Bakersfield who couldn't run a smoothie shop'?" I asked once he was out of hearing range.

"Because the dirtier this gets, the harder it's going to get for you. Even if he weren't better at slinging mud—and we have a couple decades' worth of evidence that says he is—even if that weren't true, it's going to be two on one in there. Move too fast or aggressively, and she's going to use it to knock you off balance."

"She's just a principal, you know." My readiness to go toe to toe with Chad had me primed to take on all comers. "It's not like she's going to *A Few Good Men* me. I think we might be giving her too much . . ."

A flash of déjà vu shot through my body just then as Tori looked over my shoulder, her entire demeanor stiffening in the process, like on that day at Coffee Brewers.

"Mr. Parker, Ms. St. James."

Deidre Weekler was in the building.

Tori had told me Liz and a couple of other parents had confronted Ms. Weekler about the list when she got back from that conference. She had apparently looked over the handout for a few seconds and hadn't missed a beat, saying the photo was clearly a fake, perhaps one cooked up by the same campaign that had posted a letter online of its candidate giving the finger to a piece of paper. After all, she had concluded, if something like the list were real, did they really think she would've given anyone access to it to begin with?

Parents had continued to grumble, but Ms. Weekler appeared to have played them to a stalemate, at least for the time being. And if she'd had motivation to install a puppet as head of the parent board before, how far would she go now?

When she walked by Tori and me into the gym, it was in a perfectly tailored blazer, well-cut pants, and a pair of what must have been five-inch black heels. I knew even less about fragrances than I did about the geography of California, but she sliced through the stale cafeteria funk on a subtle wave that was floral and refined, with a dash of broken dreams.

"Just a principal?" Tori said.

"Point taken."

We waited a few more seconds and then followed her into the gym. There were 50 folding chairs set up in five rows of 10, and almost all of them were already filled. A few parents I didn't recognize were milling around in the back row. Chad was talking to a guy I straightaway dubbed Man Bun off in a corner.

The familiar trappings of the bookfair were gone, including the table where I had staged the greatest coup in the history of elementary school parent politics a few days before. Now there was an enormous drop cloth running the length of the back wall of the gym, brushes, rollers, and paint cans and trays arranged along it. All the grades would be painting a mural together to mark the school's 25th anniversary. Lulu was thrilled. It did make me wonder, though, whether they ever actually used the gym for, you know, gym.

It wasn't until after I'd taken all this in that I noticed the layout of the stage. In my mind, I had always pictured it as Chad and me up there facing Ms. Weekler, who would be seated at a table on the floor, her back to the crowd. Instead, there were three podiums, the one on the left angled slightly toward the other two. My name was on the one on the right, his the one in the middle. So not only would Chad be the literal center of attention, but I'd also be taking direct shots from a full two-thirds of the stage. I felt like they had backed me into a corner, and we hadn't even started yet. Ms. Weekler really didn't like leaving things to chance.

I smiled all over again at the thought of leaking her list, and that helped. It had to be eating her alive.

Tori and I chatted about nothing in particular while we counted down to 6:00 p.m. I was as prepared as I was going to be, and even if I had wanted to go over strategy one last time, doing it so close to my two combatants felt like an unforced error waiting to happen.

Tori suggested we do a post that featured a picture of the rows when they had filled—there were even a few people who had to stand—captioned with "Full house for AAPB debate night. Hoping there's not a candy bar round."

That was as "real dad" as you could get. Eleven people liked it in the first five minutes, among them Liz and Molly (from the bookfair), both of whom I was happy to see walk in while we were standing there.

There was Lana from the zoo field trip too. Good: sympathetic faces in the crowd were good.

I did wonder why one seat in the front row was empty and marked as "Reserved." Maybe it was just to get in my head. Or what if this was the Sidney thing? Chad had gotten one cardboard cutout made. Maybe he'd gotten another one of Sidney, and they were planning to sit it there to taunt me.

Okay, that might be a stretch, even for them.

And if Ms. Weekler and Chad had conspired beforehand, they didn't while we were in the gym. They didn't interact once until she summoned both of us over, right before we'd be starting.

"Well, this is it," I said to Tori. "Wish me luck."

"Screw luck, Jack. You're so ready for this. He can't smile his way out of everything."

From our respective parts of the room, Chad and I began to converge on where Ms. Weekler was waiting, a little five-step staircase leading up onto the stage. I heard my name thrown around in the crowd in what sounded like positive tones as I went. I have to say, I felt presidential—setting aside that I was in an election where Tori and I had spent an entire email chain developing a position on an existing AAPB proposal to change the name of "Spirit Week" to "Alpacapalooza." (I was pro.)

Still. I had gotten into this thing to beat Chad. And if anything, my desire to do so had only gotten stronger. It was just that, amazingly, so, too, had my desire to be president of the Active Alpaca Parent Board.

That would always sound funny.

"Gentlemen, welcome," Ms. Weekler said. She was disconcertingly nonhostile. "We're going to be taking the stage here in just a moment. I'll go on first, then introduce the two of you, starting with Mr. Parker. Mr. Parker, you will be at the podium on the far side of the stage. Once you have both taken your spots, I will explain the rules you have agreed upon to the audience, and then we will begin. Any questions?"

"Nope," Chad said.

"I'm good," I said.

"Good. Now, let's not forget why we're here, and have a good, clean debate"—she lined me up from behind those tortoiseshell frames—"that stays focused on the issues."

I met her gaze head-on. "I will if you will."

It came out as a challenge.

It was.

CHAPTER 24

Ms. Weekler was wrapping up describing the debate rules. They were simple: one of us would get asked a question and have a minute to give our answer, and then the other one would also get a minute to rebut or respond. Who went first would alternate on a question-by-question basis. I was only half listening because I was still basking in the glow of my applause having been noticeably louder than Chad's when Ms. Weekler introduced us.

"Let's get started, then," she said. "We flipped a coin earlier to see who would get the first question, and Mr. Henson won, so we will begin with him."

I snapped back to reality and caught her eye just before she turned to Chad. Her expression remained as impassive as before, but now it felt a lot more sinister.

No coin had been flipped. She was messing with me, prodding me, in a way no one but the three of us up there could see. Not even Tori, seated straight in front of me in the first row, would know this was a lie. She would just assume that's what we had been doing when Ms. Weekler called us over.

But we had also prepped for this. Like Tori said, two on one. We knew that was what this was going to be.

"Mr. Henson, why are you running for president of the Active Alpaca Parent Board?"

He wasted no time getting that hand to his chin.

"That is a great question, Ms. Weekler. And first of all, I want to thank you for giving us this platform here tonight to discuss the issues that matter to Willow Road parents. I, for one, don't think this election would've been complete *without* a debate."

I remembered Kayla's recon on how Chad had reacted to finding out about the debate at the carnival. I started to shake my head. Then I heard what sounded like a set of keys clatter against the hardwood of the gym floor and looked down to see Tori picking them up while hitting me with her strongest "keep it together" stare. So I did.

"Because at the end of the day," he concluded, "it's all . . . for the kids."

"Very well put, Mr. Henson. Mr. Parker, care to respond?"

"Uh, yeah—why wouldn't I?" God. How did they already have me on the defensive?

I took a beat. No superdad, just real dad. Just talk.

I turned from Ms. Weekler to the audience. "Hi, everyone." I kind of exhaled it, which got an appreciative chuckle. "First, I want to thank *all of you* for coming out here on a Thursday night. I know it's not easy. My wife is out of town for work, and trying to coordinate with my mom and the kids just to get out the door reminded me why Kayla and I haven't had anything resembling a social life in six years."

That got a bigger laugh.

"I'm running for AAPB president because I really believe the board has the power to make the school better for everyone—the kids and the parents, obviously, but the teachers and the staff too. When our outgoing president, Elena Choi, endorsed me—like how I slipped that in there?"—more laughter—"when Elena endorsed me, I knew . . . that . . ."

My brain glitched, even as some of them were still laughing.

Sidney Edmonds was taking that empty seat in the front row.

Not a cardboard cutout of Sidney Edmonds. The man himself. In the flesh.

The stage lights felt like they were setting my skin on fire as 5 seconds of dead air became 10. I was suddenly aware of sweat, which had appeared out of nowhere, dripping down my back. I knew they had talked to him, but this . . . I hadn't seen him since the day he'd fired me while the business I had helped to build smoldered in the background. Now he was staring at me again, dragging my short-comings as a leader out of my memory and dumping them into my present.

"Is that all, Mr. Parker?" Ms. Weekler asked. She sounded satisfied. And like she was a mile away.

"Uh . . . yeah . . . I . . . uh . . . was just going to say . . . I think she thought I could do the job." Sidney rolled his eyes.

"Great," Ms. Weekler said. "Because the next question is for you. Most of us know you as the man who was fired for burning down a building while eating a Chocsplosion! candy bar. What would you say to people who might not trust your leadership abilities as a result?"

I was still frozen. Tori had followed my eyes and seemed to have put together what was going on. I could sense her in my peripheral vision, trying to will me out of it. We had practiced my response to almost this exact question with Brooke playing Chad. I knew we had. I just couldn't grab onto it. All I could think of was the microwave and the cigarettes and the firefighters and the failure and the embarrassment and the drive to that gas station and telling Kayla.

Kayla.

That night I had asked her whether I should ask Tori to be my campaign manager, she had told me Chad didn't stand a chance. I did remember that.

And then I came back to life.

"Well, it wasn't the *whole* building," I said, turning to face her. I held there for a second or two, several parents clapping and whooping in approval. Or maybe it was relief. I wasn't going to be picky about it.

I looked back out at all of them. "Plus, technically speaking, I was let go because I wasn't laying people off like my boss"—glance in Sidney's direction—"wanted me to, not because of the candy bar or the fire. But as for the question, I was working for Mouth Inc. then because they had bought out a company called Scrub. You all remember Scrub, right?"

I returned to Sidney before delivering the next line. "That electric toothbrush that no one, *especially* Mouth, could compete with?"

Man, did that feel good.

"What most people don't know is that I was director of corporate strategy at Scrub. I was part of the original group that founded it and built it into what it was. What happened that day with the microwave that caused the fire was a mistake, the biggest one of my life. It happened. But since then, I've been home raising our two kids, Lulu and Klay, and I'm confident my experiences, all of them, make me the right candidate to be president."

I considered whether to end my answer there or go for the dagger like I had in our prep, like Brooke had begged me to. It was still early, and I had just gotten my bearings again.

But I was feeling it.

"And as long as we're on the subject of trust, I'd like to know how we can be expected to *trust* Mr. Henson after the text messages he's been sending."

He didn't flinch.

"So I used the school directory to reach out to some parents," he said. "How is that a big deal? I, for one, think the president of the Active Alpaca Parent Board should be accessible."

"It's a big deal because no one but the principal's office is supposed to have access to that list. It's a big deal because you implied you'd already won the election."

"Did you ask Ms. Weekler for the list?"

I humphed into my microphone. "No, I didn't ask her for it."

"Well, that's all I did. I'm sure she would've given it to you if you had asked."

"Of course, I'm sure she would've. Just like she would've given me her notes about what she thinks of all the parents. Since you two are such good buddies, did she happen to share those with you too?"

There were some oohs of assent from the crowd while he took a moment to ponder whatever lie he was going to spin.

"Jack, we've known each other since high school, right?" On a scale of 1 to 10, he was dialing the pity face up to a 20. "And I have to say, I never got a conspiracy theory vibe from you until tonight. I thought we were going to talk about the issues."

"That's an excellent point, Mr. Henson," Ms. Weekler said, jumping back in. "And you haven't had a chance yet to give your answer about whether people should trust Mr. Parker's leadership abilities. Would you care to do so now?"

"Thank you, Ms. Weekler. But no, as I said, I'd like to get back to the issues that matter to Willow Road families."

From somewhere in the crowd, there came a very audible "Give me a break" followed by a cluster of muffled laughter.

And this time, Chad did flinch.

"I would remind our audience that they are to refrain from commenting during the debate," Ms. Weekler said, looking down over her glasses in their direction. "Now then, Mr. Henson, if elected president, what changes, if any, would you make to the school's annual candy fundraiser?"

"I'm glad you asked because I have some exciting news to share. You mentioned Mr. Parker's memorable history with Chocsplosion! a couple of minutes ago. Well, I'm pleased to announce that Sidney Edmonds—the CEO of Mouth Inc., where my wife, Cassie, is a *vice president*—has offered to donate all the Chocsplosion! the kids can sell, free of charge!"

I could see some of the parents were impressed.

"Now, you may be asking yourselves, Why would Mr. Edmonds do such a thing?" Chad continued. "Doesn't he hate Chocsplosion!? The answer is yes, yes, he does. But when I explained to him how *bad* Mr. Parker felt about burning that office down, he wanted to give him some closure. And what better way to do that than by turning the candy bar that caused so much friction between them into something positive . . . *for the kids*."

Chad proposing a Chocsplosion! candy sale was laughably predictable, and I knew Sidney couldn't stand me, his glare confirming that the years had done nothing to tamp down his anger. But how on earth had Chad roped him into this? I wanted to know because of course I did. Right then, though, it didn't matter.

"Mr. Parker, your response?"

"First, I'd hope that Mr. Edmonds's *generous* offer would stand regardless of which one of us is elected president. However, what I'd really like to talk about is something that impacts all Willow Road families: the technology fee. Or what my opponent likes to call the technology 'tax.'"

"Great, let's do it," Chad said.

"As you might know, he has proposed that any family who wants to should be allowed to opt out of paying this fee, which is twenty-five dollars per student per year. If you're like me, you may not even have been aware there is a technology fee because it's folded into the materials fee we pay. But while this program exists under the radar, it has a big impact. It was developed by our own teachers, and it allows all kids at the school to have access to a tablet, even if their family can't afford to buy one. Letting people who *can* afford to pay opt out would make that impossible."

Chad huffed. "Well, Jack, twenty-five dollars is a lot of money to some people, and I—"

"You're right," I said, cutting across him, "it is. That's why families with kids on free and reduced-price lunches are automatically exempted from having to pay it. So you didn't do your homework before proposing this, or you did and you just don't care. Either way, it's unacceptable."

I could tell both he and Ms. Weekler had been caught off guard, so I kept going.

"Just like it's unacceptable that we send kids home from the book-fair without a book. Like many of you, including Mr. Henson, I had the opportunity to volunteer at the fair earlier this week. And on the one hand, it was a great experience to see so many kids so excited about reading. But I also saw some kids unable to purchase any books while others walked out with their arms full.

"Reading should never make a kid feel bad. So if I'm elected president, what I'd like to propose is a modest five-dollar bookfair fee modeled after the technology fee. We'd split that money up evenly among all the kids, so they'd all have a chance to buy a book or two. No more, and no less. Everybody gets the same."

My campaign had never had less to do with Chad than it did in that moment.

"Uh, that's called *socialism*, Jack," he said.

"Uh, it's really not." Burst of applause.

"Gentlemen," Ms. Weekler said with enough of an edge to warn us, all of us, that she was still in control. That was what she was going for, anyway. I knew she was worried. She and Chad had come close to knocking me out at the beginning, but I had rallied, and now I had them on the defensive.

Tori and I traded a quick glance. We both could tell Ms. Weekler was about to throw another haymaker at me. And we were right.

"Mr. Parker, we've received complaints in recent years about the school district's approach to lockdown drills. Some parents feel we do too many and are scaring the children unnecessarily, while others think we should be doing more. How would you approach the problem of gun-violence preparedness?"

"A question about gun violence," I said. "Wow. That's quite the follow-up to Mr. Henson's stumper about the candy sale."

I waited a good five seconds for that laughter to die down.

"Look, I'm going to be blunt: I don't know what the right answer is. The fact that we have to talk about gun violence at a debate for an elementary school parent board is sad. What I do know for sure, even after only being a parent at this school for a month, is that we have great teachers here. And, as the voice of the parents, the AAPB should seek out the teachers and listen to what they have to say about it. They're the ones whose opinions I'm most interested in."

"The teachers?" Chad countered, not waiting for Ms. Weekler to tag him in. "I don't know about the rest of you, but the last time I checked, the teachers work for us. Those are our tax dollars paying their salaries. They're not going to tell me what's best for my kid."

I could see a few people in the crowd nodding in agreement, but he was teetering, his inner goblin begging to come out and soak up the stage light. The right push would bring him out in full force.

"Let's move on to a new question, Mr. Henson," Ms. Weekler said.

"I'd like to hear the rest of his answer about gun violence and/or teacher pay," I interjected. "He sounds pretty passionate about both."

Chad wheeled to face me, looking ready to unleash, but he wasn't fast enough.

"I'm the moderator of this debate, Mr. Parker. You'd do well to remember that."

There were a couple of light boos from the crowd. She sent a death glare their way before turning back to the stage.

"Mr. Henson, how would your experience as an entrepreneur in the fast-paced environment of Southern California benefit the Active Alpaca Parent Board?"

This was it, the moment of truth.

While he took a few more seconds to collect himself, I stood there, waiting, still unsure whether to bring up Sunset Smoothies. I figured I wouldn't know until I heard his answer.

"In the startup world, we have a saying: 'Don't wait for someone else to do what you could do yourself.' I had to learn the ins and outs of all the facets of my business in order to build it into a success, and then, as it got bigger and bigger and bigger, I had to find ways to instill that same mantra in my employees as their boss."

Here he paused to insert an "aw, shucks" chuckle, before adding:

"And I tell ya, making the decision to move on was one of the hardest things I've ever had to do. Because I wasn't just their boss—I was their mentor. I was their general. But I was reading the Steve Jobs biography then, and in the end, I knew I had to have faith that what I had taught them would stay with them long after I was gone. That's the kind of leadership I'd bring to the Active Alpaca Parent Board."

"Thank you, Mr. Henson." She looked as delighted as she had introducing him at orientation, but her expression cooled when she remembered I was there too. "Mr. Parker?"

I looked at Chad. I almost felt bad for him. He really seemed to believe every word he'd said.

"I just . . . I guess it feels weird to me to try to argue the details of Mr. Henson's business record. I've known erratic CEOs"—smile for Sidney, his hold over me officially broken—"and I've known absolutely brilliant entry-level engineers and designers. For me, so much of it comes down to how someone is as a person. So whether Mr. Henson was running a Fortune 500 company or, say, managing a smoothie shop"—smile for Chad—"I'd remind you that he left Southern California, moved here, and is now running for elementary school parent board against me, a guy famous for starting a fire and eating a candy bar. Not to drone on about it, because *droning* on is the worst"—oh, was this sweet—"but neither of us is going to be confused with Steve Jobs anytime soon."

Even though he had gone first on this question, Ms. Weekler gave Chad a window to respond. But he didn't budge, his face looking like mine felt when I saw Sidney walk in. It was obvious he wasn't keeping Bakersfield, Sunset Smoothies, and his flying Mucho Mango Madnesses a secret just from us.

He was keeping it a secret from Ms. Weekler too.

"Mr. Henson?" she tried after he didn't say anything.

"Hmm?"

"Would you like an opportunity to respond to Mr. Parker's comments about your experience?"

"Oh, uh . . . no, I'm fine."

Her unflappability twitched. "Are you sure? Maybe something about the negotiation skills that allowed you to get the highest possible price when you sold your business?"

He looked at me. I smiled at him. Bigger this time.

"Nope, I'm all set, thanks."

"Really, Mr. Henson, I think you ought to . . ."

"It's not his turn," Liz Morrison said from the second row.

"What was that?" Ms. Weekler said, scanning the audience, desperate to single out the culprit. Liz threw her a bone and stood up.

"I said, it's not his turn, *Deidre*. Stop giving him extra chances. Unless you want to ask him what he knew about your little list."

A murmur spread throughout the parents. While this was happening, Tori, from her seat one row up and three places to my left, took out her phone and started recording a video. Her instincts as a campaign manager proved to be spot on yet again.

"*Mrs. Morrison*, I have already warned all of you about . . ."

"It's not his turn," a few more people echoed.

"Ladies and gentlemen, this is hardly the way to conduct yourselves as an audience. It's disrespectful to me and to the candidates."

As far as I knew, Liz wasn't aware of what had happened between Ms. Weekler and Elena's husband, despite Liz and Elena nominally being "best friends." It was hard to tell how she might have reacted to that news. But if Ms. Weekler had escaped Liz's wrath once, karma seemed dead set on not letting our dear principal go two for two in that department.

"As disrespectful as you implying we're dumb or have no lives?"

"Mrs. Morrison, I'm not even going to dignify that with a response."

"No?" Liz fired back. "How about the library, then? Don't you want to tell us who has 'an unhealthy relationship with their bichon frise'?"

Ms. Weekler huffed. "As I've told you, that list was clearly a fake. Your behavior right now is entirely out of line."

"That may be. But that doesn't change the fact that it's still not his turn."

A large proportion of the crowd assembled in the Willow Road Elementary gymnasium had heard enough, and the chanting began.

"Not his turn!"

"In all my years at Willow Road, this is the most disgraceful behavior I have ever witnessed—from parents or students!" Ms. Weekler bellowed.

"Not his turn! Not his turn!"

Chad appeared to be swaying slightly from side to side, while Ms. Weekler was quickly losing her chance at restoring any semblance of order. So she kept going.

"Oh, spare me!" she yelled. "I've heard half of the people in this room make jokes about that bichon!"

"Not his turn! Not his turn! Not his turn!"

"And like it's a *big* shock one of your husbands wanted to sleep with me! Have you seen the way they look at me? You people need to grow up!"

This time, the chanting did stop. Ms. Weekler's breathing was heavy. Chad had the tensed look of a man ready to run, but she looked out at the crowd like she had vanquished an inferior yet nettlesome foe.

"Oh, go to hell," someone said from the back.

Chad summoned all the indignation his lack of character could manage.

"How dare you speak to a woman like that," he hissed into his microphone.

Reminded of his existence, the crowd seemed to regard him with a sort of malicious curiosity. That was when I learned that if you're going to hand out swag bags with T-shirts in them, you shouldn't tie those shirts into rolls unless you're prepared for the possibility, however remote, that they will be chucked at you end over end as you flee from the stage.

The shirts were aimed relatively evenly between them, but as Chad had farther to go to get to the stairs, he took the brunt of the heavy fire.

When they were gone, everyone was kind of looking around at each other while taking a collective breath. Sidney, Man Bun, and the other Chad supporters had slipped out, but it was still a good-size group.

Eventually, all eyes came back to me, the one still standing, at my podium on the stage.

"Good thing we didn't ask them about changing Spirit Week to Alpacapalooza," I said.

It took a while for the clapping and cheering to stop.

CHAPTER 25

As resounding a success as the debate had been, the election wasn't for another five days. There were people planning to vote who hadn't been in that audience (and some who had been who would stay loyal to Chad). And while we did have the video Tori got of the parents turning on him and Ms. Weekler, culminating in my hero shot, we had agreed not to post it anywhere. When we talked to the parents afterward, there were a few who had begun to freak out about there being physical evidence of them throwing projectiles, even soft ones, at the school's principal. As a former viral sensation, I got it.

That said, Ms. Weekler screaming that all the dads wanted her wasn't a good look for her either. She must have seen Tori recording, or else someone had told her about it, because later that night, we received an email from her requesting that, in the interest of all involved, we not publish the video.

I wouldn't say Tori and I used that to strong-arm her, but we weren't in a hurry to disclose that we'd decided not to use it. We had been waiting on Ms. Weekler to rule on several proposals we'd made regarding voting procedures, and it was reasonable to assume she would give them fuller consideration if she thought the video was still in play.

Our main concern was making it easier to vote, so we had pushed for online ballots and/or letting people cast them at end-of-the-day pickup in addition to the traditional morning drop-off window.

Friday afternoon, the day after the debate, Ms. Weekler sent Chad and me an email with her official ruling. Attached to it were the Active Alpaca Parent Board Bylaws, a document that somehow numbered 20 single-spaced pages. She directed us to Article II, subsection A:

II.A. Presidential Elections

To vote in an AAPB election for president, the prospective voter must be a legal guardian of a current Willow Road Elementary student *and* cast his/her ballot at the appointed location on school grounds between 7:30 and 8:30 a.m. on the day of the election. No other forms of voting will be permitted.

However, Ms. Weekler went on to note in her email that "in light of last night's events" and in the absence of any rules to the contrary, she was willing to grant a third request we had originally planned to make from the debate stage but had ended up submitting with the others: that I be in the room when the votes were counted.

"I am hopeful that this consideration will allow us all to move on and leave this regrettable incident behind us," she wrote in conclusion.

"Sounds good to me," I wrote back. "And looks like amending the bylaws will be the first item on my agenda." Smiley emoji.

Still, on balance, this was a blow to my chances. My message figured to resonate most strongly with working parents. But the only ones who could vote were those who could spare the 15 minutes first thing in the morning. That would eliminate a number of people doing drop-off on their way to work and all but rule out those whose kids went to before care or rode the bus.

There were 400 or so students at the school, for a total of somewhere between 400 and 800 parents and guardians. We knew from Elena we should expect the total votes cast to be around 100, which was a little higher than we'd first thought. Even if I could count on, say, 30 or maybe 35 from debate-night attendees, we'd still have to sway some of the people who'd been inclined to vote for Chad simply because they'd seen Ms. Weekler anoint him at orientation. It was going to be close.

"Was that Kayla?" my mom asked me as I put my phone down after reading Ms. Weekler's email. She had offered to stay until Saturday morning, and we were sitting at our kitchen table drinking coffee while Lulu and Klay played some sort of game that involved throwing their lovies up in the air, calling them by the wrong name, and then laughing uncontrollably.

If no one's crying, you don't ask.

"No, she's been in meetings straight through," I said. We still hadn't talked since she had left. She had texted the night before to see how the debate had gone, and we'd traded updates about her work and Lulu's school day when we got home that afternoon. All of our messages were one sentence (or less). The fight was still too fresh, and I couldn't have summed up that debate in a text if I'd tried. Given how tight the race was, I also didn't trust myself not to sound off again on her not being there to vote. "This was actually the principal at Lulu's school. Tori and I had asked for a few things related to the voting, and Ms. Weekler finally responded."

"And?"

"We got one out of three. So not a total loss. But we need all the help we can get."

She registered the information but didn't say anything, choosing instead to take another sip of her decaf.

"Thanks again for being here," I said.

"I'm glad I was able to do it. You're lucky I didn't have book club. If you had asked me earlier, I would've been able to reschedule, but not the week of."

"But you *didn't* have to reschedule. So it was fine."

"I know. I'm just saying it *could've* been a problem."

"Well, I'll tell you one thing that *was* a problem: me for Chad at the debate. I don't know if I'm going to win the election, but I owned him last night. It was a thing of beauty."

"Why did you wait so long to tell us you were running?"

After having kept it under wraps for weeks, I no longer felt like holding back. I'd won the debate and exorcised my Sidney demons. It was time to pull the Band-Aid off with my mom too.

"Because I hadn't planned on telling you about it at all."

"Why not?"

"I guess it didn't seem like the sort of thing you'd really understand?"

"Give us some credit, Jack," she said with an air of dismissiveness. "We know what a parent board is. We're not that old."

She was going to make me spell it out.

"Yeah, no, I know you do. I just mean that I didn't think the two of you would get why *I* was doing it." I briefly thought about leaving it at that, but I'd already come this far. "You know, because I'm a man."

Saying it out loud to her felt strange. It didn't just bring back memories of the weekend we'd told her and my dad Kayla was pregnant. It went back longer than that.

I knew this girl in college named Simone. She was premed and wanted to be an oncologist and to this day is one of the smartest people I've ever met. We bonded over our mutual fear, possibly irrational, of Nickelback world domination and tried dating for a few months. But while we always had a blast hanging out together, the physical-attraction piece just wasn't strong enough, not for either of us. Nothing like seeing Kayla across the room at that party.

Although we had given up on being a couple, Simone and I had stayed friends, close enough for me to make a point of introducing her to my parents and brother on graduation weekend. When Simone didn't volunteer it on her own, I told them how she was going to Johns Hopkins for medical school and would probably one day cure cancer. Mom and Dad showed the appropriate level of interest, Simone and I made plans to meet up at a party that night, and Scottie threatened to disown me if I left him at the hotel with our parents. Then they all did the "congratulations / nice to meet you / you too" thing, and she went on her way.

Later that day, my mom brought up meeting her and asked if we were dating. I said no, we were just friends.

"See, Frank?" my mom said. "I told you not to worry."

"Uh, worry about what?" I asked.

"A girl like that, Jack," my dad said, almost wincing, "she's so . . . career oriented. Good luck with that."

"What're you talking about?"

"Dad's Guide for Dying a Virgin," Scottie had offered. He really was good people, my little brother. It was the way my parents held him up that drove me nuts.

"Let it go," my mom had said. "We're having a nice time. Like you said, you're just friends."

My freshman-year roommate and his parents walked up then, and the conversation shifted quickly to full-on nostalgia mode. I had been annoyed, but I told myself I wasn't going to waste my last weekend of college arguing with my dad over his archaic views on gender. I'd have ample opportunity to do that in the years to come.

Except I hardly ever talk to my dad, and when I do, it's abundantly clear I'm incapable of changing his mind on anything. Circling back to his reaction to Simone had always felt like it would be a punishment, and that was before Kayla had said she was going to keep working and he had looked at her like he would a salesperson who'd disregarded his

"No Solicitors" sign on the front porch. When I walked out of their house that weekend, I hadn't been able to imagine a scenario where I would try to explain to them why I wanted to stay home. And I never had. Perhaps that was a moral shortcoming on my part.

But my mom and I were in it now—just as Lulu appeared, asking me for lemonade because she was "dying of thirst." I could tell my mom was distracted by what I'd said because she didn't try to get the drink for Lulu herself like she usually would've. I didn't know if her impulse to take over had to do with giving me a break, since I did it all the time, or an inability to accept that refilling cups and changing diapers was how her son spent his days.

"'Dying of thirst'?" I repeated as I made my way to the refrigerator. "Don't you think that might be an exaggeration?"

"I'm not exaggerating, Daddy."

"Well, if it's that desperate of a situation, I think I should at least get a *please*."

"*Please* can I have some lemonade, Daddy?"

"That's better. And yes, you can." I opened the door but didn't see the lemonade where I expected it to be. I began inventorying our drink options. Just like those old SunnyD commercials, there was some pop, orange juice, and purple stuff (two-week-old sangria that I really needed to dump) plus milk, apple juice, and the last two cans of hard seltzer. That was it.

"Actually, it looks like we're out of lemonade," I said.

"But I really want lemonade."

"I know. But we don't have it right now. We have to go to the store tomorrow, so we can get it then."

"Tomorrow? Tomorrow is forever!"

While my daughter was objecting to how time worked, I retrieved a pen from the junk drawer to write on the notepad magneted to the fridge. "See? I'm writing it on the list so we don't forget."

"But I'm thirsty *now*!"

"Good news, then. We have orange juice, apple juice, milk, and water. You can have any one of those."

"But I don't want any of those!"

"Well, that's all I got, kid."

"Fine. I guess I won't have anything to drink, then."

She went back to Klay and was trying to teach him how to do a somersault on an oversize pillow by the time I rejoined my mom at the table.

"You know, I think it would be easier if she'd just admit she wasn't that thirsty to begin with," I said. "That's all. Just, 'Daddy, you were right—I was exaggerating.'"

"Don't hold your breath," she said. "I'm still waiting on an apology for that fit you threw when I didn't get the right kind of Rice Krispies."

"Uh, that's so not the same thing. And neither are Rice Krispies and 'toasted rice cereal.'"

That succeeded in easing some of the tension in the room.

"So you don't think your dad and I understand why you'd want to be president of the PTA?"

"Honestly? I don't think you get why I'm a stay-at-home dad. Like, any of it."

"I'm not going to lie to you: it's taken some getting used to."

"*Have* you gotten used to it? When I called to ask you to come here, you told me to ask Scottie for career advice."

"You know he prefers Scott now, Jack."

"Yeah, that's not happening."

"You and your brother," she said, chuckling. "To answer your question: yes, your dad and I have gotten used to it, for the most part. Although one of us more than the other."

Not having a lot of experience with forthright conversations with my mother, I felt myself doing a dance, wanting to get the most out of this that I could without doing too much too soon and shutting it down. The similarity to the strategy I had employed the night before at the debate was obvious. Unlike Chad, however, my mom was not a weasel, and I didn't want to hurt her if it could be avoided.

"You mean Dad's not bragging about my sick nurturing skills?"

She smiled. "I suppose you could say that. You really are great with them, though. Even watching you just now with Lulu."

"Really? Because that felt like a stalemate at best."

"But that's so much of what parenting is. You do the best you can, and then you move on to the next battle. Because there's always a next one."

I looked at her.

"What?" she asked.

"This. Why don't we talk more like this? You've never said anything like that to me, but it's so true. And it's something, an experience, a frame of reference, that you and I both have."

"You don't need my help. I see you with them, and it amazes me."

"But why? Why does it amaze you? I mean, I've been a dad for, like, six years now. Dealing with surly children is the first line of the job description."

"Maybe being hands on as a father is natural for you, but it wasn't for us. That's just how it was. Our husbands went to work, and we took care of the kids. Unless you got divorced. And I'll tell you something. Those were some of the best moms I ever saw. I don't know how they did it."

"See? Something else we agree on."

I picked up her now empty cup and went to make her another. Kayla and I had upgraded from a regular Keurig to one of those home espresso machines a few months earlier, and even if we were still dealing with pods, I pictured Brooke saying there was something sacrilegious about using it to make decaffeinated coffee. But I wasn't about to let this conversation stall over a lack of my mom's preferred beverage.

"Didn't that ever bother you?" I asked when the drip had started. "That decision basically being made for you?"

"What did it matter if it bothered me? It was 1984. I had a baby at home and a high school diploma. It wasn't like I was leaving loads of money on the table."

"But it did bother you?"

"Sure. Sometimes. I just didn't dwell on it. Because it didn't even feel like a real option."

"That's really depressing."

"Eh, you weren't so bad," she said with a smirk.

"I'm no Scottie, though." Okay, so I really was putting it out there. All of it.

"Why would you say that?"

"Just the way you and Dad talk about him. It's like he's the star and I'm . . . I don't know. *The other one.*"

The coffee finished brewing, and I set it down in front of her. She grabbed my hand.

"I'm so sorry if I've made you feel that way, Jack. That was never my intention."

"I know."

"Truly."

"I know, Mom."

She let my hand go, and I sat down.

"And I am proud of you," she said after taking a sip. "Maybe I don't always say that, but I am."

"Thanks."

"Your dad's proud of you too."

"I don't believe that for a second."

"You're not hearing me: I didn't say he *understands*. I said he's proud of you. He just doesn't know how to say that."

"That kind of sounds like semantics." No point in sugarcoating it now. "And this whole 'the man's supposed to be the provider' thing is just so stupid."

"Look, he had this image in his head of who you were going to be. He didn't go to college, but he thought you would end up as a CEO or a doctor or a lawyer."

"I did for a while too. Well, maybe not a lawyer. But something."

My mom sized me up in a way I couldn't remember her having done since I was a teenager. It was her "If you're scamming me, I'm gonna know" look.

"So you're telling me it never bothers *you* that *you're* the one home with the kids instead of Kayla?"

"There are times when I miss working, yes. But that has nothing to do with Kayla. It has everything to do with only being able to muster so many thoughts about who the best member of the PAW Patrol is."

"I'm being serious," she said.

"I am too. I'm proud of my wife. And I know you don't like this word, but she's a *goddamn boss*."

"And how about you? Are you proud of yourself? Of the kind of husband and father you are?"

Somehow, I had never thought to ask myself that question before.

"Yeah. I guess that I am."

"Then can I tell you something?"

She slid her chair back.

"None of the rest of it matters," she said.

She stood, placed her hands on my shoulders, kissed me on the forehead, and then went to play with her grandkids.

CHAPTER 26

My mom didn't leave until around eleven o'clock Saturday morning so I could sleep in. I thanked her again for helping so much with the kids and for having that conversation with me. She brushed off my acknowledgment of it, almost like she didn't want to risk starting another one. I also might have been reading into what was really her just trying to get out the door. She and my dad had early dinner plans she didn't want to be late for—something to do with a two-for-one buffet at a casino. Related: my parents didn't gamble.

That suited them somehow.

It left me to wonder what, if any, impact having had that talk would have on our interactions going forward. I'd invited her to come back at Halloween to see the kids in their costumes, and to bring my dad. She clearly appreciated the idea, although she wouldn't go so far as to say yes to it. But even if the impact turned out to be negligible, it had been worth it to me. Not so much because she had told me they were proud of me but because I felt like I'd said something I had needed to say for a long time, sort of a planting-the-flag moment for all the decisions Kayla and I had made about how we wanted to live our life together.

Was I proud of who I'd become, my mom had asked me. Discovering my answer was yes had felt like a weight being lifted.

"Did you have fun with Grandma?" Kayla asked Lulu and Klay from her hotel room before we got ourselves together to go shopping. I had texted her to see if she could FaceTime with us almost as soon as my mom had driven away. She was in Minneapolis for a few more days, and it sounded like when she wasn't in meetings, she was prepping for meetings. Making a call like this was a risk with the kids, who sometimes had a harder time with her being gone if you reminded them she wasn't there. Plus there was our fight and my continuing frustration over her being unable to vote. But she had been gone more than 48 hours by then, and I really needed to see her for a minute, come what may.

"How's everything?" I asked her when our children ran off after about 30 seconds to retrieve the new lovies my mom had given them. They had insisted Kayla couldn't wait until she got home to see them.

"Eh, okay." We had continued to text, mostly stuff about the kids, with a few updates about our own things mixed in. I knew she was cautiously optimistic about the firm's chances of landing the client, and she knew the debate had exceeded all my expectations. However, as hard as it was, I remained committed to not telling her about the parent uprising. The only way to do that justice would be in person. As long as we didn't pick up where we had left off right before she went to the airport.

"I'm tired," she said, running her fingers through her hair and then leaving them on top of her head. "It's just a lot. Especially after we . . . you know."

"I know."

"But the debate was good?"

"Yeah. Really good."

We both waited for the other to say something else.

"Listen. I wanted . . . ," I started.

"Jack, it's been . . ."

"Oh, sorry."

"No, you go."

I heard a hurricane of "Mommy! Mommy!" and "Look at mine first!" approaching and knew our time alone was almost over.

"Shit," Kayla said. "My phone's ringing. I have to answer this. Hold on a sec."

She must have been talking to us on her iPad because now I was watching her on the phone. Lulu and Klay showed up, bearing matching stuffed dogs, as Kayla explained to whoever was on the other end of the call that they would have to wait while she said goodbye to her kids. My heart hurt for her as I watched her get pulled in opposite directions by work and family while she sat alone in a hotel, and FaceTiming with two kids shouting over us wasn't the way to talk about what we needed to talk about, anyway.

"Ooh, I love your puppies," Kayla said. "What're their names?"

"Mine's Sandra," Lula said, suddenly and uncharacteristically bashful.

"Aww, like your teacher. What about yours, Klay?"

"Doggie!" he exclaimed, thrusting it toward the screen and covering the camera.

"Should've guessed." Kayla was smiling but with a hint of sadness. "Okay, Mommy's gotta go. But I'm so glad I got to see you. I love you so much."

"But we just started talking," Lulu objected.

"I know, baby. I'm sorry. I'm just trying to get all this work done, and . . ." The emotion got my wife, the noncrier, midsentence, and the tears quickly followed. "Then I can come home, okay?"

She and I had to figure this out. For all of us.

Klay didn't quite register what was going on, but Lulu started crying, too, and more than a little of me wanted to follow suit—for my kid wanting her mom, for me missing my partner, for what was unresolved between us, and for her struggling so mightily as she watched us from far away. I was hit by the reality that no matter how exhausting and thankless it could be at home with the kids, when so much felt ragged and frayed, home was the one place you wanted to be. Not on the road, living out of a suitcase. I certainly wouldn't want to be in Kayla's position. At that particular moment, I was sure she didn't want to be in it either. It was one of those times when you don't care what you've been fighting about because you just want to make it better for the other person.

I couldn't do much, but seeing her kids fall apart wasn't going to make things easier.

"All right, let's say goodbye to Mommy," I said over Lulu's crying. Klay did understand that and now joined in with her, so I had to almost yell my follow-up of "Tell her that you love her!" They obliged, although the manner in which they did suggested they might be uniquely well suited to careers as professional mourners.

I turned the phone toward me and took a step or two away from them. "Hang in there," I said.

She wiped her eyes. "You too."

We hung up, and I lingered on the empty screen. Should I have said "I love you"? Unlike my parents, Kayla and I said it to each other all the time, just not reflexively at the end of calls like some people. But given the circumstances, maybe I should have. One more thing to think about for the three and a half days until she got back. Ugh. How was it still that long?

I looked down at my children, whose grief showed no signs of letting up. I needed something to change our moods, and the standard Target run wouldn't do it.

"Hey, do you two want to go to the farmers' market?"

The crying lessened.

"Can we get some . . . of that fresh-squeezed . . . lemonade they have?" Lulu asked through her tears.

"Of course we can. And we can eat at the food truck in the middle, too, if you want."

The grieving period was over.

I had actually been thinking of suggesting we go there even before we'd called Kayla. The farmers' market was a hot spot for Willow Road parents on a Saturday morning, so it might give me a chance to do a last round of in-person campaigning. And for all I knew, Chad was already there, about to post a photo of him and Crispin trying the vegan brie with hashtags like #dadlife and #forthecows. Cassie wouldn't be there with them—she was probably at a gas station, refilling her tank for the third time in five days.

Lulu used the drive there to press me on why we hadn't yet scheduled another playdate with Crispin. She hadn't asked about this in a while and now was doing so right after I had been thinking about them, so the only reasonable conclusion seemed to be that my daughter had recently harnessed the power of her brain into impressive telepathic abilities. That, or it was just a coincidence.

"We'll see," I said as the gravel of the market's parking lot crackled beneath our tires. The place was at its most crowded before noon, so by the time we got there, at 12:15 p.m., it was busy but not overwhelmingly so. Better yet, there was no sign of Chad's BMW. Blowing off Lulu's request would prove exponentially harder if we ran into them in person, never mind the election and my general aversion to seeing him. I just had to wait her out, which I knew I could because some of my best parenting happened when my kids had no idea I was disregarding their opinions.

I really hoped that telepathy thing wasn't true.

We got out of the van, Klay with significant assistance from me despite his insistence that he would "do myself," and I grabbed both of their hands before setting out. We'd start with lunch so we didn't have to leave what we bought in the car and because a touch too much of my emotional stability that afternoon was wrapped up in the grilled cheese at the food truck. It was simple enough—melted gouda with tomato and caramelized onions—but we were talking churro levels of goodness.

On our way to the truck, I spotted and said hi to a few Willow Road parents. The scenario was kind of perfect: my kids loved the grilled cheese, too (sans the onions), and once they could sense it was almost within reach, they were practically dragging me to it, leaving little time for small talk. So it was a "Thanks for coming to the debate" here, a "Don't forget to vote Tuesday before school" there, and then me moving on with two kids at my side. It didn't matter that the degree of nonchalance I exhibited had less to do with my abilities as a dad and more to do with Lulu and Klay's own focus on lunch. As far as any observers were concerned, I was solo parenting the hell out of Saturday at the farmers' market, a task that had laid waste to far more talented caregivers than me.

After I got our sandwiches, I looked around for a spot to sit. There were only five or six tables, so it was expected that you would share with people you didn't know. I was drawn to the long one that easily seated eight but currently had just a single occupant, a woman at the end opposite from where we were standing. I was so focused on getting the three of us situated I didn't even notice who it was.

"Why didn't you tell me your plan was to stage a T-shirt revolt?"

I looked up and started to laugh. It was Elena Choi.

"Because if you had," she said, "I wouldn't have just endorsed you; I would've funded your entire campaign."

"I don't know—campaign swag is apparently a major liability with voters who have been directly insulted by their child's principal."

She very clearly enjoyed that, and I turned to Lulu and Klay.

"Daddy's going to go talk to a friend for a minute, okay? I'll be right there if you need anything," I said, pointing down the table. They had already achieved grilled-cheese nirvana and couldn't have cared less.

I got back up and walked the several steps to the seat across from Elena, who had on a striped maxi dress and a large sun hat. She looked glamorous in a way she hadn't at the going-away party and that wasn't entirely in keeping with our surroundings.

"How'd you hear?" I asked.

"Liz called me right after."

"Yeah, she was kind of the ringleader."

"I'm sorry I missed it. Honestly, the Chad thing is neither here nor there to me, but I can't believe you got *Deidre Weekler* to break."

"Well, again, I think Liz deserves a lot of the credit for that."

"Sure," she said, studying me over a can of sparkling water. "But I doubt Liz would've been so worked up if you hadn't just 'happened' to find that list at the bookfair. What were the odds of that?"

I looked away to the kids. They still didn't seem to notice I'd moved.

"Good enough," I said and then turned back to her. "The odds were good enough."

"Yes, I suppose they were." She wadded up the aluminum foil her lunch had been wrapped in. "Nothing's going to happen to her, you know. Deidre. A photo of a piece of paper doesn't prove she wrote that list."

"Yeah, but she basically admitted it at the debate."

"That's not the same thing as actually admitting it. Besides, from what Liz told me, I don't think the parents are in a rush to take that video to the school district either. And I know this may come as a shock to you, but there are some parents who pay absolutely zero attention to anything having to do with the Active Alpaca Parent Board. The open rates on our emails would make you think we were selling time-shares."

I laughed, and she continued.

"Just promise me one thing: If you win, she's going to try to reel you in, make you think you can trust her. Don't."

The clothes weren't the only thing about Elena that had changed. The sadness that had hung over her wasn't gone, exactly, but it wasn't looming in the same way. I could feel the presence that had led to her getting elected four times.

"I think it's pretty much a toss-up," I said. "I won the debate, but the voting is another thing altogether. The school certainly doesn't strive to make it easy."

Elena gave me a funny look. "I always found most parents can figure it out. At least those who care to."

It was a good reminder: even after all that had happened, Elena still had more in common with Ms. Weekler than she did with me. While Tori had admitted she had been exaggerating some at orientation when describing Elena's unflinching loyalty to our principal, there had been a large element of truth there, also. They had gotten along so well for a reason. If Ms. Weekler had cheated with literally anyone else's husband, Elena wouldn't be moving to Boston, and I, too, would be deleting her parent-board emails rather than running for the position she had held for so long. I definitely wouldn't have realized how much of an impact that position could have on people. Or on me.

"So when's the big move?" I asked, not wanting to get into a discussion about the things in the AAPB bylaws—*her* bylaws—that I wanted to change.

"Monday. The movers got everything from the house earlier in the week. This has always been one of my favorite places, so I wanted to come one last time before I go."

I had been struggling with Kayla being gone for *a few days* after we had gotten into a fight. The idea of packing up my whole life to move to another city after my spouse had cheated on me was beyond comprehension, even if it was their hometown.

"Well, I hope everything works out for the best."

"Thank you. Leslie and I will be fine. But Steven . . ." She lost herself in thought for a minute. "Steven's going to need a good lawyer," she eventually said.

"Oh. So it's, like, official?"

"He doesn't know it yet. But it's official for me."

"I'm so sorry, Elena. That . . . that sucks."

"It does. But I'm not going to be with a man who doesn't want to be with me. I am not that woman."

I tried to think of an appropriately impressed response, but she didn't wait around for one, instead standing and slinging a large brown purse over her shoulder.

"One more piece of advice," she said as she put on her sunglasses. "If you are ever going to cheat on your wife? Make sure she doesn't know your email password."

Oddly specific.

But whatever issues Kayla and I needed to work through, trust wasn't one of them. We saw through to the core of each other and loved what we found. That went an awful long way with the person you'd chosen to spend the rest of your life with. I wished the same for Elena one day.

Until then, though, the least I could do was vanquish our respective nemeses and become her successor.

Go Alpacas.

CHAPTER 27

"I've never been to school this early before," Lulu said when we pulled in at 7:15 a.m.

It was Tuesday everywhere else in the world. In the hallowed halls of Willow Road Elementary, however, it was Active Alpaca Parent Board Presidential Election Day. I felt like marking it somehow, so I got up before the kids, took a long shower, and made a ceremony of throwing out that pack of cigarettes I'd bought. Whatever the day had in store, I was ready.

"That's kinda fun, though, right?" I tried.

"Why?" Lulu asked.

"For one thing, you and I get to walk into your room together. We've *never* gotten to do that before."

"Why?"

"Because Daddy has the election thing this morning, so Ms. Sandra said you can go in early and play *Happy Numbers* on the iPad while she gets organized for the day. Wasn't that nice of her?"

"I don't like *Happy Numbers*. I like *Reading Eggs*."

"Right. *Reading Eggs*. That's what I meant."

"But you said *Happy Numbers*."

I put the van in park, turned off the engine, and savored these final few minutes with my daughter, who, even when interrogating me over the availability of her preferred educational app, was an infinitely better conversational partner than my opponent.

"I think you can do whichever one you want," I said, turning around to look at her in the back seat. "And that's not even the best part about today."

"What's the best part?"

"Mommy comes home this afternoon!"

From that point until I dropped her at her room, we talked exclusively about Kayla—what Lulu thought she had been doing in Minneapolis, all the things she wanted to do with her once she was back, how Mommy would probably like *Reading Eggs* but "really love" *Happy Numbers* because she was an accountant.

I stared at her in amazement. "You know Mommy works with numbers?"

"Uh-huh. That's what accountants do, Daddy. They account things."

It felt like I had been kissed by a ray of sunshine inside that fluorescent-lit hallway.

"I love you, Lulu."

She hugged me around my leg. "So much?"

"So much."

"I love you, too, Daddy."

I waved to Ms. Sandra, who welcomed us with a warm "There's our friend Lulu!" That's when I noticed Crispin sitting by himself and figured he was doing the same thing Lulu was. His whole body visibly relaxed when she walked in. It occurred to me then that I probably should've used the opportunity to have her show me around the room, but I would see it in a few weeks, at the parent-teacher conference.

I also wouldn't have traded the goodbye I'd gotten for anything. It was too easy to miss stuff like that when you were juggling both kids, which I almost always was when it came to Lulu since she was older and in school and Klay wasn't. Even though it had just been her and me for almost four years, I had a hard time remembering what that particular dynamic felt like. That made me a little sad. Not because I loved Klay any less than I did her; as previously documented, if I'd ever had a favorite, it was him during the 10-second window at Chad's when he'd wanted to bail. No, I think I was just grieving a little for that period of time when I was first getting to know her and getting to know myself as a dad, and I didn't like that those years had become so blurry.

At the same time, though, if it hadn't been for her going to school, I wouldn't have been in the election and I wouldn't have realized that there was something out there besides going back to work that would still let me use those skills I'd developed while working. It didn't have to be an either-or. I could be a stay-at-home dad *and* have an impact outside my house. Taking care of Lulu as a newborn had brought me back from the fire, and now being forced to let her go had taught me I didn't have to be defined by that day.

Wow. I was going to be a mess if she got married someday and asked me to give a toast. That much was clear. Then I'd remember Klay and "Doggie!" and it'd be all over.

Focus, Jack.

Election Day. Lulu was in class, and I had known that leaving Klay to his own devices in the school while I was busy electioneering would be a recipe for disaster and that I therefore needed a babysitter. For the bookfair, I had asked a dad I knew from a playgroup if he could watch Klay for a couple of hours. He was very cool about it, but I still didn't think I should follow that up eight days later with another request, especially since it would go something like, "Hey, remember how we hadn't talked in months, and I asked you to do me that favor? Well, can you do it again, only this time I'll be dropping him off at seven in the morning?"

Fortunately the campaign hadn't just given me a renewed sense of purpose; it had also given me an honest-to-God friend. Tori didn't even wait for me to ask. She had taken the morning off work initially so she could keep an eye on the ballot box and make sure Ms. Weekler didn't attempt to pull anything while Chad and I were in front of the school, greeting people as they came to vote. But with Kayla out of town, Tori had willingly taken on reacquainting herself with the rhythms of a non-potty-trained human. She was going to bring Klay to the school just before 8:30 so she could still vote. And lucky for us, Liz Morrison had already volunteered to work the coffee-and-doughnut stand the AAPB had set up just past the ballot box, so she had been more than happy to pull double duty as our poll monitor.

Everything was in place. All that was left for me to do was cast my own ballot. And then wait.

With Chad.

When people walked into the gym, there were three tables staged in a row right inside the doors. At the first, Kathy Francis checked voters' names off the official list of parents and guardians and then handed them each a small rectangular piece of white paper that served as the ballot. The second table didn't have anyone at it and was the spot for people to mark down their votes in (relative) anonymity. Ms. Weekler stood at the third, waiting for them to drop the folded pieces of paper into a lockbox. She was giving Chad an approving smile while he did so when I walked in.

"Just the two of us so far?" I asked Kathy, nodding toward Chad as she crossed me off. It was 7:30 on the dot, so this question seemed to have an obvious answer, but we hadn't talked since the Target aisle, and this was my attempt at meaningless chitchat to alleviate any awkwardness.

"You're the third, actually." She didn't look up but pointed toward my left with her pen. There, leaning against the wall, sipping a venti that was definitely not from the coffee stand and wearing an expression that suggested she was not to be trifled with, was Liz. She raised her cup to me, and I did some sort of chest-pound thing in response that I was nowhere near cool enough to pull off. We both laughed.

Kathy handed me my ballot, and I moved on to table two. Chad and I casually acknowledged each other as he left, but neither of us said anything. I supposed that would come when we were outside.

I put a check mark on the blank line next to my name—which, to my surprise, was one of three choices, not two, there being an option for a write-in candidate below me. I briefly considered saying something, but in addition to knowing it wouldn't do any good, I wasn't sure who the write-in was more likely to help, so I let it go.

"Best of luck today, Mr. Parker," Ms. Weekler said once I'd deposited my ballot in the box. "And thank you again for your discretion with the video."

It sounded sincere, and I wondered whether maybe it was. For an elementary school principal, she maintained quite the aura of invincibility, and yet over the last week, she had taken two direct hits: the "leaking" of her list and then her implosion at the debate. She couldn't prove I'd been responsible for the leak, and the other parents were the ones who had pushed her over the edge Thursday night. But there was no denying that my campaign and I were in the thick of it all. I felt like maybe, in a backward way, I had earned her respect.

Which was exactly the kind of thing Elena had warned me Ms. Weekler would want me to think in the event that I won.

"Uh-huh," I said. "See you for the counting."

I thanked Liz on the way out for being there. I exited the way I had come in so I could return to the school's main entrance, saying hello to some moms with their kids as I did. I didn't know all of them, but they all seemed to know me. It was a good sign.

When I emerged out front, I saw teachers helping students out of cars along with a few more moms and maybe a grandma walking in. I think arriving early on AAPB Election Day was an excuse for some to finally get a peek at their kids' classrooms.

It was overcast and looked like it might rain. Chad was standing to the right, under the edge of the overhang that covered much of the walkway into the building. I didn't particularly want to stand near him but knew acting like I didn't care was the power play.

He was busy chatting up a mom when I got there, and I jumped right into their conversation, telling her to make sure she grabbed some coffee after she voted.

"How'd you figure it out?" he asked me once it was just the two of us. We both kept our eyes on the drop-off activities.

"How did I figure what out?"

"C'mon, Jack. I know you didn't come up with 'smoothie shop' out of thin air."

"Aah, that. It wasn't me, actually. It was one of your posts. The Sunset Smoothies poster was in the background."

He muttered something to himself, and we stood there in silence for a bit. This wasn't that afternoon at his house with the letter. His sheen had truly been dulled this time, at least in the complicated inner universe that existed between the two of us.

"Thanks for not saying anything," he said after the first dad I'd seen walked past. "If the roles were reversed, I wouldn't have been able to resist."

"Well, that's because I'm a better person than you."

He laughed grimly. "How did you get that photo of the list?"

"Who said I had anything to do with that?"

"It was a good move. It's not like I could say anything without implicating myself. Or *her*."

"If I knew what you were talking about, I'm sure I'd say thanks."

The progression of people there to vote was modest but steady, and it picked up a little before 8:00 a.m., once the school day had officially started. Several of the parents I recognized from the debate straight-up ignored Chad when he tried to talk to them, but overall, he and I seemed to be regarded equally.

"You and Ms. Weekler," I ventured during one of the lulls, curious how much I could get out of him. "Are you two . . . you know."

"Ha—no. I really thought I had a chance too. She was flirting with me constantly. But then when I made a move, she wasn't interested. I think she's got some long-distance thing going. Some guy in Boston."

"Wait . . . *you* tried to sleep with *her*?"

"If it makes you feel any better, I'm positive Cassie is cheating on me. That day you came over with the kids? She was pissed because I'd confronted her about it."

Chad pursuing an affair shouldn't have caught me off guard. It was a pretty Chad move. And apparently he hadn't been lying about him and Cassie having problems. Then there was Ms. Weekler. Long distance with some guy in Boston. Elena implying she'd been reading her husband's email and that their marriage was over. That couldn't be a coincidence.

I wanted Kayla home. Not because I thought either of us would ever cheat on the other. Just to hug her.

"What about Sidney?" I asked. "How did you get him to agree to that Chocsplosion! thing?"

That brought a smile to Chad's face. "A master stroke. He was in town and invited Cassie and me to dinner, and the election and who I was running against came up. When I said it was you, he got all red in the face and goes, 'Did you know those Chocsplosion! *assholes* still send me ten cases of candy bars every year on the anniversary of the fire? Just to rub it in my *face*?' Apparently your video did as much for Chocsplosion! sales as any ad campaign they've ever run. It drives him nuts. *You* drive him nuts."

For the first time, I felt an actual fondness for that fire.

I'd hardly had time to process what Chad had told me when Brooke's unmistakable voice boomed out:

"Is this where I go to vote for Jack Parker for president of the parent board?"

"Yes, ma'am, right through here and into the gym," I said.

"Thank you, young man. And do you know one of the things I love about Jack Parker?" She stopped in front of me. "He's never going to call me 'ma'am' again."

I laughed. Chad failed to read the room.

"I wouldn't even need to be told once, Ms. . . . ," he attempted.

She looked at him like he had just proposed we introduce flat-Earth theory into the geography curriculum.

"Yes, Jack Parker's my man," she continued, loud enough for anyone else out there to hear, which at the moment was an annoyed-looking Man Bun—but with his hair down?—and a mom with her head buried in her phone, clearly hoping to avoid interacting with any of us. "Well, not my man, per se—I'm married to a beautiful woman, you see, one whom it only now occurs to me that I could've carpooled with this morning since she'll be here shortly. Then again, we'd need two cars when we were done, so I guess that wouldn't have worked out after all."

She pressed the buzzer to go into the school and then held the door for the two behind her. "But you know who would've known that from the start?" she said to them. "Jack Parker."

"She's loud," Chad said.

"I know. It's the best."

After reaching that peak a few minutes before 8:00 a.m., turnout began to taper off, and from 8:20 on, it was just Chad and me. Limiting the voting to first thing in the morning made it so you weren't really even giving people an hour to do it since a lot of them would have to be at work well before 8:30.

"I think I'm gonna go in," he said. We had both retreated into our phones by then, which was fine with me. It was only one vote, but I was getting jittery waiting for Tori and Klay to appear. It meant even more to me because I knew Kayla couldn't be there—like if I couldn't have *my* person, I needed the one who had been with me throughout this whole strange ride, especially here at the end.

"Aren't you going to wait for Cassie?"

"No, I don't think so." He paused on what to say next. "She just texted me. She forgot."

"Sorry, man," I said.

He slunk off, and I was alone.

I had meant it, saying I was sorry. His marriage appeared to be a train wreck, and I wouldn't wish that on anyone. Talk about appreciating what you've got.

It wasn't until I went to check again for a text from Tori, even though I knew there wasn't one, that something different hit me:

He had been leaning into his marriage problems for most of the time we had been standing there. Wasn't it maybe a little too much?

Sympathy had been my undoing with Chad before. Fake cancer, a fake apology—he could've been doing it again. He could've thought I'd feel so bad for him that I'd go in and tell Ms. Weekler I had changed my mind and was dropping out.

But even if this were fake—even if Cassie hadn't forgotten and just had an early meeting she couldn't get out of, even if she weren't having an affair—Chad had run out of ways to escape who he really was.

Fabricated success? Real.

Booed off stage at his kid's school? So real.

Rejected by his kid's principal? The realest (or else the biggest self-own of a lie of all time).

It wasn't an exaggeration to say the only way for Chad Henson to be considered a winner that day would be if he got the majority of the votes cast for president of the Willow Road Elementary Active Alpaca Parent Board.

It didn't matter if he'd decided at the last second to pretend one more time that his life was sad. It had been for a long time.

A deep breath passed through my lips. My stomach began to settle. What had been a growing nervousness twisted into a hum of excitement, of curiosity. Vindication wasn't waiting for me in that ballot box. I had already gotten that.

Now I just wanted to win.

CHAPTER 28

"Mr. Henson, Mr. Parker—if you're both ready, I'll count the votes."

The three of us were sitting in Ms. Weekler's office. Tori had made it in time, but I'd never seen her come in. She had been cutting it close due to a Klay diaper mishap on their way out of the house, so she had gone straight to the back door of the gym, which was much closer to the parking lot. Liz had heard her knocking that turned into pounding and let her in with two minutes to spare. She had voted with my son on her hip and was now entertaining him in her car.

I really owed her a spa day or something less creepy for a male friend to give her.

"How is this going to work, exactly?" I asked.

"I'll pull them out one at a time and show them to you both and then place them in your respective piles as appropriate," Ms. Weekler said. "When I've pulled them all, I'll add up the totals, and then we'll have our winner."

I eyed her hands, resting on the still-locked box. It felt like she was explaining a game of three-card monte to me. My suspicion was not lost on her.

"You'll notice that I do have a master's degree, Mr. Parker," she said, looking to a framed diploma from Northwestern on her white-plastered walls; it was next to a poster of that famously magnificent Barcelonese cathedral. "But you're welcome to double-check my math when the time comes. You, too, Mr. Henson."

"That won't be necessary," he said.

"Speak for yourself," I mumbled back.

By then, I was more than accustomed to the way she could fix onto you from behind her glasses, almost like she was wielding a tractor beam, but it still commanded my attention whether I wanted it to or not. A hint in the air of the same fragrance from the debate and an especially intense selection from Mozart playing on a speaker I couldn't see only heightened the effect.

"Mr. Parker, I do hope that if you're victorious today, you and I can get on the same page, so to speak. As I've said, serving as president of the Active Alpaca Parent Board is a large responsibility, one that requires considerable collaboration with me as the school's principal. I'd be counting on your . . . professionalism . . . in our dealings with the school district in particular."

"Yeah, I heard it's a big year for you there. Five-year review and some angry teachers, right?"

In the subtle hint of a sneer that crept across her face, I thought I saw both that newfound respect I'd sensed earlier and a deepening desire to stab me with her stiletto. Be that as it may, she let my remark pass without further comment.

"Let's get started," she said.

Her hand disappeared into a drawer on the left side of her desk and reemerged with the box's key. Seconds later she was showing the two of us the first slip of paper, and it was decidedly anticlimactic.

"Write-in for Trish Merletti," she announced with a roll of her eyes. It was possibly the only thing in the world that would've made all three of us laugh.

The next vote went to Chad.

The three after that went for me.

Then two more for him.

One for each of us.

And so on.

I started out trying to keep track of each of our counts but lost it fairly fast, especially since write-in ballots kept popping up every now and then. After about five minutes, all the ballots were on her desk in three piles, with his and mine appearing to be very much the same size.

She went to the write-ins first and quickly added them up: seven. Trish got the most, with three, and no one else received more than one.

"All right, Mr. Henson's pile."

The slips were face down, but she flipped them over and placed them face up as she went, almost like she was dealing an interminably long hand of Texas Hold'em.

"Forty-eight. Forty-nine. Fifty. Fifty-one. Fifty-two. Fifty-three votes for Mr. Henson. Mr. Parker, would you care to recount?"

I shook my head, but just barely.

"Very well. On to yours."

I watched her hands, accented by well-manicured white nails, begin slapping my votes down in front of me. It was too close to call, but something inside me told me I had this.

She hit 30 and then 40 and then 50.

And then she hesitated.

I looked up from her hands. We both knew now.

There were definitely more than three votes left in my pile.

"Fifty-one. Fifty-two. Fifty-three. Fifty-four. Fifty-five. Fifty-six. Fifty-seven. Fifty-eight. That's fifty-eight votes for Mr. Parker."

Chad sat there, stunned. I was quiet too.

"I lost," he finally said. "I can't believe I lost. *To Jack Parker.*"

"You didn't," I corrected him. "Not yet, anyway."

"What?"

Ms. Weekler looked at me. "I see you took the time to familiarize yourself with the entirety of the AAPB bylaws."

"No, just the rest of Article II."

"Someone tell me what's going on," Chad begged.

"One of us has to get a majority to win. Otherwise it goes to a runoff."

"But you did get a majority." His expression changed. "Wait. Didn't you?"

"A majority of *all* the votes cast," I clarified, "including the write-ins. I got fifty-eight out of a hundred and eighteen. I missed it by two damn votes."

"Very good, Mr. Parker," she said, clearly pleased to have order restored.

"That was a clever little trick you pulled there."

"Actually, a write-in option is on the ballot every year. If you don't believe me, you can ask your good friend Elena Choi." We were both briefly distracted from the task at hand by her trying to read my face for just how much I knew.

"So when's the runoff?" I asked.

"Yes, the runoff. I'll be frank with you, Mr. Parker: I didn't expect you to do even this well. Nevertheless, because you've continued to make it abundantly clear you have no interest in working together, I knew I needed to come prepared."

She returned to her desk drawer and handed me a letter written on Willow Road Elementary letterhead. It was addressed to me, from her, but unsigned.

"You said you wanted to change the way we run the bookfair, yes?" she said. "Make it more equitable?"

Was she really about to do what I thought she was?

"If you concede the election, it's done."

Yes. She was.

I could feel her watching me for a reaction as I skimmed through the letter, which was only a few paragraphs long. It established a new committee, independent of the parent board, that would assume complete control over the bookfair, with me serving as its chair. The committee's charge was to "transition the bookfair to a model of community-based financial support."

"And if I don't concede?" I said, putting the letter down. "You seem to have forgotten I'm winning."

"Oh, you got more votes *today*. But you and I both know that's not *winning*. The runoff is another thing entirely."

"That I could win."

"Or you could lose. But that doesn't matter. The only way the bookfair changes is if you drop out. Because even if you did manage to win the runoff, Mr. Parker, you need to understand that nothing happens in *my school* without *my approval*. And I can tell you right now that your proposal goes nowhere with you as AAPB president."

She and I were engaged in a staredown, but Chad's eyes were so wide I could see them from the corner of mine.

"What about the technology fee?" I asked.

"Cutting that has never been on the table," she said.

"Deidre, are you sure we should—"

"Shut up, Chad," I said. "The grown-ups are talking."

There was that begrudging respect again. "Further antagonizing the teachers is not in my best interest," she said. "And as hard as this may be for you to believe, I am still an educator and do care about the education these children receive."

I sat back in my chair. Was I really considering this? I mean, the entire conversation was insane. My kindergartner's principal was basically offering to bribe me so that I'd throw a parent-board election. Insane didn't even begin to cut it. It was patently absurd.

Yet it was also probably the one and only way I could make an actual difference at the school. And did I really want to spend the next nine months fighting with Deidre Weekler, day in and day out, all to accomplish nothing? What would that mean for Lulu and the rest of the kids?

"Why isn't it signed?" I asked.

"I sign it once you've agreed to my terms, and we send the email to all the parents announcing your decision."

"Do I get to say I got the most votes?"

I couldn't help it.

"That hardly seems wise. But we will announce that I have so much faith in your vision for the bookfair that I've appointed you to lead this new committee."

How she was running an elementary school and not in an abandoned factory ordering someone's kneecaps broken was baffling.

"So, do we have a deal, Mr. Parker?"

"I don't know yet."

"I see. You should know that my offer is good for twenty-four hours. We can finalize it tomorrow morning after drop-off. Otherwise, I will announce the runoff election."

She took the letter, slid it back into the drawer, and rested her hands atop the desk, interlacing her fingers as she did. Her body was telling me what words were not: it was time for me to go.

I stood to leave while Chad stayed put, which tracked perfectly with everything else about this race.

"I'm going to get what I want, Mr. Parker," she said when I reached the door. "It's just a question of whether you get something too."

Chad opened his mouth to speak but thought better of it.

"I think I already did," I said.

Less than 20 minutes later, I had finished telling Tori everything that had happened that morning. We sat in the front seat of her car while Klay miraculously remained distracted by a pile of board books.

"What did you already get?" she asked me.

"Huh?"

"What you said at the end—what'd you mean?"

"Oh. Well, closure with Chad, for starters. I mean, he looked absolutely pathetic in there. And as we've learned, that's a lot closer to who he actually is. Plus, not for nothing, I did get more votes than he did. But even more than that, I feel like I've gotten a piece of my identity back. Being a stay-at-home parent doesn't have to mean I don't get out there and mix it up with the rest of the world. This is a chance to make an actual difference for the kids at this school. I honestly didn't know I had something like that in me anymore. And you, as much as anyone, helped me realize it."

That answer did not satisfy her.

"What does you getting more votes matter if no one but us and him ever knows?"

"Aren't we the only ones it should matter to? And he was my nemesis, so really, shouldn't it only matter to me? As long as I know?"

"Oh God—spare me the 'I'm a better person for it' ending, Jack. I didn't do this for a moral victory."

I had expected her to be frustrated or angry. But not with me.

"I thought you thought all of this was stupid," I said.

"A lot of it is. Especially when people like Chad or Ms. Weekler or Elena are the ones in charge. But decency's got to win sometimes too. Otherwise what's the point?"

She stopped, and I waited. There was more, but she was taking a moment to reset herself.

"Remember that friend I told you about at dinner?" she asked. "The one in high school who freaked out when I told her I was gay?"

I nodded.

"The part I didn't tell you is a story only Brooke knows. This girl's name was Tori Wilcox. People had called us The Two since eighth grade. We were inseparable. And then . . ." She put her hands together, almost like she was praying. "She told me that being The Two only made it that much worse.

"'People are going to assume it's some sort of lesbian thing,'" Tori said, doing a high-pitched impression of the other Tori. "She wouldn't even speak to me. But she talked a lot *about* me. And there she was, the one giving the speech at graduation about class unity and moral character, blah blah blah. Meanwhile, I didn't even get to go to my own prom."

"Tori, I'm . . . I don't know what to say. That's so messed up."

"It is. But that's not why I'm telling you. I'm telling you because this is what people like this do. They have zero regard for anyone but themselves, and they get their way because they just don't care. And if we don't stop them sometimes, when we can, they run everything."

She stared out her window, and I thought about how to respond.

Tori was right. Obviously. But even if I hadn't thought that, I, of all people, wasn't going to tell her how to feel about what had happened all those years ago. The whole reason we were sitting there in the first place was the degree to which my past had been hanging over my pres-ent—and unlike me with Chad, hers wasn't just about the past. Because although I had never been judged for who I was or who I loved, I'd be shocked if in Tori's life, there had been only one Tori Wilcox.

"I'm sorry," I said when the silence had stretched on for a while. "I shouldn't have said this didn't mean anything to you or that it was just about me."

"No, I know. I didn't take it that way. But thanks."

"It's amazing how someone like a Tori Wilcox or a Chad Henson can affect us for the rest of our lives, you know? I mean, he's a philan-dering failed smoothie-shop owner, and she's probably a . . ."

"An average, run-of-the-mill mom," Tori said. "I've looked her up a couple of times. Nothing exciting. Nothing terrible. Fit as ever, which is super annoying. But nothing special."

"And even as unremarkable as they are as human beings . . ."

" . . . what they thought or did manages to stick with us."

Neither one of us said anything else until Klay dropped one of his books and discreetly asked me to pick it up by yelling "Daddy! Book!"

"I haven't decided what I'm going to do," I said after I'd handed it back to him.

"Of course you have. You're going to take the deal. I could tell as soon as you described it to me." She paused, then added, "It's what I would do too." The disappointment was evident in her voice. "You'll get more done with this one thing than you would in an entire year of trying to work with her. And it comes with the added bonus of sparing you an entire year of trying to work with her."

"Yeah," I said quietly. "And hey, we'll always have the debate."

She chuckled. "There is that."

"Also, at the risk of making it awkward, I feel like I got a pretty great friend out of this. So. Yeah. That's pretty cool."

"Me too."

Tears seemed like a real possibility for both of us, so I maturely changed the subject to the steady rain that had grown from a mist when I'd gotten into her car. My van was in the same lot but on the other side, and she offered to drive us over to keep us dry.

"Ready to go home, buddy?" I said, twisting to buckle Klay into his seat and then buckling my own seat belt for the 30-second ride. As Tori put the car into gear, I was about to tell her that I would call later, when I had officially made up my mind. She had been correct about how I was leaning, but I still wasn't ready for it to be a done deal.

Before I could say anything, though, I saw an email notification pop up on my phone.

I didn't recognize the sender's name but opened the app thinking I'd delete it, the urge to battle inbox clutter being something I was physically incapable of resisting. But then the subject line caught my eye:

Meadow Park School District.

The email was about the length of Ms. Weekler's letter, and by the time we had come to a stop, I had finished it.

I looked out past the front of the car toward the playground, the windshield wipers squeaking from side to side.

"Well, this is interesting," I said.

"What is?"

I handed Tori my phone so she could read it for herself.

CHAPTER 29

"Mommy!" Lulu and Klay shouted together before Kayla had even emerged through the door leading in from the garage.

"Where are my babies?" she yelled back with a huge smile, dropping her suitcase to the floor as they ran to her across the kitchen. It was just after 5:30 p.m., and to welcome her home after the trip that had concluded with a major deal she'd orchestrated, I was making her favorite meal: mac and cheese.

That was what our children had insisted it was, anyway. When I suggested Mommy might not want something involving a packet of cheese sauce following six days of travel, I was admonished to "just trust us, Daddy."

Once they released her, we met at the end of the counter.

"Hi," I said simply but so, so gratefully.

"Hi," she said back. I knew she felt the same.

We kissed, and I wrapped her in my arms. She noticed the box next to the stove.

"That sounds delicious right now."

"Ha—well, I was told it's your favorite. And the best way to officially say congratulations."

"Thanks, Jack."

I studied her how you do after you haven't seen someone you love in a while. Her hair was coming out of her ponytail, and she was a little sweaty. There were bags under her eyes. And I was pretty sure she had on the pants she had when she left on Thursday.

"It's good to see you," I said.

"You too. I missed this." She tugged at the holey Gus Macker 3-on-3 Basketball Tournament T-shirt I'd had since I was 15 and had refused to throw out on at least a half dozen occasions.

"So?" she said when I turned to pour the macaroni into the pot of boiling water. "You won? But not really?"

I had told her over text about the runoff but hadn't gone into all the details. It was complicated enough on its own, and we hadn't had a chance to talk about the debate yet—which would put Ms. Weekler's backroom bookfair deal in context—or that my dad had texted me that afternoon to ask how things had gone.

I hadn't even made sense of that one.

"Yeah. The whole thing is . . . I don't know where to start."

The end of my sentence was drowned out by the kids returning to the kitchen, insisting Kayla go see what they had built out of stuff from the recycling bin—picked when I hadn't been paying attention.

"All right, everyone," I said over the top of them. "Here's what's going to happen. Lulu and Klay, show Mommy whatever it is you've built."

"It's a doghouse for our lovies," Lulu said.

"Doggies!" Klay added.

"Great," I continued. "Then, if Mommy wants, she can go take a quick shower and put on pajamas like the rest of us."

"Yes, Mommy would very much like that," Kayla said.

"I thought you might. Then we're going to meet back here in about fifteen minutes and have dinner. After that, you two"—I pointed at the kids—"are going to bed so Mommy and I can have a real live conversation with one another that doesn't involve typing and/or trying to talk over both of you."

"But that's so early," Lulu cried.

"It's not *that* early. And I'm guessing that since she's been gone a few days, Mommy's going to want to do both of your bedtimes."

"You guess correctly," Kayla said.

"Yay!" they both yelled.

"And," I said, Kayla the only one still listening on their way out, "Daddy's going to use bedtime to finish up something for school."

"Intriguing," she said over her shoulder.

The kids showed Kayla their doghouse (which, troublingly, included an egg carton for "holding all the dogs' pills") and followed her upstairs to play between our bathroom and bedroom while she showered. They didn't let her or me get in more than a couple of words at a time during dinner, Lulu leading the charge with Klay as her monosyllabic lieutenant. It would've been exhausting if they hadn't been focused exclusively on Kayla, who soaked it up after her time away while I relaxed in my sudden anonymity.

For the last two nights she was gone, I had given up on putting them to bed in their own rooms so I could just do one bedtime in ours. The first time, I got them asleep, went back downstairs for a few hours, and then returned to find them so sprawled out that the only spot available to me was the corner of the mattress next to Kayla's nightstand. The night before the election, I had never even made it back out of the bedroom, falling asleep with them on either side of me before 8:00. Kayla decided to take the same one-bed approach and made me promise to wake her up if it seemed like she might be lost for the evening.

I could hear the kids chattering away at her as I did the dishes and then moved to the couch to work, but they eventually quieted down. Still, it wasn't until I was closing my laptop and about to send her a check-in text that I heard her coming down the stairs.

"Yours is waiting for you in the fridge," I said, holding up my can of rosé.

"This—this is why I married you."

"I thought you married me for my tremendous influence at Willow Road Elementary School."

"Nope, it was the wine. The elementary school politics are just a bonus." She took a short detour through the kitchen before grabbing the cushion next to me, cracking open her can, and tucking her knees to her chest. "And now, I've waited long enough: tell me all of it."

"I'm going to. But before I do . . ."

"Boo."

"I'm serious. When we don't see each other for a few days like this, we're so glad to be back together that it makes it easy to gloss over that we were fighting when you left."

"So you . . . want to have another fight?"

"No, I just want to talk through the one we had. Because I don't know about you, but to me, it felt like it had been brewing for a while."

Her face softened. "Yeah. Me too."

"All right, so." I had been thinking since the weekend about how to put this and really wanted to get it right. "What you said about feeling guilty sometimes about not 'picking' the kids, and people acting weird about that? I have to apologize. It never even dawned on me that something like that would happen. Sometimes I think because I'm the one at home with them, I . . . I don't stop to think about what it's like for you, working, and I forget the rest of the world doesn't always look at it the same way we do. And that's totally unfair of me, and I'm sorry I haven't been seeing it."

She didn't respond right away, and I wondered if maybe I needed to try again.

"Thank you for saying that," she said before I could overthink it any more. "Really. Just because I want a big job doesn't mean I can't still be jealous of you building blanket forts with them. Wanting one thing doesn't mean I can't miss the other."

"I've been realizing that myself. And you should also know that in the course of telling my mom how proud I am of you, I referred to you as a 'goddamn boss.'"

She almost spit out her wine.

"How did that come up?" she managed to choke out between coughs.

"When I told her that anything I missed about working had nothing to do with *you* working. Oh, and that I didn't believe her when she said my dad was proud of me, which may be the reason he texted me today to ask about the election."

Kayla stared at me. "The next thing you're going to tell me is that you called her out for all the Scottie stuff."

"Yup, did that too."

Her eyes got even wider. "Seriously, what was going on while I was gone?"

"This election—I don't know. It woke me up. I'm home because I want to be home. I *do* fit here, and I don't want to go back to work. Not even a little bit. And I'm okay telling you that now."

"Why weren't you before?"

"Because I felt like I was letting you down by not being the guy you married. This wasn't our plan back then. I wasn't going to stay home. Then I burned a hole in my office and my career, and my confidence was shattered. When the kids were really little, I think I was able to push that out of my head because of how much they needed me. And it turned out I was *really damn good* at the dad thing. But with Lulu going to school and needing me less, I started to question myself and my worth all over again."

"You being here with them *is* worth a lot, Jack. I can't tell you how much the way you take care of them means to me."

"I know. Thank you. That's why I'm in no rush to leave it behind. But the election reminded me—hell, it retaught me—that I'm also still really good at other stuff. Not having a job hasn't changed that, and running for president let me tap into that stuff in a way I haven't since Scrub."

She took a long drink of her rosé, keeping her eyes on me the entire time.

"This renewed confidence is unquestionably getting you laid tonight," she said.

"But the kids are in our bed."

"I'm sorry, do you *not* want to have sex with me in the office?"

"I do now," I said, making like I was going to stand up.

"No, no, no." She grabbed my hand and pulled me back down. "We need to talk. You said so yourself. And it's my turn now. I couldn't care less about you not working, or this not having been our plan when we started out. The only thing I care about is you finding what you want." She gave me a mischievous smile. "That's the luxury of being married to a boss, right? You don't have to do something you don't want to just to get paid?"

I smiled back. "Among other things, yes."

"And what I said about you only wanting to not lose to Chad—that was a low blow."

"Thanks. I mean, it started out that way, but it definitely became something else."

"I also know how much I've been working is a problem."

God, was I glad to hear her say that.

"Honestly? Yeah, it is. And not just for me, and not just for them"—I nodded toward the kids asleep upstairs—"I think it is for you too."

"It is. This trip was bad. I mean, professionally, it was great. But emotionally, I felt so far away from the three of you, and I hate that. So after we closed the deal . . ."

264

"After *you* closed the deal," I objected.

"Sustained," she said, smiling. "After *I* closed the deal, Patrick asked me what I wanted, and I told him there was no reason I couldn't work from home one day a week so I could see my family more. I also told him I wanted to travel less—especially now that my husband is going to be president of our daughter's school's parent board."

"You really said that?"

"Hey, you're not the only one who goes around bragging." She reached for the zip-up sweatshirt she had brought down with her. "But I suppose in the interest of being totally transparent, I should note that I did start out by saying a bonus was in order."

"Like I said: goddamn boss."

It was a happy, familiar feeling as we tapped our wine cans together in a cheers, and I thought about just leaving it at that. But if I didn't bring it up right there and then, I didn't know when I would.

"I hope I didn't . . . you know, with the travel thing—I hope I'm not the reason you told him that."

She looked at me like I hadn't been listening to a word she'd said. "Of course you're the reason—you and those two goofballs upstairs."

"No, I know. I just mean, I hope I didn't, like, guilt you into it or anything."

"Oh, Jack," she said airily, patting my knee, "when have you ever known me to do something I didn't want to do? It's one of the many, *many* things you love about me."

I laughed. "You're right."

"Of course I am."

"Except about the parent board. I haven't won anything there yet."

"And you still haven't told me what's going on with the runoff. Or what happened at the debate."

"Aah, that's because it's a tale that could only truly be appreciated once we were face to face."

"All right, then—spill."

Reliving the debate with Kayla was almost as glorious as standing there at the end of it after Chad and Ms. Weekler had fled from the stage. When I had finished explaining the barrage of T-shirt swag, I paused to take a drink only to discover my can was empty.

"I knew you had this," she said. "Even without my vote."

That last part came out before she had a chance to realize it was going to catch in her throat, much like when she had been talking to the kids from the hotel.

"Kayla, it's okay. It's not like you chose not to be there. And I promise, it's not the reason it ended up in a runoff." I never would've guessed coming up two votes short would be so much better than one.

She waved me off. "I know. I'm just . . . sorry I wasn't." She inhaled deeply to clear a sniffle. "That bookfair idea is great, by the way. And I'm not just saying that because now we wouldn't have to remember to send money to school with Lulu."

"Thank you. It's one of the things that made this feel like it could be worthwhile beyond sticking it to Chad." I summoned my best impression of a wizened old sage to add, "And the bookfair's role in this story is only beginning to unfold."

"Where are you going?" she asked as I stood.

"To get us another drink."

"No, I'm good. Keep going."

"Well, I want another one. But I'm not leaving you empty handed." I took out my phone and cued up Tori's video from the debate. "In case you thought I was embellishing."

I had left Ms. Weekler's Mrs. Robinson implosion out of my retelling so Kayla could experience it in something akin to real time. The gasp I heard all the way in the kitchen told me when she had gotten there.

She appeared as shocked as I hoped she'd be when I returned to her on the couch. Then she whacked me on the arm.

"How did you not send me this?"

"Because I didn't want to miss the look on your face right now."

"So . . . she berated a group of parents . . . at a debate for elementary school parent board . . . by claiming all the dads think she's hot?" Kayla punctuated each piece of her sentence by gesturing with both hands toward me.

"Yes, that is in fact what happened," I said, opening my can. "Which . . ." I trailed off on purpose.

"Obviously. She's not wrong. But has anyone said anything? Like, to the school district?"

"I don't think so. She's done a good job deflecting the accusations about the list, and I don't think anyone wants to dig too deeply into how attractive their spouse may or may not find the principal."

"That's true. Not everyone is as evolved as us."

"Yet I'm about to tell you another side of Ms. Weekler's story that will complicate your feelings about her even more than her debate meltdown. Enter: Elena and Steven Choi."

Like me, Kayla couldn't tell whether Ms. Weekler and Steven Choi actually being in love with each other made the whole thing better or worse.

"Here we thought the parent board would be boring," she said.

"I know. And this all brings us to today: the election."

"My heart is literally racing." She grabbed my hand and stuck it on her chest. "Feel."

"Do you want me to finish this story, or do you want me to get distracted by your boobs?"

She swatted me away in pretend annoyance.

I told her about dropping off Lulu, my conversation outside with Chad, and Tori's mad dash to vote on time. I told her how I had realized that I didn't have anything to prove with him.

Of course it helped that if I had, the score had come out pretty lopsided in my favor.

And I told her how I had walked into Ms. Weekler's office knowing I wanted to be president, proceeded to get the most votes, and that still wasn't enough.

"You already said my vote wouldn't have won it for you, but I got stressed out about it all over again listening to you talk about her counting them."

"I know. It was intense in there."

I then broke down Ms. Weekler's deal, the expedience of which was exceeded only by its audacity, and described Tori and me all but arriving at a decision in the school parking lot.

When I was done, Kayla leaned into me, and I put my arm around her.

"I really am proud of you," she said. "I hope you know that."

"I do."

"And chair of the bookfair committee. That's not nothing."

"No, it's not."

"So, how's this going to work tomorrow? I took the day off, so you can leave Klay here with me when you go in."

"Well, there is one more thing I have to tell you." She couldn't see my face, but I think she could tell it was enveloped in a smile because she sat back up.

"What? And please bear in mind that if you drag this out any more, office sex is coming off the table."

I leaned over to the coffee table and picked up my laptop.

"Right before Tori dropped us off, I got an email. From the school district."

"Okay."

"Apparently Molly Andrews, one of the parents from Lulu's class, told them about my bookfair idea. And they *really* liked it. In fact, they want to pilot it in five elementary schools across the district, and they want me to be the one to head it up."

"Oh my God—Jack, that's amazing!" We hugged, but then she leaned back abruptly, expectant all over again. "Wait. Have you told Ms. Weekler?"

"Almost."

"What do you mean, 'almost'? How're you going to do it?"

For all her planning, all her manipulation, Ms. Weekler hadn't just underestimated me. She had underestimated Kathy Francis too. And that came at a cost.

Because now, Ms. Weekler and Chad weren't the only ones with the email addresses of every parent and guardian at the school.

I had them too.

It had taken a long time to enter them all in the bcc field, but each second felt worth it as I turned my screen toward Kayla so she could read the message sitting in my drafts.

Subject: Active Alpaca Parent Board Election Results

Hello, Willow Road Families—

This is Jack Parker, one of your two candidates for president of the Active Alpaca Parent Board.

First off, I want to say thanks to all of you who came out and voted this morning and apologize to everyone who couldn't because of the limited options for doing so. Making it easier to vote is one of the things I hoped to change as president.

Also, a special thanks to my campaign manager, Tori St. James, who may never speak to me again for calling her that. ☺

I'm writing to let you know that although I received more votes than my opponent, Chad Henson, I didn't get to a majority (there were a few write-ins—which, hey, you do you). According to the AAPB bylaws, that means Chad and I go to a runoff.

However, as luck would have it, today I was also contacted by the Meadow Park School District. They heard about my proposal for community-funded bookfairs and want to pilot the model in five of the district's elementary schools, Willow Road included.

I've been offered a position as a special adviser to lead this and other projects, and I'm happy to tell you I've said yes.

While this is a nonvoting volunteer role, it's designed to give us something we haven't had before: a direct line to the district's decision makers.

If you have particular issues you'd like to see the school district take up—or even ideas or concerns about our own school you've found difficult to raise in the past—consider this email an open invitation to reach out to me directly. I'm not quite sure what this will look like yet, but I'm here to help.

Lastly, and given everything else, it only seems fair to let Chad assume the role of AAPB president and avoid a runoff. For those of you, like me, who were concerned about his plan to change the administration of the technology fee, please know that Ms. Weekler has gone on the record as saying those changes will not be implemented.

Beyond that, I look forward to working with the two of them on any business they have with the school district.

Thanks again, everybody.

Jack

Kayla looked at me when she finished reading, jaw dropped, before reading it again.

When she was done for the second time, her mouth was still open. But now it had rounded into a smile, while that spark I loved bounced around her eyes.

"I told you," she said.

"Told me what?"

"That he didn't stand a chance."

"Yes. Yes, you did."

She handed the computer back to me. I hit send.

And then we didn't talk about Chad or Ms. Weekler or elections for the rest of the night.

SIX MONTHS LATER

Life as a nonvoting special adviser to the school district's council members was good. My parents had started telling people I was on the school board, which was inaccurate, but I got the sense it was because they didn't get the distinction, not because they thought it would only be worth mentioning if they inflated it. Scottie, whose insane schedule ensured our communication was sporadic at best, texted me out of the blue one day:

Mom's talking about you like you're a Kennedy.

I'd also gotten an email from the son of a woman in her book club who was staying home with his first child and struggling. My mom had passed along my info because I was "better at it than anyone she'd ever known."

Camelot or not, my charge with the school district was to talk with other parents. I got to help where I could, and, unlike the Kennedys, I got to do it without once being accused of being a corrupt politician.

Some of my fellow parents still left something to be desired.

My first meeting was in mid-October, when the council told Chad we had a district-wide contract for the candy sale and that he couldn't just have Willow Road kids sell Chocsplosion! instead.

"That's really interesting," he said, going to the chin-scratching-nodding thing. "But you know, one thing I found from my time in business is that sometimes rules are made to be broken."

"Not this one," the woman who had recruited me to the position said. "Anything else?"

By the time the spring bookfairs came around, I had the pilot in place. Despite a few hiccups here and there, the council considered the project a huge success—which, admittedly, was thanks in part to it not generating any more complaints than the old model. We were moving forward with plans to introduce community-funded fairs in all the elementary schools for the fall.

Lulu and Crispin continued to be good friends, and we did do some more playdates (ugh, that word), although I insisted on going to playgrounds or parks to minimize the amount Chad and I would have to interact. Kayla even came home early from work a couple of times to go in my place. She still took Klay, too, which both kids loved and gave me a slice of afternoon to myself. As if that weren't enough, she always returned with a story about Chad's life as president. Once it was him having to cut their time short so he could make 12 dozen cupcakes for a bake sale the next day. His two volunteers had gotten into an intractable dispute over whether the one making the gluten-free option was still required to split the cost 50-50, even though the gluten-free cupcakes represented only 25 percent of all the cupcakes. Another time it was about how a mom from school had basically accosted him while he sat on a bench and demanded to know (a) why he hadn't made any progress on his promise to put a gourmet-snacks bar in the cafeteria and (b) what he personally was going to do to defend prayer in the nation's public schools.

"You missed out on some fun, fun times," Kayla said after relaying the bench story to me.

Other than emails she sent to all the parents, I hadn't heard much of anything from Ms. Weekler since I left her office the day of the election. I wasn't going out of my way to avoid her; there were just limited opportunities for us to cross paths, which I was sure she, like me, was fine with.

I did know that Liz had launched a petition calling for her removal as principal. I had clicked the link when she sent it to me but didn't sign, and the last time I checked, there were only a few dozen names on it. Perhaps not coincidentally, there was significant overlap between them and the people who had used their Chad T-shirts as projectiles at the debate.

I hadn't told anyone on the council what Ms. Weekler had yelled at everyone that night, and no one there had asked much about the race for Active Alpaca Parent Board president. But when Ms. Weekler's upcoming five-year review appeared on our agenda in March, it seemed some version of the information had found its way to them even without the benefit of a video.

Listed prominently among their topics to discuss with her?

"School Election Irregularities."

Guess I wasn't too nice to ever win anything after all.

ACKNOWLEDGMENTS

I have to start by thanking you, the reader, for spending time with this story. I never would've gotten it to you without the support and encouragement of a lot of amazing people.

To Jessica, my agent. You signed me as a joke writer who thought he was meant to do essays, all the while knowing there was a novelist in there somewhere. Thank you for your vision, your patience, your guidance, and most of all, your friendship.

To Chris, my editor. You understood what I was trying to do with this book from the first time we talked, and you gave me the guidance to make it stronger. I am indebted to you, Jen, Elyse, Stephanie, Philip, and everyone at Lake Union for turning *Schooled* into a reality.

Mom and Dad, you always insisted I could do anything, and you made sure I had every opportunity to try. Thank you.

Sheila, this book wouldn't have come together the way it did if you hadn't encouraged me to keep writing in the early days of the pandemic. Rein, you don't pay insincere compliments, so you telling me this was going to happen meant more than I can tell you.

Nonna, you aren't here to see this, but somehow, I think you know.

To my *Seinfeld* DVDs. You taught me so much. And to Kevin. You made it through all of them (and lots of other stuff) with me. I couldn't have asked for a better friend.

To J. and A., the two therapists I've worked with at different points these last 11 years. I'll never be "cured" of anxiety and depression, but I am living with it far better than I did thanks to the two of you.

To Susan, Kate, Joey, Mallory, Sam, Aunt Lia, Uncle John, Ryan, Brian, Molly, Dixon, Chris A., Chris E., Josh, Pat, and so many others. Some of you are family. Some of you are friends. You are all my people. Believe me when I say I know how lucky that makes me.

Buckner and Roxy, I don't get why the Parkers don't have a dog either.

Henry and Caroline, I literally could not have written this story without you. I am so proud to be your dad. When you're old enough to read this, I hope you'll feel the same about me. I love you both. Now put the LEGOs away.

Jenny, I didn't even know books were my dream when we met. And then six or seven months in, you told me I should try writing one. Now here we are 16 years (and some hits and misses) later. Thank God it didn't take me that long to propose. I love you.

Finally, to Jack. You're not real, but getting to live inside your head has given me more than I ever could have asked for.

ABOUT THE AUTHOR

Photo © 2021 Erin Ponisciak

Ted Fox is the author of the jokebook *You Know Who's Awesome? (Not You.)* and once solved the *New York Times* crossword puzzle forty-six days in a row (not a joke). He lives in Indiana with his wife, their two kids, and two German short-haired pointers who are frankly baffled there aren't more dogs in his books. The recipient of a prestigious "No. 1 Dad" keychain, Fox was widely recognized as having the best swaddling technique of anyone in the family when his kids were babies. And not just the immediate family—grandparents, aunts, uncles, everybody. Anyway, *Schooled* is his first novel.